VIRGINIA FOX
ROCKY MOUNTAIN YOGA

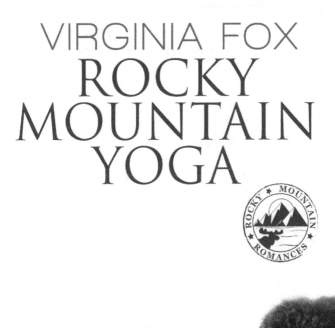

DRAGONBOOKS
PUBLISHING HOUSE

DRAGONBOOKS
PUBLISHING HOUSE

Names: Fox, Virginia, author.

Title: Rocky Mountain Yoga (Rocky Mountain Romances, Book 1)/ by Virginia Fox.

Description: First Edition. | Boulder, Colorado: Dragonbooks, 2022.

Summary: When a yoga teacher grabs her poodle and flees the big city—and her shady boyfriend—for the Rocky Mountains, she's in for a whirlwind of adventure, misadventure, and romance as she sorts out her life.

Subjects: BISAC: FICTION / Romance / General. | FICTION / Romance / Contemporary. | FICTION / Women.

ISBN 979-8-9862800-9-7 (Paperback) | ISBN 979-8-9862800-8-0 (eBook) LCCN: 2022920299

Editor: Elaine Ash
Associate Editor: John Palisano
Cover Design: Juliane Schneeweiss
Interior Design: Jennifer Thomas

ROCKY MOUNTAIN YOGA

CHAPTER ONE

"WHY CAN'T I FIND anything in this purse!" For the third time, Jasmine shook her large shoulder hobo for the key to the yoga studio. But there was no telltale jingle. Her boss, Keith, would be cranky if she opened late. As a wannabe social media influencer in the yoga world, Keith was on top of his clients' every desire.

Jasmine resisted the urge to dump her purse out on the sidewalk and sift through the jumble. But that wouldn't do, not on this prime shopping street in the lower Queen Anne district of Seattle. No, she had to head home and hope the key was on the entry table in her apartment. Just great! Now she had to pray that the traffic gods of GPS would be merciful. She turned on her heel and ran back to the parking garage. At least it wasn't drizzling for once; a pleasant exception in rainy Washington state.

Rambo, her black standard poodle, had already been dropped off at the dog sitter. That was one thing to be thankful for. Fifteen minutes later, she pulled up in front of her apartment building. Ignoring the no parking sign, she left her emergency lights flashing and sprinted up the stairs. On the third landing, she stopped briefly to catch her breath. *You should be used to living on the fourth floor by now,* she scolded herself. Not to mention that she taught yoga for a living. She straightened her back, ready to tackle the last flight of stairs.

THUMP! The noise came from overhead, the direction of her floor, followed by the murmur of voices. She narrowed her eyes. Her boyfriend Gavin was home, that was expected. But company this early? It was a miracle Gavin was out of bed at ten a.m. A thought popped into her head; was another woman with him? *Please, please no.* She fervently hoped there was an innocent explanation for the noises coming from her apartment. The last thing she wanted was to catch Gavin cheating.

With a queasy feeling in her stomach, Jasmine crept up the stairs. She was glad she was wearing sneakers as usual. Not very fancy, perhaps, as Gavin always liked to remind her, but unlike high-heeled shoes, the sneakers didn't make a sound on the floor of the stairwell. She could make a near-silent approach. When she arrived on her floor, the voices were clear. They didn't sound female. Those were men's voices. Maybe Gavin's friends had made an uncharacteristic early call. Her inner clock chimed, reminding her there was no time to lose if she wanted to make it back to the yoga studio on time. Going to open the door, she noticed it was ajar. That's why she could hear the voices so well. *What the heck?* Her thoughts were interrupted when Gavin spoke up.

"I told you, no personal contact. The risk—someone who knows me could see you. Surely you're aware of that."

"That was before you failed. We don't like fails."

She did not know this voice.

"Not printing on time—big fail," agreed a second unfamiliar voice. "You made this a personal visit, dude."

The uneasy feeling in her stomach intensified, and hairs on the back of her neck stood up.

"Listen, you'll get the real money." That was Gavin's voice and he sounded nervous. "I just need a few more days and I'll have my girlfriend soft-boiled. I know she has cash, the real stuff, sitting in an account that she doesn't need."

Money she didn't need? Jasmine's cheeks grew pink with anger. That money was exactly three thousand dollars and eighty-seven cents. She'd saved it over two years of working nights, weekends, and days off at the homes of well-heeled clients, teaching them yoga and relaxation techniques. It was a little nest egg for herself and Gavin in case things got tough. Or they wanted to start a family. Which Gavin obviously didn't want, if he was so free about dispensing her money to strangers. Fortunately, she'd had enough sense to follow her grandma's advice to save it in a separate account.

The first strange voice snapped her out of her thoughts and made her blood run cold.

"We launder at flea markets and farmers markets, dude. The stuff needs to be printed in time before the weekend starts. You want to walk in with a twenty, buy something for a buck, and get the real stuff in change. If you're gonna launder, you got to make the stuff on time."

A twenty? Launder? Did he mean money laundering? Fake money? As in counterfeiting? How had Gavin gotten involved in this? She leaned forward to listen. The overstuffed hobo on her shoulder tipped forward and bumped into the door. It swung open. Three pairs of men's eyes shot over at her. Two bull-necked strangers radiated malice out of every pore. They didn't look like they'd shaven for a couple of days. Maybe the last time they'd seen a shower was even longer. Gavin looked annoyed.

"Oh, hello everyone. I'll be right back, just have to get something," she said in a put-on cheerful voice. Friendly. Naive. Harmless. They had to buy that, didn't they?

"What are you doing here? I thought you'd be at work by now!" Gavin's frightened voice offered no reassurance.

"That's no way to talk to your girlfriend," Stranger Voice No. 1 chided Gavin, giving a snarling smile that made Jasmine's stomach turn.

"What a happy coincidence," Stranger Voice No. 2 agreed. "Now we can settle the real money thing. Always happy to help solve problems." He cracked his knuckles to demonstrate.

Uh-oh. Retreat! screamed all the alarm systems inside Jasmine. The key to the studio lost all importance. She took two cautious steps backward.

"Hey! This little one's gonna split! Stop her!" shouted Stranger Voice No. 1, reaching behind his back to pull a frighteningly real-looking pistol from his waistband. Gavin seemed frozen, he made no move to stop anything. Jasmine never expected Gavin to be a knight in shining armor, but she never expected a wet dishrag either.

It was one against three and every woman for herself. Jasmine dashed out of the apartment and raced down the stairs as if all the hounds of hell were on her heels. She was quick and agile thanks to years of training and her small, slender stature. Unlike the two gorillas chasing her, who were cursing loudly and bumbling on the stairs.

She covered the four floors in no time, gaining precious seconds.

On the ground floor, she flew out the door and jumped into her old car, which she had fortunately forgotten to lock. As the two thugs piled out of the building entrance, she drove off, tires squealing.

A few streets away, Jasmine slowed to the legal speed limit and tried to get her thoughts in order. She still couldn't quite grasp what she had just witnessed. Her live-in boyfriend, Gavin, involved in a counterfeit money scheme? She broke out in a sweat thinking of his cold stare while the two guys were about to grab her. But what if this wasn't anything like it seemed? Gavin was her *boyfriend*. Maybe there was a reason for his reaction.

While she was driving along, torn with conflict and confusion, her phone started to ring. With one hand she dumped the hobo upside down so everything tumbled out on the passenger seat. The cell phone buzzed at her, its screen blinking "Gavin." She pushed *Speaker*, but all she heard was scuffling and static. Then the signal died.

Her attention turned back to the road. In a panic, she had blindly crisscrossed the neighborhood. Should she contact the police? At the next street corner, she saw a sign for a police station. An empty parking space seemed waiting for this occasion and helped her decide. She pulled the car in and sat for a moment with the engine running, taking a deep breath. It was like being in the wrong movie!

Jasmine shook herself like a wet cat and reached for her purse. Before stepping out, she took a good look at the entrance to the police station—and stopped. Out the door came none other than Gavin, engaged in a friendly conversation with a police officer. She took her hand off the door handle and huddled deeper into the car seat. She was half a block down—it wasn't like her car was directly in sight. She watched as the two patted each other on the back in male solidarity. As the officer stepped back inside the building, Gavin's gaze roamed the area, looking for something. Her? Had he known she'd go to the police? If what just happened was innocent, what was Gavin doing schmoozing a police officer? The timing was odd, very odd.

Jasmine pulled her head down even further. A surge of adrenaline made the blood rush in her ears. Cautiously, she peered over the dashboard and saw Gavin walk over to a waiting car. Stranger Voice No. 1 and 2 were in the front seat. Gavin got in the back.

What was she supposed to make of what she had just seen? She had no idea if corruption was an issue in the ranks of the Seattle Police Department. But seeing Gavin speaking directly to a cop as thugs 1 and 2 looked on halted her decision to report the incident right now. Especially parked right outside the police station, where they seemed to be waiting for her to show up.

Jasmine rubbed her temples; the whole thing was crazier by the second. She was a peace-loving person, she abhorred violence. Nor did she have any secret fantasies of being a heroine. She was absolutely not made for that. She gritted her teeth. Time for a new plan.

When the gun guys and Gavin left the parking lot and disappeared around the block, she picked her cell phone out of the pile underneath her purse and called

Pat, a longtime friend whom she trusted one hundred percent.

When Pat answered on the other end, her heart lifted. "Hey Pat, listen, I need your help. Can you pick up Rambo for me at Kathrina's Dog Sitting?"

"Sure," he answered promptly. Fortunately, Pat was self-employed and had the freedom to slip away now and then. "What's the matter? Your voice sounds like you just finished a sprint."

"Almost. I'll explain everything later. Meet me at Westcrest Dog Park in two hours?"

Pat seemed to accept that he'd get no more info out of her for now. Relieved, she lowered her shoulders, which, she noticed, were pulled up almost to her ears from the tension.

"See you later." She ended the call. *Whew.* Time to move on to the next problem. Soon, she was on the freeway heading south. The destination was a shopping center on the outskirts of Seattle. Gavin would certainly not expect to find her there.

A few impulse purchases later included a big sack of dog chow with rice, sweet potatoes, and wild game, plus an important visit to the bank, Jasmine collapsed on a bench outside the shopping center eating a veggie dog. After devouring the last bite and wiping her hands on a napkin, she reached for the phone again.

"Hello, Nana!"

"Granddaughter! Jaz! Well, this is a pleasant surprise!"

Jasmine laughed tensely.

"When are you coming to visit me? The weather is getting nice."

"I was thinking, like, two, three days."

When her grandmother didn't answer right away, she added the question, "I can sleep on the couch. Any spot will do. Or is now not a good time?"

"It's always a good time," her grandmother hastened to assure her. Jasmine heard Nana take a deep breath on the other end. "It's just that I don't live at my house anymore. The place got lonely over last winter, and Nadine invited me to come and spend a few weeks at her place nearby. I guess you could say staying with her got to be a habit."

"That was the smart thing to do, Nana."

"My house has been empty but I never turned off the power. I was just waiting for…well, I don't know what I was waiting for. You're welcome to stay there. The keys are where they've always been. Come whenever you want."

"Thank you, Nana. It will be so great to get away." She made a face at the double meaning of "get away," glad her grandmother couldn't see her in person. If Nana only knew the getaway she was making! Jasmine made a bit more small talk and ended the call.

Her thoughts jumped to Keith and the studio. It was way past opening time, he'd be in soon. She made a quick call to Caitlin, the next instructor on the schedule, and fudged a bit of truth, saying she'd been called away suddenly by a family matter. Could Caitlin go over to the studio early and meet Keith there? He had his own key, and the boss would have to figure out what to do after that. He was constantly complaining about the rising cost of contractors, so unfortunately he could pay her little more than minimum wage. Yet he wouldn't have a business at all if she didn't take care of all the lessons while he gave private sessions to female customers in particular need of enlightenment—mostly married women. She was just a part-time freelancer at the studio, no employment contract, therefore no notice period.

Truthfully, Seattle was starting to lose its appeal. Not its proximity to the Pacific, of course. She was sure she would miss the ocean. But the city and its accompanying hustle and bustle were getting on her nerves. A change of scenery might do her and Rambo some good while she got to the bottom of this Gavin fiasco. Whether she was in real danger or whether she wasn't, Grandma had always said never to take chances. Get to a safe place first and let everything else take care of itself.

So, off to Independence, Colorado—a small town in the Rocky Mountains.

CHAPTER TWO

THIRTY-SIX HOURS and one time zone later, Jasmine pulled onto the weedy entrance drive that led to her grandmother's house. Rocky spires rose in the distance under a bright full moon. Her body felt every one of the 1,200 miles traveled in record time. Beside her, the phone flashed with many text and voicemail messages, most of them from Gavin. She hadn't read or listened to any of them yet, afraid she might have a weak moment and reverse her promise to reach safety first, before sorting this out. Pat would have filled Kathrina in on the sketchy details, so they wouldn't worry about her for a few days. Meanwhile, she had stayed off social media and her favorite sites, afraid that Gavin might see her on there and confront her in public.

The experiences of yesterday still sat deep in her bones. She wanted to put as many miles as possible between her and Seattle, as quickly as possible. She hadn't felt her butt for hours, either. Rambo, sitting next to her in the passenger seat, must have felt the same way.

"How's my boy?" she asked, tousling Rambo's black curls. He licked her hand briefly and then turned his attention to the new surroundings outside the car.

Jasmine ran a tired hand through her blond chin-length hair—which was doing its own version of a getaway, sticking wildly off her head—and opened the car door. Rambo jumped out and she followed. The crisp night air of the Rockies welcomed her. Shivering, she leaned inside the car once more and grabbed a sweatshirt from the back seat. Here in the mountains, the nights were chilly, even in summer. Early spring was cold for Pacific Northwest folks like her. With a groan, she slipped into the garment and turned to her grandmother's old, well-worn house.

For the area, the house was spacious. Built in log cabin style, it stood weathered but still solid and proud. During the day, you could see the mountain stream that ran a hundred yards behind the house and the incredible surrounding rock peaks. Behind the house was an old barn that once housed hay in the winter. Under the silver moon there was not as much to see, only the murmur of the water could be faintly heard.

Jasmine trudged toward the front door. During the summers she spent here while her parents traveled the oceans, she helped her grandfather with barn chores or her grandmother around the household. In total there were eight bedrooms. Four of them had their own fireplaces to conserve gas and electricity.

Jasmine's great-grandfather, who built the large house, had a great sense of family. The name McArthy was originally from Ireland, not to be mistaken for McCarthy, the more common spelling. Her grandmother had grown up as one of seven children. By now, only Nana lived in Independence. The real name was Independence Junction. It wasn't the real Independence, which had long been abandoned and was a ghost town. The rest of the family was spread out all over the states, visiting each other for the holidays.

Rambo nudged her with his wet nose. He had completed his first inspection tour and wanted to know what was happening next.

"Well, then, let's see if a bear has taken up residence during Nana's absence," she said to him. She could hardly wait to put the clothes on her back in the washing machine. Tomorrow, a shopping trip into town would be a priority.

In a few steps, she arrived at the front door, Rambo close on her heels. A familiar reach up to the door ledge revealed the house key. Nice that some things never changed. She unlocked the door and slipped inside. In the dark, Jasmine groped for the light switch. When she didn't find it right away, she impatiently turned on the flashlight function of her smartphone. Even in the low light, she could see dust floating in the air. The kitchen seemed crammed with stuff—cartons, empty glass bottles for canning, more pots and pans than one person could possibly use. Grandma always did hate to throw anything out. Not sure of what she might find, Jasmine opened the fridge to see what was there. Empty. She opened the freezer on top and a cloud of frosty air escaped. She waved her hands at it. The cell phone light revealed frosted mystery lumps. Tomorrow, cleaning and groceries in town were on the to-do list.

Nana had many great qualities, first and foremost a huge heart, but she no longer cooked. After Grandpa passed, she announced that her time as a farm wife was over. Cooking was for special occasions and holidays from now on. While Jasmine's footloose mother couldn't wait to get away from this "hick town" and had never looked back after leaving in her twenties, Jasmine had always loved Independence. She could have fled to Florida, where her parents had their primary residence. But the retirement apartment complex hadn't appealed. She knew no one there. Plus, Mom and Dad were currently sailing the seven seas, investigating warm and cold ocean currents. Environmental causes had always been important to them, maybe even more important than their daughter. In return, she had always been close to Nana.

It still felt good to be here, in this house where she had spent many a happy vacation. She almost felt something like gratitude toward Gavin. After all, he was the reason she was here now. But only *almost*. Because before she could finish the thought, Rambo growled and she froze.

Fifteen Minutes Earlier

The next acre over, Paula Carter saw the flash of headlights turning into the neighbor's property and put her hand to her shotgun. It must be midnight. Who on earth was driving this far out at this hour? The house was not directly on the main road. Besides, it was vacant right now. She watched the headlights die, and darkness enveloped everything again. Recently, Paula had felt like there were eyes on her place, watching, and it was creepy. Keeping a tight grip on her shotgun, she headed outside for a look.

Paula's patrol around the east pasture revealed nothing except an old Prius parked in front of Rose McArthy's house. Rustlers were nothing new, they'd been raiding homesteads in the area for some time, stealing chickens, goats, and produce. But were they brazen enough to park in plain sight?

When she came closer to the McArthy house, she noticed the moving glimmer of a flashlight behind one of the windows. There was someone in the house! Well, the burglars were in for something! Paula stepped up her pace and jogged toward the house. With an ease that spoke of years of practice, she slipped under the fence and approached the back door. Carefully, she pushed down the handle. She was in luck. As expected, it was unlocked. She slipped past the laundry room and pantry, and paused in the hallway outside the kitchen when she heard a growl. *A burglar with a dog?* she thought fleetingly. Never mind. She would deal with him. With one hand she felt for the light switch, with the other she held the shotgun with a practiced grip.

Jasmine yelped as the light in the kitchen snapped on overhead. She managed to grab Rambo by his collar before he could live up to his name. With the combination of an uninvited visitor and a scared mistress, he was on high alert. A woman in her early thirties stepped into the kitchen, and for the second time in forty-eight hours, Jasmine found herself on the wrong side of a gun. The woman held her shotgun with a steady hand and pointed it at Jasmine. Judging by her expression, she was seriously determined to use it.

The woman's eyes flicked to Rambo, who growled menacingly. Jasmine saw her brow furrow. The woman must think she was a burglar!

"Do you want to explain to me what you and Barbie's dog are doing here?" the woman said stoutly. "Or should I shoot you right now?"

Paula had kept her voice level, but the intruder was becoming angry. She launched a counterattack, "Explain? I don't owe anyone an explanation. Especially not people rude enough to point a gun at me. I happen to live here! Unlike you…"

The overgrown poodle snapped in agreement and braced himself against the collar.

Paula looked at her in disbelief; this intruder seemed to not grasp the gravity of the situation. With her left hand, Paula pulled a cell phone out of her pocket, keeping the shotgun steady. "We can solve this problem the easy way or the hard way."

"There is no problem here that needs to be solved. This is my house and you are not invited. End of discussion," the stranger retorted.

Paula ignored her. "The hard way, then. I'll call the sheriff." The sheriff was her older brother, Jake. He would not be pleased, but she couldn't help that. He would be even less pleased if she took matters into her own hands—more than she already had. She pressed the speed dial button and waited for her brother to pick up the phone.

"Paula? Has something happened?" Jake answered worriedly after the third ring.

"Good evening, Sheriff." Paula figured the thief didn't need to know that the sheriff was her brother. She could almost hear his frown on the other end. Jake would wonder why she was being so formal and know something was up. "Nothing has happened yet, but you'd better get here before there's trouble."

"To your place at the ranch?" He didn't dwell on asking the circumstances. There was a brief silence and she could imagine him massaging the bridge of his nose. His word for her was "impulsive," and that was when he was in a good mood. Now, at midnight, and on what Paula knew was his first night off in five days, he would probably use more colorful adjectives.

"I'm at the neighbor's—Rose McArthy's house. I caught a thief, or at least a squatter, in the act—" she paused in mid-sentence and watched in disbelief as the intruder opened drawers in a nearby sideboard and got out a length of twine. She tied it to the dog's collar and announced, "I need some stress remedy for my dog. I use the homeopathic drops distilled from flowers. Very effective." Then she pushed Paula's shotgun aside with an outstretched arm and said, "I'm going outside to my car. Put that thing away, would you, please?"

Paula followed her movements, speechless. She resolutely shoved the gun back toward the stranger's face, causing her to recoil in fright. That prompted a round of fresh barking from the poodle. Paula hollered into the phone at the same time, "You better come quick, Sheriff! Before I take matters into my own hands and smack our spiritually concerned thief. She's about to get a lesson in how we deal with uninvited guests in the mountains." Paula noted that the bandit was looking a little pale.

"Just breathe," said a tinny-sounding voice through the phone speaker. "I'll be there in fifteen minutes. Don't do anything rash!"

"Yes, yes." Paula rolled her eyes.

CHAPTER THREE

JASMINE KEPT HER EYE on the gun as she stroked Rambo. Her hands were shaking. With exhaustion as well as fright. Maybe it was just as well if the sheriff showed up. At least she could get this woman out of Grandma's house. She thought longingly of the homeopathic remedies she had in the car. A few drops would calm Rambo's stress. And hers. She summoned up all her courage for one last attempt to clear things up. She extended her hand in greeting. "We haven't even introduced ourselves yet, I'm—"

The shotgun thrust out and back again. "Save the fairy tales for the sheriff," the neighbor said gruffly, "and put that dog in a closet or something. If you can even call that overgrown fuzzball a dog."

That was enough for Jasmine. A stranger insulting her dog was not acceptable. Twice was an outrage. She straightened up to her full, admittedly not very impressive, height, and took a step forward without a second thought about the gun. "So you mean I can let him go? Barbie's dog? The fuzzball?" she asked saccharinely as Rambo let out another deep growl. "Good boy, Rambo."

For the first time, something like uncertainty showed in the neighbor's eyes. But it disappeared so quickly that Jasmine wasn't sure whether she had just imagined it. She was pretty sure this woman wouldn't shoot. Otherwise, she surely would have done so by now. Instead, she had called the sheriff. From the eye roll Jasmine had observed earlier, he was someone this woman knew well, a boyfriend, maybe. In terms of her own self, Jasmine knew she was close to the breaking point. If she didn't get some of those stress-rescue drops, she didn't know if Rambo might break away. His struggles were strong and her energy was slipping. With the law about to show up, she wanted to avoid escalating the situation with this woman, even if she did take the concept of neighborhood watch to the extreme.

Jasmine blinked, screwed up her courage, and simply walked past the gun and the woman. Rambo was in tow led by a firm grip. Ignoring the woman's protests, she went down the hall and out the front door. Outside, she made a beeline for the car, shut Rambo safely in the back, and started rummaging through the trunk. Too late, she remembered leaving the stress remedy in the glove box. She closed the trunk and already had her head inside the front of the car when the self-appointed officer of the x-treme neighborhood watch caught up. No matter. She finally had her remedy within reach; she wouldn't surrender without a fight.

Jasmine finally had the little bottle in her fist when she was jerked around rudely by the shoulder. She promptly hit her head on the door frame—hard. For a moment, she saw stars. But she didn't loosen her grip on the bottle in her hand.

Uh-oh, thought Paula. She hadn't meant to do that. She had forgotten the hands-on grip on the head, like you always saw the cops do on TV so the prisoners wouldn't bump their heads. Although the cops were usually trying to get people into the car, not drag them out. One idiotic thought followed another as she tried to figure out how to get out of this one without her brother, the sheriff, having a crisis. He could be a real stickler for the law sometimes.

The intruder had recovered enough by now to stand up. She reared up in front of Paula and angrily tapped her chest with an index finger. "That's it. Of all of us, you need this rescue remedy the most. Not that you deserve a single drop!" With her empty hand, the wannabe booster rubbed the spot on her head that had gotten clunked.

Paula took a step back, dumbfounded, the shotgun useless at her side. She wasn't clear on exactly what had happened, but somehow she had lost control of the situation. She was pretty sure by now that the woman was harmless. Even though she would never have admitted it, especially not now that headlights were appearing on the road that ran along the property. Her brother would be here in a moment, and she could relinquish responsibility for the lawbreaker.

Jake couldn't believe his eyes as his front headlights fell on the scene in the drive of the McArthy house. His sister stood eye to eye with a petite blonde in lavender yoga pants. Her blond hair was a tangled mess, and if he judged her silhouette correctly, the yoga pants she wore were not only a fashion statement, but had actually seen the inside of an exercise studio. This was supposed to be a burglar. At least that's what his sister believed, if he interpreted the murderous look in her eyes correctly. Unfortunately, he knew better.

Jake had spent his lunch break at Independence Junction's only diner. The diner, along with a bed-and-breakfast, belonged to the Disney Sisters, also known as Miss Daisy and Miss Minnie. Not only did the diner serve the best burgers in town, it was also the best source for information. You could call it information or you could call it town gossip. Whatever you called it, a small-town sheriff found it invaluable. While eating lunch, he'd run into Rose McArthy and knew that a granddaughter was on her way for an eagerly awaited visit. The granddaughter's name he'd forgotten. Miss Yoga, whatever her name was, definitely had a right to be here. His sister, Paula, always did pick the biggest *faux pas* to jump into with a running start.

Without turning off the engine, he got out of his vehicle and, keeping in the light of the powerful headlights, approached the two women who were still glaring at each other. Something struck him as strange about the way Paula was behaving so calmly while the stranger, with her head tilted way back, dripped some kind of liquid into her own mouth from a bottle. Jake sincerely hoped it wasn't illegal.

"WHAT'S GOING ON HERE?" a male voice boomed.

Jasmine's nerve endings tingled when she heard the voice. *It had to be the sheriff*, she thought with relief and tilted her head down to look. He was already closer than she thought, so she bumped full force against his broad chest. Embarrassed, she tried to back away, but he held her by the upper arms.

"Whoa. Not so fast. What's that in your hand?" He grasped her wrist and turned her hand over so he could see the bottle.

"It's for my dog. He's been going crazy over this, this, *neighborhood-watch extremist!*" Jasmine pleaded, jerking her head at the shotgun nut. The sheriff took the bottle from her hand, read the label, sniffed the contents, and handed it back.

"I'll take that," he said to the nut, taking her weapon, dumping the shells out, and laying it aside. He came back to stand beside Jasmine.

"Are you going to arrest me now?" Jasmine asked, voice cracking. "My dog didn't do anything wrong!" Rambo had taken to barking again, from inside the car.

The lawman bent at the waist and tapped on the car window. "Hey boy," he said. "How are you doing in there?"

Rambo whined, sat down, and wagged his tail.

Blinded by the spotlight, Jasmine couldn't get a good look at the sheriff. But he sounded young and reasonable, and Rambo had just given him a vote of confidence.

The man chuckled softly at the dog, who was scratching at the window to get out and play.

Jasmine couldn't help but throw her opponent a triumphant I-told-you-so-my-dog-is-great look.

The other woman's posture remained stiff and annoyed. "While this is all cozy, I'd like to point out that you're flirting with a ranch raider right now!" she huffed at the sheriff.

He gave her a stern look over Jasmine's head. "A ranch raider in yoga pants? With a poodle?"

This question earned him a surprised look from both women. Unconcerned, he shrugged his shoulders. He didn't register any shame for noticing Jasmine's clothing. His expression said he was an officer of the law, paid to notice details. Or something like that.

The security lunatic gritted her teeth. "Sorry I didn't take the time to do a clothes analysis. I was busy dealing with the fact that someone was sneaking around the house. You have to admit, that looks very suspicious!"

"Hey! I couldn't find the light switch on the first try!" Jasmine protested. "It's been a long time since I was here. I didn't know vigilantes lived next door."

Jake interrupted them both. "Meet Paula, my impulsive sister." That earned him a scowl, which he studiously ignored. "And Rose McArthy's granddaughter."

Jasmine gave him a puzzled look. He already knew who she was? And this exhausting woman was actually called Paula?

"I met your grandmother at the diner this afternoon," he added by way of explanation. "I'm afraid I didn't catch your name when Rose spoke of you. I'm Jake Carter."

"My name is Jasmine. Friends call me Jaz." *Oops.* Once again, her mouth was faster than her brain. It was far from certain whether this brother and sister act would advance to the Jaz category. She hoped her reactions would return to normal after some sleep. She was proud that most of the time she acted very calmly and thoughtfully. Zenlike. Admittedly, her Zen had been conspicuously absent in recent days. Jasmine took a step back. This time the sheriff let go of her.

"Nice meeting you," she nodded to him, ignoring his obviously mentally confused sister.

"And now, if you'll excuse me—" She rummaged in the front of the car for her bag and headed for the house, dog in tow.

Paula clamped her mouth shut and gave Jake a bitter look. "Can I have my gun back, please?"

He picked the gun and shells off the ground and handed them over.

"Don't even think about it," she hissed as he started to say something. Before he could close his mouth, she had disappeared into the darkness.

Jake watched her go, not in the least surprised at her quick exit. He would have done the same in her place. He stretched and took one last look at the McArthy house. So, he had met the lovely Jasmine. The night's excursion had not been in vain. Now he had an excuse to call on her. Since his sister would certainly not apologize, he'd have to do it for her. What wouldn't he do for family? He grinned to himself and strode over to his four-wheel drive to go back home.

Jasmine watched the SUV from the kitchen window until Jake's red taillights were swallowed by darkness. What a day. So much for the idea of showing up here inconspicuously. By tomorrow, all 784 residents of Independence Junction would know that Rose's granddaughter was back. She smiled wryly. That was both the beauty and horror of a small town like this. Everyone knew everyone and stuck their nose into everyone's business, wanted or not. The best example of this was Paula with her watchdog ways. Jasmine wrinkled her nose. She definitely liked the brother more.

CHAPTER FOUR

Jasmine woke with a start. Her phone was on silent, but that didn't stop it from flashing at her in the dark like emergency lights on an ambulance.

Gavin.

Again.

With a sigh of resignation, she clicked *Play* on the most recent message. Gavin's voice sounded small and insectile coming out of the tiny speaker in the dark room.

"I've had time to calm down, you've had time to calm down. This is all a silly mistake."

He sounded so reasonable.

"Why aren't you calling me back? What don't you understand? I explained—"

Rambo *ruffed* at the sound of Gavin's voice.

"Surely we can talk about this like reasonable people."

You didn't seem reasonable when your pal pulled a gun on me.

"Jasmine." Gavin's voice dropped in register, which she always found so attractive. Her stomach fluttered. "We have so much between us. Can't we get past this? Like I said, I can expla—"

"RUFF!!"

Rambo jumped off the bed where he had kept her company all night and barked like a wild thing. What was going on now? She rolled out of bed, grabbed the sweatshirt off the floor where she'd carelessly dropped it before falling into bed, and pulled it over her head.

"Ruff, RUFF," Rambo warned.

The soles of her feet touched the cold wooden floor. She shuddered. Rambo leaped to the bedroom door. She let him out, and he charged ahead. She followed the frenetic barking to the front door. Once there, she heard a vehicle pull away. A big truck, judging by the roaring engine. People here in the Rockies didn't seem to have much use for energy efficient cars, yet.

Carefully, she opened the door, her hand tight on Rambo's collar. Her eyes fell on a brown paper bag lying on the top step of the porch, next to it a thermos with a yellow sticky note attached. The items certainly didn't look dangerous. Curious, she picked them up to carry into the house. Judging by the smell coming from the bag, it had warm biscuits inside. The vacuum flask smelled of rich coffee. Her mouth watered.

Rambo had calmed down by now and was more interested in the bag than in potential burglars. She reached for the yellow slip of paper and detached it from the thermos. A slight smile played on her lips. Maybe a certain sheriff had made the effort. She hadn't really seen him because of the headlights. The last time a man made a special effort to be nice seemed like a distant memory.

She read the sticky note in her hand:

Welcome to Independence.
P.

She stared at the clear but unmistakably feminine lettering. *Oh.* She hadn't expected that. Not a complete apology, but pretty much. What a surprise. She shooed away the quiet disappointment that the message wasn't from the sheriff. What was his name? Jack? Joe? Something with J. Whatever, his sister had made an apology-offering and that was a lot better than an enemy neighbor. An apology from Paula was likely a rare event, extremely rare. Which made it all the sweeter.

She pushed the front door shut and burrowed into the bag. It held still-warm homemade buttermilk biscuits with organic butter and honey on the side in separate little containers. Sinking to the mat, she devoured both biscuits, dipping them into the butter and honey instead of taking time to get a plate and butter knife from the kitchen. She was starving! And this was her kind of food. Paula was quickly redeeming herself as a human being.

The thought of seeing Paula and Jock—John?—again made her shoulders tighten. She couldn't see anybody while dressed in these grubby clothes on her back. One more day and they'd start to smell, if they didn't already. She had nothing else to wear!

Jasmine hurried to the kitchen, put down food and water for Rambo, and then made a beeline to the laundry room on the main floor. She stripped off every stitch of clothing, put it all on the fastest wash cycle, and then ran back upstairs to rifle closets and bureau drawers. She came up with a warm hand-knitted sweater with a diamond pattern in rose and cream wool around the neck, and a cozy housecoat of Nana's. But not much else. A shopping trip to town was mandatory as soon as her pants were dry. Surely she could get in and out of town without being noticed. Especially if she wore the knit sweater on top. Nobody would know she was wearing the same things she'd driven cross-country in.

Just as the main-street stores were about to open, Jasmine drove toward the center of the small town. The plan was to duck into Johnson's Sporting Goods, get a few pairs of tights and long T-shirts, and then hightail it to Nana and Nadine's with no one the wiser. It would be nice if she could get a call in to Gavin before the visit, but he'd be in bed till ten a.m. at least. And he always took a half an hour to wake up. No sense trying to call and work things out with a sleepyhead. She would wait till ten-thirty. Just to make sure, she placed an alert on her phone.

Rambo sat in the passenger seat and held his head out the window. His long ears fluttered in the wind. Approaching the center, she slowed the car before stopping at the town's only traffic light. Things had changed in recent years. Instead of three warped, weathered buildings, there were now six or seven storefronts lined up on each side. Someone on the street she didn't recognize gave a cheery wave. Jasmine absently waved back. Ahead, she spotted a bookstore with an attached bakery, a gallery, a flower store—the light jumped to green and she continued on her way. Past the diner with a bed-and-breakfast on the side, and the community center with its quaint bell tower. The sandstone of the town hall gleamed, and the diner had a new coat of paint. Perhaps the idea of opening a little yoga studio wasn't as absurd as she'd thought.

The Prius swung into the large gravel lot that served as town parking, and Jasmine got out. Unlike Seattle, parking here was still free. Steps from the door of Johnson's, a car slowed on the street.

"I'd recognize those yoga pants anywhere," a male voice hollered.

Jasmine froze and then turned around. Walking beside her on the leash, Rambo jumped up and wagged his tail like crazy.

It was the sheriff. With a delighted smile lighting up his face.

O-o, she thought.

Rambo was beside himself with joy, and Jasmine realized she was expected to walk out to his vehicle and say hello. In the middle of the street! No problem, there was no traffic anyway.

She plastered on a smile and stepped out. "Hi, Jason!"

The smile fell from his face. "Jake," he said flatly. "It's Jake."

Her smile wavered. "My mistake. So much going on last night, you know."

"True that," he said good-naturedly. "What are you doing out so early?"

"Just looking around. You know," she said, realizing she'd just used "you know" twice in a row, like she was trying a little too hard to be nonchalant.

His eyes twinkled. "Because if I didn't know better," he said, "I might think you were on a shopping run for some yoga pants."

The blood rushed to her face. "Well, so what?" she sputtered. "I mean—"

"RUFF!" Rambo to the rescue. He jumped both paws on the SUV door, begging for a head scratch. Jake obliged, watching as she struggled for composure.

"Thought you might be headed to your grandmother's," he said easily, giving Rambo a good ear massage. "Where she's been staying, I mean."

"Yes, I was, I am," she managed.

"Got the address?"

The note Nana left in the kitchen mentioned no address. Jasmine realized with a sinking heart that she had no street, just a P.O. address for mail. Finally her brain kicked in. "All I have to do is call. I was reaching for my phone just as you drove up."

The sheriff looked like he was weighing another crack about shopping and yoga pants but thought better of it. "I'll take you there," he said kindly. "Follow me."

She was about to say "*No, no, don't take the trouble*," but she knew arguing might trigger more tortured conversation. Jasmine closed her lips firmly, nodded, and went back to her car. It figured he knew where Nana was. In a small town everybody knew where everybody else lived.

She was acutely aware of Jake waiting patiently until she had Rambo stowed in the car. He seemed a little surprised when he saw that the dog was allowed to sit in the passenger seat—he actually raised an eyebrow. But he didn't make an issue. In Independence, people had their dogs sitting up front all the time. But most of these were working, homestead dogs, trained to sit quietly and not distract their owners. Jasmine knew a big, unruly dog like

Rambo in the front seat of a small car wasn't particularly safe, not for her and not for the dog, but it made her feel less alone.

As she followed the big SUV out of town, Jasmine couldn't help but notice that new storefronts were far from the only changes. On the sides of the green mountain slopes were new houses, many of them log-cabin style, with lots of glass. They weren't quite as glamorous as those in Aspen or Breckenridge but still very nice.

Further ahead, she spotted a turnoff with a sign reading "Elementary School." The next sign said "High School" and "Athletic Field." So many changes since she'd been here as a teenager. *Wow.* The road surface changed from tar to gravel, and the little Prius shook like a smoothie in a blender. Rambo gave her a worried look and lay down. If she really planned to stay here longer, she might have to consider something more solid. She looked at the big back end of the sheriff's SUV and sighed.

Finally, the sheriff slowed down and put his turn signal on coming up to a private driveway. Jasmine flashed her lights to let him know she understood this must be Nana's turnoff. He drove a little further and turned around. When he drove past again, he tapped the rim of his Western-style hat in farewell. She waved back. Nice of him to take the time to show her the way. One of the advantages of living in a small town.

BLIP! BLIP! The ten-thirty alert flashed on her phone. But this was no time or place to hash things out with Gavin. She swiped away the alert. It would have to wait.

CHAPTER FIVE

She had hardly knocked when Nana swooped her into a hug. "You're really here. I still can't really believe it!" she cried. "You could have gone to Florida, but instead you came to me."

Jasmine hugged her tight. "Yes, I am. I'm here. Barely."

"Whatever do you mean, Miss Jasmine?" Nana's blue eyes flashed with amusement. Her seventy-two years did not show at all. She was still as petite as she had been in her youth, and she wore her silver-gray hair done into a long French braid.

"I didn't pack as well as I should have," Jasmine mumbled.

Nana took a good look at her. "I recognize my sweater." she said, tweaking the handknit wool between her fingers. "It suits you."

"I hope you don't mind—"

"Shush, you're so used to Seattle you must have forgotten how cold it gets here." Nana turned and led Jasmine into the kitchen. It was fragrant with the smell of cherries and peaches.

"Are you canning?" Jasmine ran her fingertip along the edge of the large cooking pot and pinched a little of the sweet delicacy that was about to transform into Nana's famous jam. Her grandmother may not have been a big fan of cooking now that her days as a farm wife were over, but when it came to canning fruits and vegetables, she was an artist.

"I had all this fruit in the deep freeze. It's time to use them up," Nana announced. Then her tone changed. "Heard from your mother?" The question was accompanied by a meaningful glance.

"Not so much lately. I guess it's hard to send cards from an environmental tracking vessel."

"Your mother always did have that Don Quixote touch to her personality. I have no idea where she got it from." Nana gave Jasmine a wink. "Now tell me everything."

Over the next hour, as pots chugged and steamed, Jasmine related a curated version of events, designed not to alarm a doting grandmother. She mentioned that she and Gavin were in the process of working out an understanding of sorts. Maybe a misunderstanding, kinda. She still had to get his side of things.

Nana stirred her pots and considered this. "What does he think of you coming here without him?"

"Umm, he doesn't know exactly."

Nana's spoon left the pot and hovered in the air. She made a long nod with her head. "I think this is done," she said. Jasmine didn't ask if she meant the pot of fruit jam or her relationship. In fact, she didn't really want to know.

At that moment they were interrupted by the sound of the front door opening. Shoes clicked across the wooden front-entry floor, and Nadine walked in. She was dressed very smartly in a fashionable pantsuit, her brown hair streaked with silver strands worn in a chin-length bob. She looked as if she had come straight from an important meeting.

"You remember Nadine?" Nana said, delightedly. "Nadine worked as an elementary school teacher until she retired."

Nadine smiled warmly. "The retired part ended when I accepted a position as a principal."

"The town has grown so," Jasmine marveled.

"More and more children are born in Independence or moving here. We saw the writing on the wall a few years ago, so a few parents and the city council banded together to start an elementary school," Nadine said. "Now kids can spend at least the first couple of school years without being bussed out."

"Makes sense." Jasmine frowned. "Independence seems to be booming. With the economy the way it is in Seattle, I was afraid of the opposite."

"The popularity of Breckenridge, Aspen, and Vail brings more tourists looking for a little more authenticity than the glitzy ski towns offer. Prices aren't quite as high. You can't imagine how much a coffee costs in some places," Nana enthused.

"Oh, I bet I can," Jasmine answered.

Nadine grinned. "Don't worry. On the surface, everything sounds perfect, but we have our difficulties and quarrels just like other places. Enough about me, let's hear about your plans. Do you have any yet?"

While Nana had slowly approached the subject, Nadine got right to the point. Jasmine took a deep breath and let it escape slowly as she gently stroked Rambo's fur with her foot. He had laid down at her feet after his initial exploratory tour of the house. "I'm just here for a few days but got the idea that there might be room for a yoga studio in town. What's the current population anyway? I had seven hundred and eighty-four in my head."

"We've grown almost twice that," Nana replied. "I think at last count it was one thousand, four hundred and thirty." She had a hopeful look on her face. Almost as though she had some kind of agenda.

"What is it, Nana? Why are you looking at me like that?"

"I'm just excited, that's all. I have an idea, a business idea for the old house."

Jasmine took a seat on an oakwood kitchen chair, to listen.

"Now that I'm living here, with Nadine, I have no inclination to move back to that big empty house," Nana said with a toss of her French braid. "The big question is what to do with it?"

"Err, it's not exactly empty," Jasmine started.

"I may have collected a few things over the years since Grandpa passed. So many people went on to meet their maker and the families asked me if I wanted things. I didn't have the heart to say no."

Jasmine didn't have the heart to tell her the place needed a good clean out, either. She was glad when Nana continued her original train of thought.

"According to my research there are all kinds of resorts and dude ranches around here. But, no exercise resorts. I've got a huge empty house and a talented granddaughter who specializes in yoga. What more could I ask for? We could have hot yoga, Pilates, Zoomba, maybe even burlesque lessons, or Zuu, which is very good exercise, they tell me."

Jasmine's mouth fell open in a little "O."

"Whatever the ideal mix would be to get an exercise resort off the ground."

Jasmine said a little prayer of thanks. At least Nana was open to suggestions. Scaling back on the scope would be a good first move.

Nadine chimed in, "You know how all those city people are stressed from work? Daily meditation and exercise in our fresh mountain air would work wonders."

"What do we know about it?" Nana replied. "I'm just an old woman from the mountains. But you are young with all of life ahead of you. This might be just the thing to get a fresh start."

Jasmine tried to sort out all the information in her head. From a small yoga studio to a full-blown hotel and exercise resort with extras, in sixty seconds. All this from a creaky old place that "needed a little work" to put it nicely. She wasn't quite sure if Nana was going to hire her, or if she was going to work for herself. And who was going to take care of the guests? Who would cook? Clean? Make the beds? She also had no idea what permits would be required, and creating a business plan wasn't one of her strong suits. But rather than ask a bunch of difficult questions about something that was never bound to happen, she smiled and said, "Let me think on it while I'm here over the next few days."

"Of course," Nadine replied.

Nana, on the other hand, seemed almost a little disappointed that she didn't drop everything and start making plans.

Nadine noticed Nana's disappointed look, and gave her a gentle nudge.

"Ouch. What was that about?"

"Jasmine likes the idea, but she's only known about it for ten minutes. She needs time to consider."

Jasmine stood up and kissed Nana on the cheek. "Thank you for the lovely welcome. I'm glad to be here. But I have to do some shopping before the sidewalks are rolled up."

"We're modern now. We're open until six o'clock," Nana teased back. Then she jumped up and said, "Ooh, wait! There's no need to go shopping." She bustled out of the kitchen and returned with two bulging green garbage bags.

"We cleaned out the closets," Nadine said. "This clothing was supposed to be donated."

Nana held them out. "There are things we just can't fit into anymore. Take them home, go through them, and take what you want. When you go into town the next time, take the remainder and drop them in the bins marked Clothing Donations beside the diner."

Jasmine took the bags eagerly. There were few things she loved more than thrifting. This windfall was almost as good. She woke her sleeping dog, said goodbye, and headed out to the car. On the way home she opened the window a crack to let in the fresh air that carried a hint of pine resin.

Checking left and right for signs of shotgun-wielding neighbors, Jasmine pulled into the driveway of Nana's home. "As soon as we unload these groceries, it's walk time," she said to Rambo. He jumped to attention.

Minutes later they strolled along a creek and crossed it at a spot where a few large stepping-stones allowed their feet to stay dry. Overhead, the big blue Colorado sky had fluffy clouds scudding across its endless expanse. Jasmine almost felt relaxed for the first time in days. She resolved to go to bed early and resume her usual yoga routine tomorrow, well rested.

Rambo barked, bringing her back to reality. He was standing in front of a fence, obviously wanting to know if he should slip under it or walk along it. The fence told her she had to have been on Paula's land for several minutes. Hopefully she wouldn't be met with a load of buckshot right away. To be on the safe side, she decided to follow the fence for a bit and then turn back. She whistled up Rambo and they had just started moving when she heard a shout. She looked around and saw Paula running across the pasture toward her, waving. Waving was good, Paula couldn't wave and shoot at the same time. To be on the safe side, she took a step back as Paula thundered up. Her reddish-brown hair was askew, like she'd bolted out of the house.

"Wait."

"Yeah, yeah, no problem," Jasmine muttered softly. "Like I'd dare run away."

"You look pale. For goodness' sake, I just wanted to say hello—"

"The prospect of being shot has an effect on my circulation at times."

Paula's face fell. "I thought we cleared that up."

"You mean in the universal I-brought-you-coffee-and-biscuits language?"

"So you got them? Was the coffee still hot?"

Jasmine studied her face. It seemed like Paula actually cared.

"I did. And just in time. I was starving."

Paula's face relaxed. "I'm glad I could do you a good turn. Did you get back from your grandmother's okay?"

Jasmin's mouth fell open. "Are you clairvoyant?"

"No," Paula answered. "Jake called and said he'd taken you there."

"Right. That small-town communication thing. I still need to get used to it."

"We're friends now, aren't we?" Paula said, a little anxiously.

Jasmine considered her. "Who's going to say no to a friend who can handle a shotgun and deliver coffee and biscuits?"

A smile escaped Paula's lips before she regained her natural obstinate streak. "Better not get used to it. This service only comes around on special occasions."

Jasmine smiled good-naturedly.

"How are things inside the house? It was shut up for a long while."

"It's coming along. Things accumulate over a lifetime. Grandma always did hate to throw anything out."

"That's her generation, yes."

"It's not a hoarder house or anything, there's no garbage—"

"Let me give you a hand."

"Oh no, I can't have you—"

"Of course you can. The barn can store everything. You need room to maneuver."

"Well, I mean, right now?"

Later, I have to go to high school. Softball practice is starting up again and I'm the coach. I coach the girls."

"Wow. I'm impressed. I wouldn't have guessed you liked working with kids."

Paula shrugged her shoulders sheepishly. "It's not a big deal. I played softball myself in high school. Besides, they're not little kids, they're teenagers." She let her gaze wander off. "I remember very well what it's like to be fourteen and feel like the whole world doesn't understand you." She turned her gaze back to Jasmine. "Yet I come from a big loving family. Imagine what it's like when that's not the case."

"Then you also have kids from difficult backgrounds on your team?"

Paula nodded. "Not exclusively, but some. I was just trying to say, though, being a teenager is hard. And while a lot of teachers act like they've never been one, I can empathize with them pretty well. Otherwise, I treat them more or less like my dogs and horses. Friendly, but firm. It works pretty well." She grinned.

Jasmine also had to grin. "I'm going to assume that you phrase it a little differently for the parents."

"Sure. I'm pragmatic enough to take advantage of a little diplomatic psychobabble. You're welcome to come watch us work out these days. You might even have some tips for our post-workout stretching."

BLIP! Jasmine's phone sounded in her pocket. She fished it out. It was Gavin. *Can we talk? Please?* It was time for the showdown.

"Gotta go, Paula. You're a mean biscuit slinger, I'll give you that." Jasmine gave the friendliest smile she could muster and followed Rambo as he bounded in the direction of the house.

CHAPTER SIX

ONCE INSIDE, she got Rambo settled with some fresh water and a treat. Then she hauled the garbage bags full of clothes upstairs and set them beside the closet. That was a chore for later. She sat on the side of the bed, took a deep breath, and clicked Gavin's number. He answered on the first ring.

"Jaaaaaz, babe, where you been?"

"Gavin, I'm not going to answer questions. You are."

"Did you listen to my messages? I explained it all out."

"As a matter of fact, I didn't. I've been in too much shock."

"Over what?"

Jasmine grunted. "Over getting held up in my own apartment, maybe?"

"Baaaaabe. We were *acting*. It was a scene from acting class. The guys thought you were an actor, too, and decided to improv."

Jasmine was too stunned to respond. "Acting class?"

"You knew all about it. Remember the cash you gave me for Benjamin Alderichberg's masterclass series? It's part of that! We're helping to develop the script."

"With real guns?!" She jumped off the bed and started to pace the room. Rambo appeared in the doorway and stayed standing to watch.

"Real? Who said anything about real? Those were stage props. We had to sign them out and everything. They're going to be used in the show."

"The show? What show?"

"At the Seatac Playhouse in August. The venue is already booked. If you had just slowed down and not run off—"

Jasmine massaged a temple with her free hand. This was all so…

"Come on, Jaz, where are you? Come home. I want everything to be like it was."

"What about soft-boiling me? What about my money and all that?"

"It was already in the script!" Gavin's voice rose in frustration. "The character was talking about his girlfriend. Not you!"

"Let me think about this," she hissed into the phone, and hung up.

She threw herself on the bed and beat it with her arms and legs. Her nails tore at the patchwork quilt. She bit the pillow and then screamed into it.

Rambo watched everything with surprise.

Jasmine snatched up her phone again and clicked the most recent call showing. It dialed.

Gavin picked up immediately.

"What about the cop?" Jasmine shouted.

"What cop?"

"The cop at the police station. You were talking to him. Very buddy buddy."

"You were there?" he said, incredulously. "What were you doing there?"

I was about to report you, hung wordlessly in the silence between them.

"For your information," Gavin snapped, "he's an actor, too. He's in the play. We were letting him know you might come by."

A sob convulsed out of her.

"I was trying to help you, Jaz," he said, "from looking like a blond idiot."

She flinched.

"I was trying to save you from being embarrassed. Do you believe me now?"

She hiccuped in response.

"You were supposed to be at work. You weren't supposed to surprise us."

All the air went out of Jasmine. It was true, Gavin had signed up for expensive acting lessons with a master coach. Her bank account was lighter because of it.

"Just come home," he said, softly. "What about Keith? Are your clients covered?"

Jasmine mumbled something about Caitlin.

"I'll go and talk to him. I'm sure he'll be reasonable. When can you be back?"

"I'm at Nana's—"

"Out in Colorado for crap's sake? In that cow town? What was it called?"

"Independence Junction. Independence for short," she sniffed.

"Leave now."

"I can't leave now. Nana expects a visit."

His tone changed. Soothing. "Then take some time. Relax. Come home feeling good." His voice dropped in register. "Don't forget I love you, Jaz."

And before she could stop herself, she said it too. "Love you, Gavin." From his end, the call disconnected.

Rambo gave up his sentry at the door and entered the room. He walked over and licked her hand. "You like him, too, huh?" she said.

Miss Minnie Walker's diner was an institution in Independence. Her sister, Miss Daisy, ran the bed-and-breakfast. Together they covered all the dining and hotel needs of the little town. Because of their two names, everyone called them the Disney Sisters. Rather than being offended, they wore the name like an honorary title. It was easy to underestimate them. They were both rather short and portly, their white hair up in a bun, and they exuded a motherly caring. But woe to anyone who did not behave according to their very own code of conduct. Then a steely backbone emerged. Since practically all the residents stopped by at least once a day, whether as guests, employees or suppliers, they were always well-informed. Even the NSA could learn something from them.

Jasmine pulled up in front of the Clothing Donation bin right next to the diner. Sorting clothes out of the bags at home, right after Gavin's call, gave her time to think. There wasn't much in the bags that suited her, but the items that did were serviceable. She had salvaged a couple of pairs of leggings that would tide her over a few days, sweatshirts, T-shirts, socks, and a beautiful feminine dress in soft yellow that was bound to please Gavin, since he complained about her lack of dress-wearing on a regular basis. All she had to do was pick up some underwear and a sports bra in town, and she'd be set for the rest of this short trip.

She heaved the green bags into the bin and shut the pulldown door with a *clang*. Backing the Prius behind the bin, she made sure she didn't block anyone's access. Essentially, she was parked right outside the door of the diner. *Enjoy it*, she told herself. *You'll never find parking like this back in Seattle.* Snapping Rambo's leash into his collar, Jasmine guided him out of the car, and then hopped up the steps onto the diner's porch and eased through the swinging doors.

Years back she'd gotten in good with the Disney Sisters. They were dog-friendly, and they were always a dependable resource when you might need something, whether it was a place to stay, food, or information. As long as you were honest with them, paid the bill, and left a tip, all was well. Oh, and one more thing; lived life according to their ideas. The sisters often dispensed life advice and direction, whether it was a relationship that they felt needed a new lease on life or some other situation. She experienced all of this firsthand as a kid.

Whenever Jasmine spent summers here at Nana's in Independence, she often hung out at the diner. That was the place where, at least until nine, there was something resembling a nightlife, and also the place where there was always sure to be something to eat. Nana had many good points and wondrous qualities, but cooking regular meals wasn't a strong point anymore.

The minute she crossed the threshold, Miss Minnie gave a joyful cry and pressed her against her impressive bosom.

"Child, what took you so long!"

Jasmine tried to answer, but after her face was lost somewhere in the fullness of the patroness of the restaurant, it proved impossible. Fortunately, Miss Minnie didn't seem to expect an answer.

"I already baked your favorite pie today. Apple cinnamon. By the looks of it, not a moment too soon." She held Jasmine an arm's length from her and eyed her disapprovingly. "Tsk, tsk. Always these young women with their diet craze. Way too skinny. Yet everyone knows that men like something to touch!"

After this pearl of wisdom, Minnie slid her lost-and-found foster daughter onto one of the red vinyl-covered chairs.

Jingling Rambo's leash Jasmine asked, "Is it okay if he comes in, Miss Minnie?"

The dear lady turned exuberantly to the dog. "We don't want the place full of critters, but he looks clean and well-behaved. Besides, this is a special visit." She led the way to a booth where Rambo plopped down on the floor, under the table. Jasmine bent down to scratch his big fluffy ears.

"You definitely like it better here than in the big city, don't you, big guy?"

He panted, pulling up the corners of his mouth slightly so it looked like he was smiling. She grinned back.

"Sorry to disappoint, but it looks like we're going back to Daddy." *We're just going with the flow*, she told herself.

Miss Minnie snapped her out of conversing with the dog by placing a piece of the still-warm apple pie in front of her and filling a cup with steaming coffee.

"Now eat." Miss Minnie patted her back solicitously before putting down a bowl of water for Rambo. She turned her attention to another guest.

Jasmine had just shoved the first bite into her mouth—a burst of warm fruit and buttery sugary pleasure—when Minnie turned around again.

"Unless you're going to stay," she boomed.

Jasmine laughed. "Maybe when I retire." Even the thought was making her homesick for Seattle, and as she said the words, she knew something was wrong. Something inside her heart. It was that unfinished business with Gavin. Wrapping Rambo's leash around the table leg, she slid out of the chair and hurried back to the restroom. It was spotless and smelled of potpourri. The frosted window was open a crack to let in the pristine air. On autopilot, Jasmine pulled out her phone and looked up SeaTac Playhouse. Clicking the tab marked Show Schedule she blinked as the box popped up: *The SeaTac Playhouse is closed for renovations. We look forward to seeing you for our Christmas Voices program when we reopen.*

She attached the link to a text and sent it with no explanation to Gavin's number. He wouldn't need a text to feel the scathing anger behind the message.

She had just sat down again at the table when *BLIP!* an answer came back.

It just happened. We're looking for a new venue. For sure we're getting our deposit back from the playhouse.

So. There. Her intuition knew. *It didn't seem like an answer from a guilty man,* she thought. A guilty man would protest, come up with something elaborate. Maybe the website had just changed its notice. Possibly. Gavin still deserved the benefit of the doubt.

Or did he?

She finished her pie and resolved to drive to Nana's where she'd tell the whole story. But after a huggy goodbye to Minnie, as soon as she was in the car, she pulled her phone back out and did a search for the name *Benjamin Aldrichberg*. His website had an email contact form to fill out, but there was also a phone number.

The elderly thespian picked up on the first ring. Jasmine figured at the prices he charged, he probably wanted to catch customers "while they were hot."

"Benjamin Aldrichberg," a smooth, time-mellowed British voice intoned.

"Hello Mr. Aldrichberg. This is Jasmine. I'm calling about the play."

"Oh yes, my dear. Nice to hear from you. What can I do for you?"

"I was wondering what new venue you were looking for—for the play."

"Oh yes, the play." He paused.

Jasmine felt her heart rise a little. Of course Gavin was telling the truth. The kindly old man was going to sort this out and put everything back to rights.

"What play, my dear?"

"The play that the acting group is workshopping. The script—my boyfriend, Gavin Smith, is part of that group. And I saw that SeaTac Playhouse just close—"

"Gavin Smith you say?"

"Yes, Gavin. Blond hair, about twenty-five." She trailed off.

"Gavin Smith, Gavin Smith…" the thespian mused. "No, I don't know of any Gavin Smith."

Jasmine felt the bottom drop out of her stomach. Words failed.

"My dear? Are you still there?"

"Yes." It was a dry little croak.

"Are you aware that the SeaTac Playhouse has closed for renovations? There are no plays going on, or being workshopped. In fact, I am on hiatus."

"But what about Gavin Smith? You don't remember him? Maybe there's a list, just to jog your—"

"My dear, I know all my students. There is no Gavin Smith." He must have heard her choke on some tears because he added, in a kindly voice, "I'm very sorry."

BEEEEEEEP!! HONK!

Lower Queen Anne was bustling as Gavin hopped off his shiny new e-bike outside the yoga studio. The citizens of Queen Anne were out and about; driving, bicycling, jogging, eating, and dog walking. Gavin leaned the e-bike against the sidewalk bike rack, and peered into the storefront glass of the studio to see who was inside.

As soon as he got Jasmine's last text, Gavin knew that the acting story might not hold. He had to get Jasmine back to Seattle, but he also had to get his hands on her money since the counterfeiting scheme was a little harder to get off the ground than he'd realized. The best way to do that was to get her to transfer cash out of that savings account of hers into her own checking account, which he *did* have access to. But there was no money in the checking at present, she'd emptied it before she ran.

He put his hand on the door of the yoga studio, imagining the things he was about to say to Keith, the owner. Words like *mentally unstable*, *stress meltdown*, and *emotional wreck* came to mind. After all, Keith had proof Jasmine had run away from her job. Now, Gavin needed that job gone. Because if Jasmine had no job, she had no income. And when she had no income, she'd have to transfer the dough into the checking account to *get* it. And then he could grab it.

With a suitably serious look on his face, Gavin breathed in the exhaust-perfumed air of the busy street, and walked into the studio.

Jasmine had been crying inside the car, behind the Clothing Donation bin, for going on an hour. Sooner or later somebody would come along who recognized her, maybe even that cocky sheriff with his smart remarks about yoga pants. She simply had to pull herself together. She wiped her eyes and searched for messages or texts from Caitlin or Keith. There were some, but they were old. The story seemed to have morphed into being called home to Colorado all of a sudden. Family emergencies did happen, after all. Nobody had texted in the last twelve hours.

On a whim, she went to the Queen Anne Yoga website and browsed the team page, looking for her picture, her bio, any touchstone that anchored her to the life she lived in Seattle. But there was nothing. Her picture had been taken down, all traces of her name and job were scrubbed. Something beyond her control seemed to have made a decision. A final decision.

Her life in Seattle was over.

She bowed her head and wept while Rambo whined.

CHAPTER SEVEN

ONE WEEK LATER

The homeless child had drifted around the homestead community for a week now. Well-filled garbage cans were stocked with plenty of good edible food, and as long as she let the animals get used to her when they were outside, before walking into their hobby barns, they didn't spook or give her away. The cold nights were difficult to deal with and that's why she had this particular homestead picked out as a good place to hole up. The next acre away was a huge, semi-occupied old place, but it was locked up tight as a drum. Besides, there were no animals to keep the barn warm, and no garbage cans to snack from.

The place was a newer, much smaller house. A woman lived there. A woman with a shotgun, who was often away from the house for hours at a time, just like she was now. Then, the girl was free to nap in the warm barn, drink water, and eat whatever she'd pilfered from the garbage bins, in privacy.

The girl crept closer to the paddock where an old Quarter horse and a Shetland pony whisked at flies together. When the palomino Shetland saw her it broke away and danced sideways across the paddock, tossing its cream mane and tail, which contrasted with its butterscotch coat. With a little whinny it bucked its back legs out.

FAAAAAAAART!

The girl rolled her eyes. Horses and their high-spirited farts. They came with the package.

She held out a small handful of feed and the animals ambled over to take the snack. She was family now, as far as they were concerned, so they made no move to stop her as she slipped through the railings of the fence and walked across their enclosure to the barn. Cradling a half-sandwich rescued from the trash, she disappeared behind the sliding barn door. The horses went back to sniffing at the dirt under their feet, and watching the acres of pasture behind them.

Inside the four-horse hobby barn, the girl seated herself on a bale of straw and tucked into the sandwich. It was filled with tuna salad, and the bread was only a little stale. The lettuce was wilted, but still green and not turning rotten at all. She devoured it and then licked the plastic wrap clean of every smudge of mayo. She balled up the wrap and tucked it into her pants' pocket. "Leave no trace" was the way she operated, and how she remained undetected for such a long time.

The girl went into an empty stall and kicked a layer of straw into the corner to make a bed. She lay down, breathing in the smell of sweet hay and clean animals, and slept. She was fourteen years old.

Jasmine scrolled her phone through the list of moving companies that serviced from Seattle to Colorado. The prices were making her seasick. They wanted thousands for the trip. She needed her things around, and she needed to be done with the apartment shared with Gavin. But getting her things packed and moved was going to take a chunk of money. A chunk she needed, as she was now out of a job and looking at setting up a new venture in Independence.

Needless to say, Nana was on cloud nine. But Nana had the sanitized version for her staying, not the unvarnished unpretty version.

She and Rambo had established their morning routine. As soon as Jasmine rose, she greeted the first rays of sunlight that ventured over the surrounding mountain peaks with sun salutations. Then she sat on the porch with a cup of tea while Rambo held his own version of a morning ritual that involved all the trees in the immediate area. She hoped the cottonwoods that grew near the creek and the surrounding gnarled pines were strong enough to handle the intimate dog attack.

She'd already had a conversation with Pat and offered to pay him to rent a van and move her stuff out. Pat had the freedom—as a self-employed architect with his own small business—but he needed to be in Seattle to "rustle up" business, as he put it. His words rang in her ears, "The booming economy hasn't gotten around to me yet."

Then she sat with Nana's project for a while. Until now, she had not made it her own. Nadine was very careful to ask only in the most casual way about her progress with the project. Jasmine appreciated that very much. She didn't appreciate the many new ideas and suggestions. If she heard the phrase, "We thought you could also…" one more time from Nana, she would scream. Most of all, it made her want to hurl all her misgivings at them. But of course she didn't. They meant well and only wanted to help.

When she was stuck, she tried to find inspiration in a short meditation. But since she definitely lacked the inner peace to do so at the moment, her thoughts tended to dash in all directions like a group of chickens gone wild. Refuge at Nana's old house offered a place of peace and quiet but she couldn't successfully apply the serenity to herself. It was frustrating.

Stubbornly, she returned to the list of moving companies on her phone until her head was smoking from all the potential problems and obstacles that came up. A round of power yoga was definitely needed in the near future.

Paula, who had lent a helping hand to move more clutter over the past few days advised, "You need to talk to your grandmother. Tell her and Nadine your worries. Otherwise you'll burst."

When Jasmine complained about not being able to say anything in public because of the town's "bush phone" Paula rolled her eyes and said, "Might not be the worst thing for them to find out you're too much of a coward to voice your concerns."

"I'm not," Jasmine claimed irritably.

"You are! I admit that a dose of your composure and restraint would do me good. But what you're doing—keeping it all bottled up and going in circles mentally—that's not healthy either. Every once in a while you have to be able to pound the table and stand up for what's on your mind. Your version of that is probably an honest conversation. However you go about it, just do it. It's high time."

Jasmine could feel her spirits sinking and she couldn't afford that. Her mindset had to stay buoyant; had to keep moving forward. She whistled up Rambo from where he was snoozing on the floor and headed out to the diner.

Just walking in the door gave her a lift. The Colorado Caffeine Company serviced the cafe with fresh-roasted beans every week. The smell was heavenly. Fruit pies were cooling on the counter and pancakes sizzled on the griddle. Daffodils and tulips adorned every table.

So far, Rambo had not worn out his welcome, so Jasmine walked him in on the leash, and let him settle at the counter under her feet.

"Cuppa joe?" Daisy called out.

"Tea please, Miss Daisy," Jasmine answered. She noticed a man also sitting at the counter, at the end, watching her. He was a dapper little man, at least in his eighties, with a neat mustache. Rather formally dressed for a diner. He wore a bow tie. He knew she'd caught him looking, and he spoke. "Isn't that Rose McArthy's granddaughter?" he said in a clear voice. "I believe it is," he said in answer to his own question.

Jasmine smiled and nodded politely. This was Mr. Wilkinson, the unelected mayor of Independence, and at least as well informed as the Disney Sisters. "How are things going, sir?" she said.

He came around and slid onto a closer stool. "I have good problems, young lady. Do you know what those are?"

"Not really," Jasmine answered honestly.

"It means the good things have brought in newer problems, better problems than you ever expected," he said.

"Ah yes," she said. "I guess I know all about that."

Without waiting to be asked, he described his problem. "You see, I have a big beautiful house that was once the envy of the town. Now it's falling apart and needs fixing."

Jasmine winced and took a big sip from her teacup. "You need a painter and fixer-upper guy to lend a hand?" she asked.

"Painting alone wouldn't do any good. I should burn down this bottomless pit. But I just can't bring myself to do it," he concluded with a melancholy smile.

"What's the big deal?"

"It's old. Urgently needs to be restored from the basement to the roof. But I would need an expert who cares about old houses as much as I do." He shook his head. "I had two fellers come out from the big city. They said the house just wasn't worth it. As if everything only had monetary value. All the memories that live in that house are priceless, don't you think?"

"I do, I really do," she murmured. A memory surfaced; Nana said Mr. Wilkinson was loaded. An idea was beginning to take shape.

"I see that look in your eye, whippersnapper. What's on your mind?"

"Of course old houses are worth preserving if they have sentimental value or preserve cultural history," she replied.

He nodded. "Exactly. And this house offers both. But those idiots from Denver and Boulder didn't understand that." Vehemently, he put up his cane, as if to add weight to his statement.

"I do know someone, an architect, who specializes in old houses," she began.

The old man's expression focused like a laser. "Is he any good?" he asked. A sharp mind showed in the flash of his eyes.

"Absolutely," she confirmed with a laugh. "Otherwise, I wouldn't recommend him. And he knows all about getting old places named as cultural landmarks, too. Sometimes there's even funding to restore old places like that. I've been trying to get him to come out to Independence for a visit. This might tip him over the edge."

"You give him my number, young lady." Mr. Wilkinson snapped a business card out of his pocket and handed it to her. "Tell him to call anytime. I've got one of them answering machines, acts just like a secretary. Answers the phone when I'm not there. Technology nowadays, huh?"

"Agreed," she chuckled.

"My friend lives and breathes projects like this," she said.

"Well, tell him to call me up. Maybe we can get him to come out and see the old woodpile." He stood up, lifted his hat in farewell and left the diner.

Before the town's elder statesman cleared the threshold, Jasmine clicked a picture of his business card and texted it to Pat with a message.

The girl could hardly believe her luck. By chance, she'd seen where the woman left a spare key to the house. Right outside the front door on the porch, under a ceramic plant pot. The woman's name was Paula, she knew that much by now. She also knew the names of the dogs and horses. Her book, which she guarded like her treasure and carried around in her shabby little bundle, she had read so often that by now she knew it by heart. So she had nothing to do all day but observe her surroundings and hide when someone was around. In the process, she learned all kinds of things. Like, for example, that today was the ideal opportunity to sneak into the house and take a warm shower. Her first in ages.

With a shudder, she thought back to her last wash in a filthy shower at a truck stop. By a hair, some pervert had caught her there. Fortunately, she kicked him in the balls and was able to get away. Yesterday she had laid low all day, not even daring to get food out of Paula's trash can. Her fear of being caught was too great. But today, Paula seemed to be away for an extended time. For a homeless girl who could hardly stand the way she stank, the temptation of a hot shower was great.

She stepped out of the barn and squinted in the bright light. The sun was shining while clouds chased across the sky. Goats grazed in the adjacent pasture, talking back and forth with their funny bleats. She let out a low whistle. Barns and Roo, Paula's blue heeler dogs, chased around the corner and greeted her as if she were a longtime friend. She crouched down and let them lick her neck while she scratched their thick black-and-gray coats. "Well, are you going to let me in the house?"

She really hoped the dogs accepted her enough by now. Otherwise, she could forget her whole lovely plan of warm water and cleanliness. With her heart going pitty-pat, and a dog to her left and right, she walked around to the front of the house and tipped the plant pot up. A key glimmered against the wooden floor of the porch. The dogs watched her with attentively pricked ears, but could not be persuaded to come inside. With a shrug of her shoulders she entered, nerves jangling.

Before going further, she slipped off her well-worn sneakers and continued on her way in socks. No one was there, she knew that positively, but the fear of being caught was so deeply ingrained that she tiptoed. She passed the kitchen. Her eye stopped on the fridge. What could it hurt just to look? Way at the back, almost forgotten, was a takeout container with a cold meatball and a side of noodles—a feast. Would Paula notice it gone? If the plastic container disappeared entirely, would Paula miss it? Or might she think she'd left it somewhere, or already thrown it out? There was lots of other food in the fridge, it seemed like this would be easy to forget. Her stomach let out a hungry growl. The decision was made. She tore the lid off the container and devoured everything.

In the second bathroom—not the bath that Paula actually used by the looks of the shampoo and toiletries there—but a second, guest bathroom, she pulled the door shut and locked it. Curious, she looked around. The floor was wooden, just like the rest of the house. The walls were covered with iridescent blue-green mosaic tiles, contrasting nicely with the white sink and a shower with glass doors. On the floor was a fluffy carpet. But the nicest thing about the whole bathroom was that it was clean and warm. She suppressed pangs of guilt and pulled a towel from the shelf on the wall. Quickly she got rid of her clothes and slipped into the shower.

Ten minutes later she was ready and stood in the hallway, wrapped in the large bath towel. In her hand she carried her crumpled dirty clothes. Could she dare locate the washing machine and clean her clothes? She was a little worried about the length of time it would take for the wash cycle and dry time. But did she have the stomach to put those dirty clothes back on, clean as she was now? The desire for cleanliness finally outweighed the fear.

She found the laundry room. She'd seen steam rising from the vent outside when Paula did her wash. She pressed a few buttons at random, added some detergent, and hoped that the results would be clean and her clothes would be about the same size as before the wash. She threw in the bath towel, too. She could have it washed and dried and replaced in the bathroom in a jiffy. Maybe as a thank you she could keep an eye out for little jobs around the place that would go unnoticed by Paula. The first thing she would do in the bathroom would be to remove all traces. With any luck, Paula wouldn't even notice that anyone had been in the house in her absence.

A giggle escaped as she remembered the fairytale of the three bears. The bears came back from a walk and found someone had been eating their porridge and sitting in their chair. Now, she had to be careful that she didn't fall asleep for too long, like Goldilocks.

CHAPTER EIGHT

JASMINE WAS ON THE WAY to the diner restroom when *BLIP!* a text came in from Kathrina. *Can u talk?*

Jasmine called her back right away.

"Finally! Did you lose your phone? Or my number? I've been trying to reach you."

Jasmine was alarmed at the urgency in her friend's voice. Kathrina was a decidedly calm person who rarely got upset about anything.

"Gavin was here."

"Gavin was with you in the salon?" Jasmine felt a thrill of fear go through her.

"Yes. He wanted to know if I knew where you were and if I had a phone number for your grandmother. I didn't, of course."

"What reason did he give you?"

"He couldn't reach you and went on and on about love, and then he was babbling something about you owing him money." She paused meaningfully. "I found it a little hard to believe."

"Kathrina," Jasmine interrupted. "Gavin and I are done."

"Done as in over? Finito? Kaput?"

"Stick a fork in it, done."

"What a relief this is," Kathrina said with obvious emotion in her voice. "I found the money part hard to believe, and I hope I can say this now that you guys are broken up. This freeloader never had any of his own. It didn't seem far-fetched to me that he couldn't reach you, since I sent a few texts myself without hearing from you. Only one thing was strange."

"What?"

"He asked questions about where you were, where your grandmother lives, and said he couldn't find a street address for her."

Jasmine laughed out loud. "I'm really sorry. When I left, I was so rattled that I just didn't manage to tell you everything."

Kathrina seemed to regain her composure. "After making such a big fuss, Gavin turned on his heel and left my place without another word. Very rude. So how are you? I mean, is it awful?"

"It was awful. Now I'm better. You never liked him."

"That's true, though. Since you already know that, I can congratulate you without being rude." Her voice became serious. "When are you coming back? It's just not the same here without Rambo's company."

"You miss my dog. And I was beginning to think you missed me."

"You know I miss you. So, when can I expect to see you?"

"Well, um…"

"That sounds ominous," Kathrina interrupted her. "Out with it, what is it? Did you fall in love and now you're staying there?"

"Nothing like that. Although I am going to stay here for a while. The place is something special, Kat. My grandmother isn't getting any younger either."

"I'm losing you and Rambo?" Kathrina sounded genuinely disappointed.

"Hey, you could take a trip to the Rockies and give my dog a haircut," Jasmine quipped, only half joking, because Rambo really did need a trim. Plus, she had an uneasy feeling in her stomach. If Gavin sought out Kathrina, about whom he hadn't said a single kind word during their entire relationship, he must be pretty desperate. And Jasmine didn't want to put her best friend on the spot. "I want you and Pat to come out here," she said impulsively. "I'll even pay the transportation.

"What? Did you win the lottery? "

"No, there's a catch."

"Hoo boy. Let me have it."

"All you have to do is pack up a few things at my apartment and drive out. I'll pay for everything and you both can stay with me."

There was a pause on the other end of the line. "An expenses-paid vacation to Colorado? To see an old friend?"

"We'd have such a good time." Jasmine held her breath, mentally assessing all the cleaning of grandma's place this would entail.

"I wouldn't do this for just anybody," Kathrine paused, "but you do send me a lot of your clients who have pets. I owe you."

"You do not. Those clients have money and you offer the bet pet care in Seattle. That's what friends are for."

"Tell you what, I could swing two weeks away if I call in some favors. If Pat says yes, I'm in."

Jasmine had barely hung up when her phone sounded again. She was pleased to see Pat's name on the display.

"Good to hear from you!" she said, moving Rambo to one side so he wouldn't be in the way of other diners.

"Thanks, likewise. I got a call from a Mr. Wilkinson."

"That was quick. Talk about the speed of light."

"When I saw your text I called him right away and left my number. I guess he's only five minutes away from the diner so he picked up my message and called back. And you're right. I'm interested."

Jasmine heaved a happy sigh. "Fantastic. That's what I was hoping for. Completely altruistic, of course."

Pat laughed. "I'd be happy to see you again, too. But other than that, there are a couple of other things in favor of me taking a look at this house he wants to restore. There's tension between me and my business partner."

"You mean worse tension than usual?"

"I guess you could say that."

Pat had been running his own architecture firm with a good friend for a few years. Although they worked well together and successfully built up the company as a team, sparks had flown over the direction the company should go. Pat's partner preferred prestigious new buildings. Pat's heart was set on special commissions and restoration of old buildings. Jasmine heard him start pacing on the other end of the line.

"We talked about splitting up. Splitting up the company."

Ever since she knew Pat, he had lived for this company. It had to be difficult, and she told him so.

"Of course it's a difficult situation. But quite honestly, it's also time for something to change. The constant discussions are exhausting for both of us. We waste so much energy with it that we should actually be putting into the company. It seems like we've reached a point where we have to make a decision."

"What are the options?"

"Either I adapt to his plans or he walks," he replied.

"What does he think he's doing?" she said indignantly, always ready to stand by her friend. "Without you, this company wouldn't even exist."

"Sure. But not without him, either."

"Sounds like you need a break. And you need some new business. Why not do both and come for a visit? And I have a special, secret incentive."

"What might that be?"

"Not only will I pay for the truck rental, and for all gas and expenses to get here, but—"

"But what?" He was chuckling now.

"Kathrina wants to come with you."

"She'll never leave her big dog."

"I'm telling you she's in. The dog's in too."

"How are you going to put us all up?"

"Believe me, I have a lot of square feet and more rooms than all of us could ever use." She bit her lips from adding, *and most of them are jammed to the rafters with stuff.*

"Wow, I have to see this."

"But what about Gavin? Isn't he at the apartment? How can we get your stuff?"

"He is, but he goes out for long periods of time. Sometimes he stays out all night. It won't be hard getting in. Kathrina's always had a key because she cares for Rambo as his dog sitter. All I want are my clothes, my books, my laptop, Rambo's chew toys. He's got an old stick he's using right now."

"But your furniture?!"

"I'm sitting in a fully furnished house right now. Over-furnished. The last thing I need is more furniture. Leave it for Gavin."

Pat sounded like he was warming up to the idea. "In two weeks, the Indie Music Festival will be on," he mused.

"What's that?"

"Mr. Wilkinson told me about it. You don't know about it?" Pat let out his woodpecker laugh. "Breckenridge has the film festival. Independence, in keeping with the name, has the indie bands. It's a big thing out where you are."

Jasmine just shook her head silently.

"You're speechless, aren't you?"

"Pretty much. I used to live on my phone. Now I live in a small town with an information network that makes the NSA look like amateurs."

"If Kathrina can swing it, we'll come in two weeks."

"That's the best news I've had all year."

"Bye for now."

She ended the call, leaned down, and ruffled Rambo's ears. "Did you hear? Your friends are coming to visit!"

Kathrina had a *Dogue de Bordeaux,* also known as a French Mastiff. A huge beast of a dog that wouldn't hurt a fly. Except maybe drool people to death. But that didn't bother her or Rambo. He turned on his back at the happy news and thumped his tail on the floor. "I thought you'd be happy to hear that," she murmured, obediently scratching his belly.

Gavin sat in front of the clothes dryer in the basement of the apartment he and Jasmine shared until recently. His partners in crime, Skinky and Aldo, stood guard at the laundry room door. This early there usually was no one else doing a wash, but there was no way he wanted anyone walking in with a dryer full of counterfeit twenty-dollar bills going round and round.

"I'm telling you, I got played," Gavin said, carefully examining the bills. "The yoga witch left me high and dry, no money. Ghosted with her old Prius to Colorado."

"That's harsh, dude. You should take all her jewelry and sell it," Skinky said.

"She's not the jewels type."

Aldo sighed. "Women these days," he said.

Gavin leaned closer to the dryer and tested the temperature of the door. "These bills, the quality…I think we can do better."

"Who cares?" Skinky replied, flexing his shoulders. "If the buyer is happy, it's good enough."

Gavin opened the dryer door a crack and let the bills flutter to the floor of the machine. He reached in and fingered a bill gingerly. "And the paper we're using. We should use linen stock. The kind they use for fancy resumes."

"As long as the serial numbers match, that's what's important," Skinky replied. "Paper, *schmaper*."

Gavin pressed "Start" and set the green bills fluttering around the dryer drum again. "I heard that really good stuff sells two for one. Not the twenty-five percent we're doing."

Aldo snorted. "That return means you're moving big money to dudes like the mafia."

"Come on, if we print a hundred grand we make fifty. That's the kind of bucks I'm talking about."

Aldo laughed and lit a cigarillo. He blew a smoke ring and poked it through the middle with his finger. "Dream on," he said.

Gavin watched the bills flip and fly. He was definitely dreaming.

"Now, don't go before you've had a piece of lemon tarte," Miss Minnie suggested, patting Jasmine's back solicitously, and setting down a plate brimming with flaky pastry and lemon filling.

Jasmine shoved the first bite into her mouth, and was trying not to moan loudly from sheer pleasure, when Rambo jumped up next to her and wagged his tail like crazy. She turned around. The sheriff had just walked in the door. When he caught sight of her, a delighted smile lit up his face. *O-o*, she thought. Now, as she felt all his attention on her, combined with his dazzling smile, she realized that she had definitely underestimated him. Before she had a chance to stop the fluttering in her stomach area, he sat down next to her at the counter. Her poodle was beside himself with joy but Jasmine's mind was spinning. *Jason, Jonathan, Jerry, what was his—*

"So, I hear you're staying?"

She eyed him out of the corner of her eye and swallowed the bite of lemon tarte. "Sure. Why wouldn't I?"

"I don't know, maybe because you were held at gunpoint the minute you got here?"

For a moment she froze, thinking he was talking about Seattle. How did he know about that? She saw the surprise in his eyes at her reaction and ducked her head. She didn't let on and made a throwaway gesture with her hand. "I already forgot. You can get used to anything," she concluded casually.

Jake frowned. Gone was the playful grin, replaced by a serious look. "What do you mean, 'you get used to everything'? Who gets used to having a gun pointed at them?"

"Just an expression," she answered.

"I hope you'd tell me if you had any trouble. In my experience, problems have a nasty habit of following people around."

"Don't worry, Sheriff. It was just a joke." Jasmine polished off the rest of her tarte and checked Rambo's water bowl to show she was on the verge of leaving.

"It's my job to get serious when I hear jokes like that." He put air quotes around the word "jokes" to show it was anything but.

The communication device on his belt sounded. "Possible disturbance on Old Mayhew Road," a voice said.

The lawman slid off the stool. "Later."

CHAPTER NINE

The afternoon was almost gone. Jasmine was in Nana's old house, and had just finished traipsing twenty-five more boxes of stuff down the stairs and out to the barn. Earlier she had registered online for unemployment benefits, and now she was sitting in the middle of the living room on a pretty rag rug, surrounded by a heap of papers and an empty bag of chips. Because her move to Independence was coming together thanks to Pat and Kathrina, she needed to look at Nana's plan for a resort and research the venture. She was trying to find the calculator app on her phone when Rambo leaped up and ran to the door, barking his head off. A moment later, there was a knock. *Who could that be?*

She got to her feet and did a quick check of herself. Her hair was gathered back not-so-carefully with a barrette. Chip crumbs stuck to the front of her old sweatshirt and she had dust balls stuck to her black tights. Not really socially acceptable. But she couldn't help that now. Whomever was standing at the door would have to settle for *what you see is what you get*, for better or worse.

Rambo suddenly stopped snarling and throwing himself against the door. He sniffed and woofed, indicating that he knew the person on the other side and had judged them as being non-threatening.

Jasmine peered through the small panes of glass that framed the front door, and almost jumped backwards. The sheriff! *What could that man want now?* She gave herself a second lecture about pulling herself together, took a deep breath, and opened the door. He was leaning against the porch post, relaxed. Six feet tall and wore his uniform well. She forced the thought from her mind.

"Hello, Sheriff. To what do I owe the honor of this visit?"

"Just call me by my name," he said easily. "It's less formal."

"Yes, errrm, okay, I will."

"If you remember it."

She stood there blinking up at him. "Of course I remember it. I've been told a half a dozen times."

"Then what is it?"

A few more blinks. She really wasn't pulling this off well. There was only one way to go—the truth. "What I mean to say is, I've been told your name on half a dozen occasions but I can't remember it just right now." She felt her cheeks grow hot.

"And I'm putting you on the spot. It's Jake," he said nicely.

"Well, Jake," she said, recovering her dignity, "is something wrong with Nana?"

"No, no. She did send me, but this is just a friendly visit." He picked up a large takeout bag labeled *Miss Minnie's*.

"Nana sent you with this?"

"Yes. I happened to be there, also ordering takeout, and they offered it to me free if I would run it out to you."

Relieved, she dropped her tense shoulders. A beat passed, and she realized that "just a friendly visit delivering food" in Independence was code for "I'm coming inside." Small town manners, you know.

She took a step back. An amused smile formed at the corners of her mouth. "Come on in," she said, pulling the door open wide. "Excuse the mess. I'm doing a little business research." She pointed her hand at the living room floor.

"I'm not here to take pictures for *Architectural Digest*."

They both laughed, and she noticed how white and straight his teeth were. The laugh showed he didn't take himself or life too seriously.

"I'm afraid I can't even offer you anything to drink," she said, leading him to the kitchen. Rambo trotted after them, nails clicking on the hardwood floors.

Jake hefted the bag onto the large kitchen table. "You know your Nana and Miss Minnie. They leave nothing to chance." Jake pulled out two condensation-covered bottles of beer from the bag and handed one to her. He raised an eyebrow questioningly. "I take it you drink beer?"

Jasmine reached for it. "Sure. Not often, but today I'll be happy to keep you company. I don't drink a lot of alcohol and my food is vegetarian."

With a feigned look of horror on his face, he handed her a takeout box. "Seriously now? That means I can eat all my own spareribs?"

"Exactly." She lifted a corner of the box. "And I don't have to worry about you stealing my sweet potato and cauliflower curry."

He opened his container and inhaled the aroma of his spareribs and fries with eyes closed. "Ah." He opened his eyes again and looked directly at her.

Amused, she shook her head. She felt flattered that he had taken it into his head to flirt with her. But sexy lawmen weren't on the agenda for the near future. She went to a bag on the counter and tossed a few treats in Rambo's empty food bowl to keep him busy.

"Let's eat," she said, opening drawers. "I haven't brought in paper towels yet, so we'll have to do with linen napkins. Nana's finest."

"Works for me," he said.

In companionable silence they turned to the food. After several bites and satisfying sips of beer, Jake said. "What's the reason for all the papers in the living room? Or is it top secret?"

Jasmine nearly choked on a piece of cauliflower. "In this town? Top secret?"

He chuckled around the bottle of beer at his lips. "Does this have something to do with turning the house into a kind of holiday place?"

"You already know about it? Of course you already know about it. Short answer, yes."

He was watching her face, as if what he saw pleased him very much. She knew her face was expressive, and a wide variety of emotions showed unfiltered on her features. It made her a bad liar. But she'd be fine if they just stayed on this train of conversation. She had nothing to hide. About Nana's plans, anyway.

"Rose mentioned once that she had hopes of turning the place into something commercial. But mostly she told everyone how happy she would be to have you around."

Tears sprang to her eyes. She tried to hide them, unconvincingly.

"What did I say?"

"My grandmother…Nana's so sweet. She's so good to me." She trailed off. She didn't dare mention how the kind words contrasted so with the upset she'd been through the last little while. They touched her heart. Which was a little bruised right now.

He touched her hand but didn't say anything.

"Is this part of the official sheriff's service—calming down hysterical newcomers?"

He seemed to check himself and let go of her hand.

She continued, "I actually… Please don't say anything. But this resort is a big project. Very big. I had a little studio more in mind. A yoga studio to start, and then maybe adding Pilates down the road. Nana has much bigger plans, I'm afraid."

"You could always start with the smaller project and move into the bigger one."

She dabbed at her eyes. "Yes, but I have to convince Nana. You know what she's like once she gets an idea."

"I do that," he said, with a wry smile.

She averted her eyes. "If Nana's idea was for a normal center with different classes each day, that's one thing. But what she has in mind encompasses so much more. For one, there's the business side. I can tell you all about Ayurvedic nutrition, but don't ask me about a business plan or even about more detailed bookkeeping. My bookkeeping consists of income and expenses and a big portion of hope that it will be right at the end of the month."

His gaze slid from her eyes to her full lower lip and lower to her cleavage. Jasmine grew warm. Very warm. Lacking a glib answer, she looked down at her plate.

Jake watched her reaction with apparent satisfaction. They both felt the sexual attraction running wild. His stomach muscles fluttered. For the first time in his life, however, he wasn't sure the attraction was purely hormonal. He enjoyed spending time with Jasmine, and he missed her on the days he didn't happen to run into her—as long as he didn't think about his hunch that she was hiding things from him. That thought sobered him and brought him back to the topic at hand. "Aside from your new plans, which I think are great by the way, how would you divide up the house if it did end up being a tourist destination?"

Jasmine reached for a pencil lying on the table. When he realized she was about to start drawing, he interrupted her. "Why don't we walk through the house and you tell me about each room and what you thought about it? That way it will be easier for me to understand."

At the same time, they put down their plastic takeout forks. Jake placed the takeout boxes inside each other and tossed them into the trash while Jasmine wiped down the table.

"Follow me." Leading him through the house, she showed him each room, commenting on what could be done. The ground floor would serve as a dining room and lounge. Of course, some renovations would be necessary.

The kitchen, for example, would need a complete overhaul. She noticed that he tactfully restrained from saying anything about how a few remaining rooms were piled with items. He deserved a gold star for that.

"I have no idea what regulations need to be followed or how the kitchen needs to be equipped. That's one of the things that gives me a headache. I like to cook, but I certainly don't plan to cook for ten guests every day." She shuddered.

"I thought nutrition was part of your knowledge?"

"I love to cook and, yes, I have a college degree in nutrition with immersion in vegetarian and Ayurvedic cooking. That doesn't make me a cook."

Jake nodded in understanding. "But working with your chef to create menu plans would be a possibility, wouldn't it?"

"Sure. But then we're already talking about the first employee. I know as much about that as I do about cooking for paying guests. Insurance, retirement funds, and everything else I haven't thought of until now. But never mind. Let's go upstairs and I'll show you the rest."

He followed her up the stairs, enjoying the fabulous view of her swaying hips. Once at the top, he was so distracted that she elbowed him in the ribs.

"Ow!"

"You're not listening to me at all. You were a hundred miles away." She looked irritated.

"Uh, sorry," he said, with a grin that made her realize quite clearly that it wasn't entirely true.

Jasmine frowned. "What were you thinking about just now?"

His smile deepened and he leaned forward until the tip of his nose almost touched hers. "That, my yoga princess, you don't want to know. At least not yet."

Her eyes widened in surprise when she discovered the hunger in his eyes, and she hastily took a step back. *Coward*, scolded a small voice in her head. Well, then, she was a coward. Arrogant as the statement was, he was right. Despite the strong physical attraction between them, she wasn't ready to do anything about it yet. A harmless flirtation was one thing. Everything else would have to wait for the moment. First she had to get her life together.

Amused, Jake watched as Jasmine picked up the thread of conversation, but the tips of her ears stayed red. "There are eight rooms up here that can be rented out to guests. Four of them already have bathrooms, the others would have to be retrofitted with them. Again, the kind of thing I have no idea how to accomplish or what permits would be required." She dared to give him a quick glance as she opened the room doors so he could look around. "In this larger room at the front of the house, we could do a guided meditation in the morning. It's on the east side, so you can catch the sunrise."

"Peaceful," he agreed as he glanced around the open rooms. She did not open the last door. Instead, she stepped into another one with a brick fireplace. *What was in the locked room?* Jake opened the last door. Unlike the others, this one was inhabited. It looked like a hurricane had swept through. It was Jasmine's own room. Which she had, wisely, not opened. She wasn't very neat, as could easily be seen from her open gym bag and the clothes scattered around the room. From her pink sports top to her socks, practically her entire closet was spread out in front of him. She winced.

"Where's all your stuff?" rumbled Jake.

"What do you mean? This is it."

He chortled. "Don't tell me fairy tales. I grew up with two sisters. No way that's your entire wardrobe."

"It is. It's all I need."

He was risking embarrassing her further, so he changed lanes. "Maybe I know someone who could help? With the smaller, yoga studio idea, at least."

She looked at him inquiringly.

"Maybe a realtor? Someone who knows about renting commercial space."

"That might be a good idea."

They abandoned the tour and went downstairs. Rambo seemed to think the departure was a sign that it was time for his evening walk and stood tail wagging and panting in the way.

"Is he waiting for something?" inquired Jake with interest.

Lovingly, Jasmine ruffled Rambo's curls. "Walking is what he wants. He's decided it's time now. Let me just get his collar and leash and we'll be right out to say goodbye."

Jake saw that he was not being invited. A walk in Jasmine's company would have rounded off the evening nicely. It would also have given a chance to learn more about her. He'd spent eight years in homicide in Denver and knew when people were hiding something. Not that Jasmine was hiding anything, but he made a habit of routinely checking out every new citizen of Independence. It didn't take long, and it paid to be prepared.

With Jasmine, that hadn't gotten him very far. She had no record. Aside from an apartment in Seattle whose lease apparently continued, and a seldom-used credit card, he hadn't found out anything. At first glance, she appeared to be exactly what she claimed to be: a twenty-five-year-old yoga instructor who had spontaneously decided to move closer to her family. Nothing unusual, then. But her flippant remark in the diner the day before about *getting used to being held at gunpoint* made him prick up his ears. So he'd decided to do a little more research. It had nothing to do with how much he liked her laugh and her well-toned figure in the tights and yoga pants she seemed to wear all the time.

"Thanks again for the food delivery service." She fidgeted a little, switching the leash from one hand to the other. Jake could tell she was nervous. As much as he would like to assume it had to do with the emotional tension that was so evident between them, he couldn't be sure. He put on his much-tested smile to reassure her and tapped the brim of his hat. "Miss Jasmine, the pleasure was all mine."

"Thank you, Jake."

"You remembered my name. All it took was some cauliflower and beer."

This time, her laugh was one hundred percent genuine.

Man, woman, and poodle traipsed back through the house, and Jasmine leaned against the porch rail as Jake sauntered to his truck. He got in, and she waved at the retreating vehicle. It finally disappeared at the slight dip toward the creek. She hoped he put her in touch with the realtor.

Over at the neighboring acre, Paula stepped out the door, the shotgun held loosely in her hand. Night was falling and her blue heelers were barking up a storm. She'd had that funny feeling of eyes on the place again. Frowning, she took a quick look at her barn. Both dogs were barking in the other direction. She cast her eyes in the direction of Rose McArthy's property. Jasmine was letting Rambo out. Roos and Barns didn't know them well enough yet to tolerate them close to what they considered their territory.

She sighed. Time for the evening tour of the stables. Normally she didn't do it until later. But today there was a thriller on TV that she didn't want to miss. She listened for a moment, heard nothing special. The call of a cardinal punctuated the peaceful evening quiet. The nearby brook murmured. Shaking her head, she started to move.

Paula opened the big barn door and slipped inside. The atmosphere was peaceful tranquility, only the chewing of the four horses at the big trough could be heard. Rufus, her old Quarter gelding snorted, while Dolly, the Shetland pony and undisputed boss of the small herd, nickered softly in greeting. The two young

Morgan horses that completed the herd were here for training, and not quite as communicative as her own two.

It took her eyes a moment to adjust to the dim light. A movement in the back corner by the feed room made her shoulder the gun.

"Who goes there?" she commanded.

"Are you crazy? You can't shoot in here," a voice answered.

Paula blinked. Had she stumbled into a parallel universe? This was her barn. She was still in charge here! And not some homeless person. At least she hoped it was just a homeless person and not a horse rustler.

"Put your hands behind your head and come out slowly," she urged the person still standing in the shadows.

"Only if you put the rifle away," came the answer.

She didn't even think about it. Briefly, the thought flashed through her mind that the voice sounded strangely soft for a homeless man, even if the words were spoken with conviction. *Who cares what kind of voice he has*, she thought, calling herself to order. Either way, he didn't belong in the barn. Impatiently, she moved the rifle barrel from side to side in a prompting gesture.

"No," the person yelled, leaping out from the corner so they came to stand directly between the barrel of Paula's shotgun and the horses.

Only now could she properly recognize the intruder. The person was small. With ratty hair and threadbare clothing. An oversized jacket on top of everything. And a knit gaiter was pulled from below the chin to under the eyes.

"What are you doing here?" Paula demanded.

"What do you think? I'm trying to stop you from shooting the horses right now!"

This answer threw Paula for a moment. "Shoot the horses? Why would I do such a thing?"

"What are you asking me? I'm not the one waving a gun around in a closed room," the vagrant replied snottily.

Paula put steel in her voice. "Don't worry, I always hit my target. And I can assure you of one thing, I wasn't aiming for the horses."

The person trembled. Only now did they seem to really become aware of the situation. The eyes flitted frantically from left to right in search of a possible escape route.

The panicked expression in the little intruder's eyes stirred Paula. In a kinder tone, she said, "Are you a kid? How old are you, anyway?"

"I'm a woman. I'm eighteen. I'm just small," the person said, defiantly.

Paula took a closer look at the dirty jeans with the rip above the knee and the stained T-shirt. The dark shoulder-length hair looked shaggy. The eyes flashed angrily. Her gaze contained a clear warning not to come any closer. A runaway, perhaps? A teen who had been knocked around a bit? She lowered the gun. "I'm impressed that you put the horses' safety ahead of your own." This was sincere. It was rare to see such a selfless attitude. Especially toward animals. "Are you the one who's been neatening up around here?"

"Yes. I brush the horses and sweep up. In exchange for sleeping in your barn." The woman's eyes softened.

For a moment, the alertness disappeared from her gaze as she turned to look at the horses. "They're so friendly," she said, so softly that Paula almost didn't hear. Rufus, who needed attention in any form in daily large doses, came closer and nudged the visitor with his soft nose.

Paula stepped closer to the two. "What's your name?"

The unexpected question made the woman move around. Right away, she was on guard again. Her slender body vibrated with tension. She looked like a deer, ready to flee at any moment. "None of your business!" she hissed.

"No name. Okay," Paula answered soothingly.

"So, can I stay the night? Please? I can be gone by morning."

"Don't be hasty. Maybe I can help you," Paula said. "Sure, you can stay the night."

Unexpectedly, the teen ran and rammed Paula with her body.

"Hey!" Paula cried angrily, rubbing her shoulder, which had banged painfully against a stall. But before she could recover, the intruder disappeared through the barn door.

Paula dashed outside in pursuit, but there was no trace. She bit her lips. One thing she'd seen as the teen ran past was a name stenciled on her backpack— Leslie. The comparison with the deer was definitely misleading. The girl had a blue heeler soul, that was for sure. Speaking of blue heelers, where were her two dogs anyway? Calmly hanging around outside, unconcerned. Why hadn't they notified her someone was in the barn? Why hadn't they run after the fleeing woman? The only logical explanation dawned: the homeless teen had not been here for the first time. The two dogs loved people, and they almost overflowed in their efforts to please each time they encountered them. Probably Barns and Roo were already her best friends.

Paula sighed. There was nothing she could do tonight anyway. She hoped the woman would come back and or hang out for another day. The night was way too cold to be sleeping outside in the rough. And she would make a sandwich or two, and leave them in plain sight but in a plastic food keeper so no critters could get at it, in case the woman came back.

And right after, she was going to keep that date with her favorite detective and a glass of whiskey. She had earned it after this scare.

CHAPTER TEN

THE REALTOR'S NAME was Brenda and she promised to show three possible spaces that might be suitable for a yoga studio. Jasmine was waiting on the steps of the diner with Rambo, since it was an obvious place to meet, park, and depart on the real estate tour together.

"There you are," a voice said.

That voice is familiar, Jasmine's intuition said. She turned to look. Today, she had no trouble remembering his name. "Jake!"

"I was beginning to think you had vanished into thin air like an elf. But I said to myself, that's impossible! And lo and behold, I was right. Like most of the time," he teased, with a twinkle in his eye.

"Because there are no elves? I didn't know that was common knowledge now," she teased back.

Theatrically, he clutched his chest. "I'm shocked, Jaz. Of course there are elves. Have you ever looked in the mirror?"

She shook her head and bit her lips to keep from laughing out loud. "You just can't turn off the charm, can you?"

He nodded, his expression tragic. "It's a cross I have to bear every day. But what can you do?"

"Are you harassing my potential tenant?" Another voice sounded behind Jasmine. She turned and caught sight of an athletically dressed woman in her fifties. She wore her auburn hair in a chin-length bob. Her moss-green eyes sparkled with warmth and intelligence. Although the color of her eyes was markedly different from Jake's, Jasmine knew immediately that she was looking at Brenda Carter, his mother.

Meanwhile, Jake put on an innocent face. "I would never do that, Mom. I was just reminding her about our date tomorrow. Since it's my day off." There was a silent challenge in the look he fixed on Jasmine.

Dang him. She couldn't very well turn him down for a date in front of his mother, especially if she hoped to rent a space from her. So she put on a fake smile and nodded affirmatively, while secretly vowing to get back at Jake. Maybe Paula had a tip on how best to go about it.

He hooked his thumbs into his pants pockets, clearly pleased with how things had turned out. "Good, then I'll pick you up at your house at noon."

"I would rather meet with you here. I don't know yet what my schedule will be tomorrow. While I may not be saving the city from daily doom like you, I still have things to do," she replied through clenched teeth.

The twinkle left his eyes. He squeezed her hand briefly. "I know that very well. Glad it's going to work out tomorrow." He pressed a kiss to his mother's cheek. "Have a great time. I'll be in touch."

As Jake left, Brenda casually commented, "I won't use it against you if you stand him up tomorrow."

Surprised, Jasmine asked, "Really? Why?"

"Let's put it this way, he's my son and of course I think he's wonderful for that reason alone. Along with his father and brothers, of course. But I'm not stupid. I realize that he usually has it way too easy with women. Jake restrains himself in Independence, but he used to be a real ladies' man in Denver. No wonder; he's nice, athletic, and not to mention wears a uniform well. But I'd hate to see him start up with you."

Concerned, Jasmine lowered her eyes. "Did I look like I wanted to start something?"

Brenda shrugged her shoulders in amusement. "A little. But I must confess, Paula has already told me about you. I seem to remember her mentioning that you were all right and kept her older brother on his toes. From the sound of it, she's forever in your debt for that alone."

Now Jasmine had to laugh. "Nonsense. Paula is exaggerating. And yes, now he's basically tricked me into making a commitment." She wrinkled her nose. "But I have to admit, I'm, how shall I put it, not immune to a ladies' man either."

"Honest you are, too." Brenda cast an appraising glance. "No wonder you get along well with Paula. I think we'll get along just fine. Come on, we have commercial space to look at."

Truthfully, Jasmine could have made any of the spaces they looked at work. But it was a matter of finances. She decided to tell Brenda the truth. "I know the rents are reasonable but I'm afraid of signing a year lease in case I can't make it." Her voice caught a little but she recovered.

Brenda looked thoughtful. "There is another possibility. It's not turnkey, it'll take some work, but there's a vacant older building on Main Street. I can probably get you six months free rent just for taking over the utilities. By that time you'll likely know if you can make a go of it."

"What?? I can't let you do that. If this is about Jake—"

"Don't you know realtors make these kinds of deals even in the big city? It's worth it if a business client gets up on their feet. They stay forever."

Jasmine could hardly believe her ears. In a minute they pulled up to the last place for viewing. Although the windows were blocked out with brown paper, on either side were shops with windows—eye-catching and well decorated—far from cheap gift stores for tourists. Up the street was a bakery, a stationery store, a hairdresser, a flower store with colorful creations, a second-hand store for designer fashion and a gallery for western art. This place had good visibility from the thoroughfare.

Brenda stopped the car and undid her seatbelt. "This is actually owned by my daughter," she explained. "Tyler is a dancer, modern dance, and currently touring with a troupe in Las Vegas. Her old dance teacher passed away a few years ago and left her this old studio. She held annual dance retreats here. It's been empty a while." Brenda strode onto the porch, fitted a key in the lock and rattled the old tumblers until they clicked the door open. Rambo trotted right inside.

"Follow me," Brenda said. "I want to show you the second floor." Brenda's heels clicked on the stairs and Jasmine followed her up to a spacious, empty studio.

"Two thousand square feet," the realtor said. "This upper floor offers more than enough space for your plans. It's already divided into three rooms."

Rambo sniffed out every corner as Jasmine turned in a slow circle and took in the old building. The sun's rays falling through the large windows made dust particles dancing in the air visible. She sighed happily. Finally, movement was coming into her life. And for the first time in a long time, she had the feeling that she was going in the right direction. Rambo walked into a patch of sunlight on the floor and plopped down. He seemed comfortable here.

"The smallest room you might want to use as an office, and a place to store materials," Brenda continued.

Jasmine peeked into the middle room. It could serve as a dressing room, and offered enough space for a children's corner and a lounge area with sofas. Clients could meet at the end of class and relax with a beverage. The largest room would serve as the teaching space. She stretched out her arms and gave a little spin. She already felt like dancing.

"You could occupy the second floor to start, for now," Brenda suggested. "The first floor can remain the way it is, unused."

"What about your daughter, Tyler?" Jasmine asked. "Won't she be coming home and want to use it?"

"Not anytime soon," Brenda assured her. "She's traveling all over America with her dance troupe and she's very successful. But with Tyler, you never know."

A knock startled them out of their thoughts. Rambo also sat up and folded his long ears forward.

"Yoo-hoo, Jaz, are you up there?"

Her dog lowered his head back to the ground, relaxed. He knew that voice.

"Nana? What are you doing here?" asked Jasmine guiltily as the top of her grandmother's silver hair appeared on the stairs. She'd been meaning to tell Nana that she'd been mulling a smaller start than a resort, but still hadn't had that conversation. Jasmine always put off any kind of confrontation that might disappoint people. Now she had no choice but to have it out with Nana in front of Jake's mother. When would she learn not to put these things off! Oh well.

"Morning Brenda," Nana said. Turning to Jasmine she stated, "I went to the diner where Miss Daisy told me you might be visiting the old dance studio."

Sure. This was pure Independence. No wonder there was no crime worth mentioning here. Not even two hours after every event, the whole town knew about it. "I should have guessed." Jasmine shook her head in amusement. "I'm sorry I didn't let you in on my plans. You probably think I just ignored your idea for the exercise resort."

Nana took a moment to answer. "I have to admit, at first I was a bit *affronted*. I mean, the opportunity of a lifetime on a silver platter…"

"I'll leave you two alone," Brenda said, and headed for the stairs.

"Wait, please!" Jasmine started. But Brenda was gone. "It's not like that," she said to Nana.

"I know, dear. That's what Nadine explained to me when I finally ran out of swear words."

"See? Nadine gets me. I knew I liked the woman."

"Haha. She pointed out that I didn't really listen to your concerns, I just brushed them aside with more and more ideas."

That was true. Nana had a habit of brushing past concerns so they somehow talked past each other.

"In any case," Nana continued, "I decided to take the opportunity to see what you were up to." She looked at the studio with an appraising eye.

Jasmine jumped in. "The thought of tackling something as big as the resort overwhelmed me. I want to start on a smaller scale. Gather my first experiences as an entrepreneur. Try out how I can cope with the pressure."

"Thank you for being honest, dear. I appreciate you so. And now I'm going to be honest with you."

"Sure, Nana. I haven't done anything wrong, have I?"

"Not at all. This is all about me. And Nadine."

Jasmine searched her grandmother's eyes. She didn't see any anger or frustration, nothing negative. Only love.

"Nadine and I are more than roomies," she began.

A slow realization began dawning on Jasmine. "More than…" she repeated slowly.

"Yes, dear, we love each other. Please tell me you'll accept us. Since Grandpa died…" Nana trailed off. She looked as though she was struggling for words.

"Nana, there's no need to explain. I love you exactly as you are. And I'll come to love Nadine, too." Jasmine figured this must have been going on for some time. How else could it be explained that their relationship wasn't the talk of the town? Maybe it had been going on so long it was yesterday's news to the townspeople.

As if reading her mind, Nana said, "Sleeping arrangements don't have to be public, dear. Some things are private, especially at our age."

Jasmine gave her a loving hug.

"Now back to your yoga studio," Nana continued. "Your idea is a good one. First, test out your wings. I'm sure you'll succeed."

"I'm going to have growing pains, Nana. I can feel it."

"No doubt. When you're ready to tackle this, I can help." She gestured around the room. "Cleaning, painting, sanding floors, whatever comes up."

"If I go forward there's a big general cleaning coming up." She counted off on her fingers what else needed to be done. "I need a new coat of paint, I need to have a logo drawn and a sign made for the downstairs window.

"But dear, I hear you have other things to do tomorrow."

"Other things?"

"Blue River? After the tips of your ears turn red, I assume it's true that the sheriff is taking you out tomorrow?"

Jasmine rolled her eyes. "He sort of tricked me."

Her grandmother shook with laughter. "My, my, have fun. Where is he taking you? To the drunk tank at the Independence hoosegow?"

"Very funny," she said, shaking her head, and pushing her highly amused grandmother toward the stairs.

"Brenda, I think she's decided," Nana called out.

Somewhere near Twin Falls, Idaho, on route 84, Gavin got tired of tailing the Good Value rental van that Pat and Kathrina were poking along in. They and their mangy dog were packed inside with Jasmine's belongings. He'd seen them go into the Seattle apartment and watched everything go out. Clothes, linens, girl stuff, books, mostly worthless crap other than the laptop, and it was possible he might be able to steal that back down the road.

Gavin pressed his foot down on the accelerator and passed the van in a flash. In seconds, he left them in a cloud of exhaust. He would get to that little cow town ahead of them, where Jasmine's Prius would stick out like a sore thumb. All he had to do was wait at the nearest cafe. She'd be by sooner or later.

CHAPTER ELEVEN

THE NEXT DAY Jake showed up at Jasmine's house in his civilian clothes; blue jeans and a black T-shirt with a jacket over the top. Strong arms encircled her at the waist. She smiled and leaned against Jake, "If it isn't my favorite sheriff!"

He kissed the back of her neck. "Being the only sheriff for tens of square miles, that doesn't impress me much."

"Hmm. As long as you keep doing what you're doing right now, you're not going to get a better answer. Because you're keeping me from thinking that way."

"That, on the other hand, is what I like to hear." He let go of her and spun her around to face him. "Ready?"

"I hope so," she countered playfully. "After not knowing what it is, it's hard for me to judge."

"Patience, patience. Maybe you should meditate on the ride or something?" he quipped.

She shook her head in amusement. It was strange. Gavin-the-jerk had always made fun of her yoga-influenced habits. His comments stung. In the end, she had learned to be careful not to mention anything to do with it. No wonder she and Gavin had nothing much to say to each other. With Jake, it was completely different. The quips between them were more friendly banter than serious clashes.

The first stop on their excursion took them to Jake's place. "Wait here for a minute. I just need to get a few things."

So, she waited. After ten minutes, the first thing he brought to the car was a picnic basket. A fishing rod followed. Less than enthusiastically, she concluded that they were probably going fishing. He went to the house a third time. She hoped he didn't bring more hunting paraphernalia. But when he came out, he was holding a long-legged black and white cat. Not a hunting weapon or tool. He handed her the cat through the window. "Here."

She accepted the wriggling bundle of fur. No sooner had Jake joined her in the car than the cat jumped onto his lap and started purring.

"You already have a knack for us girls," she said, shaking her head.

He laughed. "I'm sorry to disappoint you. Jimmy is a male cat. Neutered, to be sure, but still."

"Are we going fishing?"

"I'm fishing, you can let your feet relax in the water while you get to watch the champion here. He loves water and he loves to catch his own meal. I know you don't really eat animals," he added. "But I thought, possibly, this might be the one time you don't mind wild-raised, hand-caught trout? If not, there are more than enough salads and other things in this basket, graciously put together for me by Miss Minnie."

"Can I still think it over?" she asked cautiously. She didn't want to throw cold water on his plans. Not after he had obviously gone to so much trouble to plan this trip.

"I want to show you what I do for relaxation. Even if you don't like fly fishing or eating fish, I'm sure you'll like the scenery by the river and that little rascal there," he scratched the cat behind the ears, "I'm sure you will."

She smiled, relieved that he didn't resent her indecision. "That definitely."

"Relax. We'll be there in ten minutes. The Blue River runs alongside Breckenridge and it's spectacular." He pointed out the window. "That's the Ten Mile Range out there," he said, indicating a stretch of rocky mountain. "The top of the peak is nearly 13,000 feet."

She stretched her legs out and drew a deep breath looking at the vista. "Funny how easy it is to take this scenery for granted when you live here. It still takes my breath away when I get up in the morning. The trees standing so tall...the light that turns the Rockies red in the early morning."

He smirked. "Sometimes I forget you're such a city kid. Didn't you ever go fishing on the summer vacations you spent here?"

Nervously, she played with her sunglasses. "As a teenager, I had much more extreme views than I do now. Fishermen and hunters were lumped together with murderers."

"And today?"

"Today I see the difference. And, of course, I've grown older and, above all, wiser," she added with a twinkle in her eye.

"Phew. I got away with that just in time. Let me tell you about fly fishing. Light baits are used, such as flies. But since flies have practically no weight of their own, the line is too light to cast them just like that. So, an additional weight is attached to the fishing line. Which requires a special casting technique. Have you seen the movie *A River Runs Through It* directed by Robert Redford?"

"Yes. Now that you mention it. The pictures of those flying fishing lines were pure poetry," she replied enthusiastically.

He grinned. "Just you wait; you'll make a fly fisherman yet."

She contorted her face in exaggerated disgust and said humorously, "Maybe not exactly. Ethical and moral concerns aside, I'm not exactly eager to gut a dead fish in any other way." She petted Jimmy, who stood on her thighs, his front paws propped on the dashboard. His whiskers trembled with excitement. There was companionable silence in the car for a moment. Jasmine used the time to look out the window and sort out her thoughts. Why did she really not eat meat? Out of conviction? For religious reasons? For health reasons? Stop. Not only did she not eat meat, she also did not eat fish. Originally, because she simply couldn't bring herself to imagine that an animal had to die just so she could eat it.

She turned to Jake, "I'm sorry. But I'm really not going to eat fish." She searched for words. When she couldn't find them, she said simply, "I can't."

"No problem," he replied calmly. "But keeping us company in our barbaric endeavor, that's okay?"

"Yeah, sure. Absolutely. Far be it from me to try to force my beliefs on anyone. I'm not even sure I fundamentally disagree with it. Hunting and fishing ensure the continuation of species. Moreover, wild animals grow up free as the wind and suspect no evil when their hour to die strikes. That's a plus point, in my opinion. I just know I wouldn't be able to down a bite while thinking about that poor fish."

"That would be a shame," said Jake. "For the fish." He reached over to his cat and petted his back. "We'll keep our fish to ourselves, won't we, Jimmy?"

They drove in silence until the trees thinned out in front of them. In more popular parts of the river were anglers, canoers, and kayakers enjoying the natural splendor. But here, they had the river to themselves. Jake parked the car beside a shallow part of the river. Large, flat stones led from one bank to the other. Jimmy jumped out and made his way straight to the riverbank.

"Beautiful woman? Here's your seat." Jake handed her a rolled-up picnic blanket, snapping her out of her musings. They got out of the car.

"Where do you want me to sit?"

"That's up to you. My partner and I, we're going fishing."

"Where's Jimmy, then? Aren't you afraid he'll run away from you?"

Amused, he pointed to the river. "Does he look like he's trying to run away?"

She had to admit this was not the case. The cat hopped lightly from one stone to the other, and tentatively tapped the water with one paw.

"What happens if Jimmy falls in?"

"It'll never happen." He winked at her. "Don't worry. The water collects by the stones in little pools. The fish sometimes rest there because the river is calmer there. Optimal hunting grounds for Jimmy."

"You have an answer for everything," she returned with amusement. "Well, here goes, you two. I can't wait to watch you show off your manly skills."

"Aye, ma'am, we will. I have to get into the water a little further downstream. Otherwise the cat will catch my line again instead of the fish. He tried that last time."

She watched as Jake stepped into a pair of big ugly rubber pants. "I thought this kind of thing only existed in comic books."

"If I don't wear 'em, I'll get wet."

"So what? Anyway, I was hoping for a striptease from you, not for you to put on more clothes."

"You don't think my fishing pants are sexy?" he asked in mock horror.

"I hope this doesn't hurt your feelings right now but, *no*."

"You wait. Revenge is sweet." He gathered up his rod and got into the water.

She followed at a safe distance. A favorite joke for men was to throw her in the water. If she was right in her guess, she wanted to delay it until after dinner. She stopped and turned around when she heard an excited meow. She saw Jimmy slap the water with his paw and actually fling a fish into the air. With a clap, it landed on one of the flat stones.

"I don't believe it. Again," Jake grumbled, turning back in the river to admire his cat's catch.

"What? You just told me yourself he was catching fish."

"Sure. But Paula bet me that he would bring home the first fish. Now I've lost again."

"What did you bet on?"

"About the biggest catch of the day today. She thought my surprise idea was stupid anyway," he admitted. "Since you're a vegetarian, she thought this was off-target. But she figured that since you weren't going to eat any, she could have some."

Jasmine bit her lower lip when she saw how unsure he was about whether she would like it here. She liked this little glimpse into his sensitive side extremely well. An interesting and endearing contrast to the confident and decisive attitude he usually displayed. A dangerously appealing mix, she thought as she felt her heart do a little leap. She walked up to the shore and carefully ventured onto the slippery stones. When she reached Jake's level, she grabbed him by the shoulder. He was so focused on his four-legged fishing partner, however, that he hadn't even seen her coming, and turned abruptly at her touch.

As his shoulder turned away, she lost her footing, grappling for the first thing that came to her fingers as she fell. His shirt. Like slapstick, they fell into the water together. Jasmine resurfaced first. Coughing, spitting and cursing. Jake had more trouble, having to get out from underneath her first. When she finally noticed his predicament, she tried to push away from him and flee to shore. But a hand wrapped around her waist.

"Are you water-shy, Jaz?" asked Jake with a big grin on his face.

She gave him a nasty look. But when she saw him like that, dripping wet and in full fishing gear, she started to laugh, which he acknowledged with a raised eyebrow. But it didn't help. She just couldn't stop laughing.

"You know, if you felt like playing with water, you could have said so right away." He cast a meaningful glance at his clothes, which were clinging to his body. "Then I'd take my clothes off next time."

When she finally calmed down, she leaned her head against his chest, exhausted. "And here I was worried you were going to throw me in the water."

"You thought you'd beat me to it?"

"No." Their faces were only a foot away. Dangerously close for a kiss.

Simultaneously they both pulled back, out of breath.

He straightened up and lifted her into his arms.

"Hey, I can walk myself!"

"I know that. But I like it much better this way. And since it almost looks like Jimmy's the only one bringing home the fish-bacon today, I'll have to prove my manly qualities another way."

With Jasmine in his arms, he waded to shore.

CHAPTER TWELVE

Every large American city has a downside of town and Denver was no exception. In the cheapest room of The Colorandan, a shabby flophouse, Gavin lounged on a lumpy bed and nursed a hot case of burning anger. The worst news of his life had just been delivered. He'd tried to use his phone to transfer money from Jasmine's checking account to his, and the transfer was refused.

The sound of breaking bottles came from the alley below his room. A stray cat screeched. Gavin leaped up and shut the window with a thump.

Up until today Jasmine's checking account had remained empty from when she'd cleaned it out and ran. But a quick check via the bank's phone app showed she'd topped the account back up with cash very recently. Gavin was all ready to snatch some spending money for himself. Seeing money had him licking his chops in anticipation. But the app mysteriously stopped working. When he called the bank, customer service informed him that his name had been taken off the account. And the situation was permanent. He couldn't get his hands on Jaz's money if he tried.

More bottles broke outside and Gavin mashed a pillow over his ears to block out the sound. The little yoga witch was serious about leaving him high and dry.

She'd also let go of the apartment, and his rent was paid only until the end of the month.

To Gavin's way of thinking, there was only one thing left to take. Revenge.

That evening, Jake stopped in front of a quaint, white-painted house in Breckenridge. With its tidy flowers and trimmed bushes, it looked like any other modest family home. Curious, Jasmine peered out the window. "Where are we? I thought you were going to take me to dinner?"

"Don't worry. I won't let you starve," he said with a wink. "Let me surprise you." He got out and walked around the car to gallantly open the door for her. Not for the first time, she thought that these old-fashioned manners, considered out-of-date everywhere else, were very charming. It had to be the yellow dress. The dress she'd rescued from Nana's clothing donation. It was silk, beautifully tailored, and it clung to her curves in all the right places. She'd found a silk-and-wool shawl in Nana's closet in burnt orange with yellow trim. It looked gorgeous around her shoulders as a wrap. With a smile on her lips, she got out.

Jake was so enchanted by her smile that, without thinking, he brought her hand to his lips and pressed a kiss to the inside of her wrist. Jaz blushed. He shook his head, an amused smile on his lips. "Come on, let's go inside before I forget what we came here for."

It was a powerful feeling to be looked at by a man like Jake with such hunger in his eyes. For this time, Jaz decided to take her own advice and just enjoy the evening without worrying about possible and impossible consequences. Jake held the door open for her and she stepped into a room that resembled a large living room. It had been converted into a small fine-dining room. Four tables of smoothly polished wood reflected the subtle light of candles. Only one table by the window was still vacant. As Jake led them to it, a man wearing a white bib apron came out of the kitchen and greeted them.

"What do my eyes behold?" the man said theatrically. "The long arm of the law, the sheriff himself. I didn't believe my wife when she told me you had a table reserved for tonight." He waggled his eyebrows meaningfully and added in a stage whisper, "In the company of a beautiful woman, at that. Aren't you going to introduce me to her?"

Jake looked tickled by the humorous greeting. "Jasmine? Meet Frank, our host for this evening."

She gave him a warm smile.

Jake helped her off with the wrap and Jasmine saw him taking in the yellow dress like he was inhaling with his eyes.

"I've been racking my brain all day," Frank said teasingly, "on how to implement the request for a vegetarian version of my menu. I suppose I have you to thank for that. Miss Jasmine?"

Jasmine squirmed under his scowl, even though he was only trying to make a joke.

"Don't do that," a tall dark-haired woman chided. She came up behind Frank and patted him affectionately.

"You've enjoyed every minute of the challenge." She extended a hand. "I'm Gail, in charge of entertaining guests, and this rude fellow is my husband, and the wizard in the kitchen."

"Frank is a star chef in disguise," Jake added, "and often misjudged here in the mountains. He's thrilled to be able to prove his skills to a worldly woman from Seattle."

At these words, Frank lowered his head in embarrassment and grumbled something that sounded suspiciously like "nonsense."

Gail helped them get seated at their table and filled their water glasses. "Are you drinking wine?"

Jake nodded in agreement.

"Very good. For your aperitif, I'll bring you a white wine from your home state of Washington. The red wine, on the other hand, is from a California winery." She placed baked bread and a small bowl of salted butter on their table. The bread was still warm and smelled heavenly. She reached for a slice and spread butter on half of it.

Jake followed suit. "There's no menu here in the real sense. Frank just cooks a three-course menu every day. When you come here, you have to eat what's on the table."

"And that works?" She was intrigued by the concept.

"Yes," he nodded at their fellow diners. "For one thing, he really does cook sensationally well, as you're about to find out for yourself. And second, the lack of space makes for a waiting list. I think that adds to the demand."

"But you got a table in a short time," Jasmine said.

"He owed me a favor," he clarified, after seeing her puzzled look.

His words put Jasmine on alert. "What kind of favor? Isn't that frowned upon in the police force? I thought it was called corruption."

Jake's jaw fell open. "What are you implying?"

"I-I've read in the papers, you know." Too late, mouth ahead of brain.

"Are you saying I'm a dirty cop?"

"No, no, I just—"

He threw down his napkin and made a move to stand up. "Enjoy your meal. I lost my appetite."

Jasmine regarded him coolly. He could go ahead and make a fool of himself. It would let her know all about his character.

"For your information," he continued, "the favor was when Gail had a miscarriage last year. I was in the neighborhood when Frank called me in a panic because all the ambulances were busy, as often happens during ski season. I drove her to the hospital with blue lights flashing. If you want to press charges against me now for abusing my authority, go ahead. I'd do it again anytime."

She felt like an idiot. Jake had never given her any reason to doubt him. Just because her experiences had made her cynical was no justification for treating him badly. She reached for his arm. "I'm honestly sorry, Jake. I made a mistake. Recently, I had a disturbing experience with the Seattle Police Department. Apparently not all officers there take their oaths as seriously as you do. Will you forgive me?"

His blue-eyed gaze softened. "Now the truth comes out. I knew there was something." He sat back down. "Did you report it?"

She shook her head. "No. Who would I trust? Besides, it's water under the bridge."

"Police corruption is never water under the bridge." He frowned. "If you want, I can look into it. A friend from my days on the Denver police force now works in Seattle."

"Later, okay? Let's not let it spoil our dinner." She sat back in relief as Gail joined them at the table with the first course on a tray.

Jake didn't look as though he agreed but he tucked it away for later.

Jasmine picked up a spoon and tried a heap of steaming corn chowder.

"Do you like the food?" he wanted to know.

"Yummy. Just delicious. How did a chef this good end up here?"

"Burnout, he says. Couldn't take the stress of being in celebrity kitchens anymore. Here, if things get too much, he sends unwanted guests out the door, or closes the restaurant for a few days and goes hiking with Gail."

Next came two hot pies, in pastry that was as light and delicate as a cloud. Jake's was filled with hearty beef goulash while hers contained assorted roasted root vegetables including sweet potatoes, onions, and fresh goat cheese. It was artfully arranged on the plate with a trio of sauces in dollops on the side.

"I think we just found something else we have in common," Jake whispered as the course was cleared. "Food."

Dessert was triple chocolatey, deeply chewy brownies accented with sour cherry compote, and Swiss-vanilla ice cream. After small cups of Italian espresso, the meal came to a close like a tastebud-tingling symphony.

"Let's go," Jake suggested with a husky timbre in his voice.

All the way home, Jasmine babbled meaninglessly out of nervousness until Jake grabbed her hand and squeezed it. For some reason, his touch soothed her and she fell silent. "Thank you for a lovely evening," she murmured sheepishly.

He winked at her. "Likewise."

Half an hour later they pulled up to where Jasmine's Prius was parked at the Independence police station house, about five miles from the McArthy homestead, Jasmine's current residence. As Jake pulled alongside her car, she said, "I still don't understand why you didn't pick me up at the house?"

"So you can drive yourself home," Jake replied.

"But why?"

"I'm certain my mother and sister told you I was a player. True, I used to be. This car situation is my way of making sure there's no misunderstanding at the end of the night. Only respect."

"I was wondering why I had no competition in town."

"The word is out about the old me. And I wanted to show you I'm mindful it's our first date."

"Cat fishing isn't a date?"

"Second date, then."

"Is the third time a charm?" she said, snuggling up to him.

"If you're lucky."

She gave a squeaky cry and pretend-slapped his shoulder. "Incorrigible!"

"Always."

A mile down the route, Gavin waited for the telltale lights of Jasmine's Prius to overtake him. His face was completely obscured by a gaiter pulled up over his mouth and nose. A beanie covered his blond hair and large glasses hid his eyes. He'd followed her from the grandmother's ugly old mausoleum to the police station and was now waiting for her return. Good thing, too, because he had proof she was cooperating with police. Worse, it seemed like there was a romance blossoming in that department with the goofy cornpone sheriff. Well, he'd show her. A good scare would do her good, and although she could never pin an assault on him, she'd suspect him as the culprit. That would make her think twice about spilling any beans about Gavin's counterfeiting operation.

As soon as the Prius went by, at a sedate forty miles per hour on this country road, he pulled onto the gravel and went after her. This was hilly country, and one side of the road was walled by a steeply treed incline. Pulling up behind her with his bright lights on, Gavin tailgated and began to honk. This should have made her speed up, but instead, she slowed and began to wave him around.

Gavin pulled alongside into the oncoming lane of traffic, taking the dangerous chance that there wouldn't be any, and drove alongside her—honking and gesturing for her to get over even though there was nowhere for her to go. Finally, he jerked the wheel and rammed the side of the Prius. *WHAP!* It hit the wall of hill and then he was past, accelerating along the dirt road.

Adrenaline pumped through his veins. He had no clue where he was at the moment. All he knew was that he had to get away from the scene of the accident as quickly as possible. He hoped the impact had been enough to get the job done and give Jasmine some good, hard knocks.

What if she was hurt and bleeding out? Without looking, he didn't have a chance to know if she was dead or not. Crap. A fatal accident didn't disappear so quickly from the daily news. With a little luck, he could attend her funeral, play the part of the grieving boyfriend. There might be money in that. He turned his concentration back to the road. Too late, the road ahead turned into a tight curve. He pumped the brakes like a madman but the car began to lurch, then fishtail. He tried to get it back on track, but—

At high speed, Gavin almost went into the hill. Instead, he ricocheted off of it and went into a spin straight down the middle of the road. Squealing and throwing smoke, the rental car spun around and around until it came to a stop, right side up.

Inside the Prius, Jasmine felt around for her purse. The airbags had deployed and were squishing her against the seat. Her mouth had taken a bump on the steering wheel. She flicked her tongue over her teeth. They all seemed to be intact. Blindly, her right hand found the purse and burrowed inside for the phone. She brought it back, squeezing her hand past the airbag to see the screen. There was only one bar of signal strength, but maybe 911 had some sort of relay system. Painstakingly, she pressed the numbers.

An operator's voice came on. "Nine-one-one, what is your emergency?"

CHAPTER THIRTEEN

"MY LIFE IS A DISASTER," Jasmine moaned to Paula. They were sitting in Paula's truck outside the McArthy house, after Jasmine had received medical treatment. Luckily, a fat lip, a ruined date, and a scratched-up Prius were the only casualties of the night. Jake was still out with the investigation.

The truck's large windshield gave an unobstructed view of the Colorado night sky—twinkling stars, bright planets, and the Milky Way had all come out to play.

Jasmine leaned her head against Paula's shoulder. She was still wearing the yellow dress, with a blanket over it. Good thing. She was sure it had perspiration stains under the arms and a damp place showing on the back. Her hair felt stringy and limp. In short, a hot mess.

"I came here with the intention of changing my life. I just want to live in peace, have positive thoughts, help people to be a little healthier."

"You must have been quite an A-hole in your last life," Paula said dryly.

"I know," replied Jasmine sorrowfully. "Tell me about it." She left the thought unfinished.

"For heaven's sake, Jaz! I was just kidding. Get a grip. It's not like you sent that maniac driver an invitation."

"I'm really glad you're here." Jasmine's teeth suddenly chattered, even though she was wrapped in the warm blanket.

"I have a thermos of tea and a flask of whiskey in here. I think both would do you good."

Jasmine groaned. "Not whiskey. I've got a lot to do tomorrow. The studio—"

"A sip or two of this might drive away the shock that's still in your bones. I can't stand the way your teeth are chattering."

Paula poured a tea shot and waited until Jasmine's face regained some color from the alcohol and the warmth of the tea. "Would you rather go in?"

Jaz shook his head. "Let's just sit out here. I have this horrible idea that if I go in the house, I'll fall asleep and have nightmares." She shuddered.

"That certainly won't happen tonight. You have not one guard dog, but two. I'll stay here."

"Really? Don't you have to check on your animals?"

"Leslie will do it."

"Leslie?"

"The young woman who is staying with me for a bit." Paula fell silent, rather than explain more.

"Let's stay here for a while anyway. I find the view of the night sky with its millions of stars immensely comforting. Makes you realize your own insignificance so beautifully. It makes the incident fade a little."

After a while Paula said, "You do realize that you are not to blame for what happened?"

Jasmine shrugged her shoulders.

"Look, Jake is out hunting that animal right now. This had nothing to do with you," Paula reminded her sternly.

Jasmine tenderly touched her swollen lip. "I hope you're right, Paula. But you don't know the whole story."

"What are you talking about?"

"I left a, a situation behind in Seattle. I hope what happened tonight had nothing to do with it. But—" Jasmine trembled.

"You mean the driver who ran you off the road might have been trying to kill you?"

"More like punish me, scare me, get back at me. I couldn't see any face, I didn't recognize the car but I have this feeling—"

"Did you tell Jake?"

"Not the whole thing, no. I was too busy putting my own foot in my mouth over dinner about police corruption."

"Oh dear. I take it that didn't go over very well."

"For a moment, it also looked like I was going to spend my date alone with my big mouth. Luckily, I realized my mistake in time. And after I nearly ran the date off the rails, I got run off the road and Jake came to save me." She giggled.

Paula eyed her skeptically, not sure if Jaz was feeling better or if she was about to have a fit of hysterics.

"I think the whiskey is reacting with the pain meds."

"Let's get you inside," Paula said. "And I think a long talk with Jake is going to be in order."

The next day, Jasmine woke up early. For a moment she lay there, trying to figure out how she felt today. She groped for Rambo in the bed and ran a hand over his flank. Thinking about what had happened last night, her stomach tightened uncomfortably and her hands balled into fists. She forced herself to take a deep breath and exhale for twice as long. In. Out. Until her breathing calmed down again. It took longer than she would have liked, but after a few minutes she felt herself relax a little. She got up and plodded on bare feet to the window. On the next acre, Paula's goats grazed in the pasture. Someone she didn't know, a young girl, walked out of the barn with some feed for the goats. Paula's blue heelers were familiar with this person and tagged along.

With Rambo in tow, Jasmine checked the swelling of her lip in a mirror, then went into the kitchen and put on some tea water. A note lay on the kitchen table.

Good morning. Went home after my brother relieved me of guard duty. Check in today and let me hear how you are doing. Paula

Jasmine glanced into the adjoining living room. No Jake on the sofa. Where was he, then? With a furrowed brow, she walked to the front door. Rambo stood in front of it, tail wagging, waiting patiently to be let out. As soon as the door was ajar, he disappeared. She stepped out onto the porch and stopped in surprise. The sheriff's SUV was parked out there, next to her dented little car. It was still drivable, and they had decided repairs could wait.

Jake was asleep in his SUV, leaning against the window. He had his left arm tucked under his head as a makeshift pillow.

Silently, she went back into the house. First she fed Rambo, who had returned from his morning excursion in time for breakfast, and then put on coffee. From the icebox she took out two large cinnamon buns. That she had these on hand was thanks to Miss Daisy, who often pressed goodies into her hand. "Here, child. See that you get something on your ribs."

She just couldn't bring herself to refuse the kind gesture. However, she didn't think the "kid" was too skinny, so she froze a big chunk of it. If it kept up, she'd have to buy a bigger freezer soon. *Or have Jake over for breakfast more often*, flashed through her mind. She could feel the blood rushing to her cheeks. Luckily, there was no one around to see it.

She peered over at Rambo, who seemed to be looking at her with amusement. "You don't count, big guy!" He put his head between his paws and gave her a meaningful look from his big brown eyes. She shook her head. Sometimes it really did seem as if he understood everything she said.

Fifteen minutes later, she had poured the coffee into a large, insulated drinking cup and arranged the steaming cinnamon buns on a plate. She adjusted the bandage beside her mouth so it covered as much swelling as possible. Then she went to the driveway and tapped on Jake's car window. Startled, he pulled up, hand on gun, and blinked. Recognizing her, he relaxed and rolled down the window. "Jaz! What are you doing up already? Is it that late?"

She felt herself start to smile and stopped it. A smile would look like a grimace with her big lip today.

He gratefully took the coffee and cinnamon buns.

"Why don't you sit with me inside?" he mumbled with his mouth full.

She climbed inside.

"How's your mouth?" he said, squinting at her face.

"Fat," she answered. "Other than that? Not bad."

He slurped at the coffee, then set it down. "We found tire tracks five hundred yards from the access road down here." He looked at her.

"What does that mean?"

"They match the skid marks the other driver made during the accident."

Jasmine just shook her head. "But what does that mean?"

"It means the person who ran you off the road was probably watching you at the house prior to the accident."

Jasmine closed her eyes and sighed deeply.

"Is there something you're not telling me?"

She sighed, "I suppose you want to hear the whole story."

Jake gave her a sharp look. "Why would you think that?"

He was being sarcastic and the barb stung. "I didn't want to get you involved in messy, personal business."

"Bullshit. You didn't trust me." His voice sounded frustrated and accusatory in equal measure.

"That too," she muttered guiltily. But then she tightened up inside. "It's not like I know you. I've been through a scary experience and a frightening experience with my ex-boyfriend. Why should you be any different? On top of that, I'm terribly embarrassed by the whole story." She almost choked on the words, "I never thought he'd track me down, either. My ex is more of an out-of-sight, out-of-mind kind of guy." She drew a ragged breath. "I still don't know how he did it."

"That's not important for now," Jake replied. "The fact is, he found out somehow. Does he have some score to settle with you?"

She wrung her hands in frustration.

"You're going to have to tell your story. Might as well tell it to me now." He took out his phone and activated the recording function.

Jasmine took a deep breath and recounted all the events that brought her to Independence. The gun incident, the overheard conversation about counterfeiting, the too-friendly officer at the police station, and Gavin's story about acting class that she had swallowed hook, line and sinker, until she'd checked it out. She pulled her cardigan tighter around her. "Do you think he's still around, waiting for the next best opportunity to jump me?"

Jake sighed. "My guess is he's not in the area anymore. The police in the surrounding towns and the few gas stations are informed and extra vigilant."

On impulse, he embraced her face with both hands and kissed her gently beside her injured lip. Frustration, lust and anger emanated from him in great waves. Overwhelmed by the sensations crashing down on her, she let her hands wander over the muscles on his upper arms. They stayed like that for a while.

Pulling away, he said, "I'll check out the rental car places next thing."

She tenderly kissed him on the cheek. Then she opened the door and jumped out.

Jake needed no introduction at Breckenridge Quality West Rentals. The manager had donated to the local charity drives that Jake was part of for years. After a cheery hello to the manager, Jake got down to business.

"Any dinged-up cars returned recently?" he asked.

"Recently? As in returned a couple hours ago?" the manager quizzed back.

"That might be my bingo."

"Follow me."

The manager led him to an economy car with a dented passenger side front bumper and tires showing skid wear.

"I'd like to see the customer information on that one," Jake said. "And I'm sorry, but as of now, the car's impounded as part of an investigation."

"Yep, understood," the manager said, unperturbed. "What kind of investigation?"

"Reckless endangerment at the very least."

"And worst?"

"Attempted murder. Have a nice day."

An hour later, using the customer information provided by the rental manager, Jake discovered the renter, Gavin Smith, was also registered at a local motel.

CHAPTER FOURTEEN

BACK AT NANA'S HOUSE, Jasmine was flying around, changing beds, and making sure the towels were clean. She had two more rooms relieved of their "extra treasures" so her guests had enough room. Kathrina and Pat had texted that they were only an hour away. Rambo knew something was up and kept checking the front door, giving soft *woofs*. Minutes later, Rambo barked in earnest and tried to throw himself through the front door. When Jasmine opened it up, a van was pulling in the drive. A door slid back, and an enormous creature leaped out. This was Kathrina's enormous French Mastiff. The dog's head was huge, like a cross between a pit bull and a bulldog. Muscles rippled underneath its shiny light-brown coat. Kathrina called him Rocky.

"We're heeeere," trilled a voice from inside the van. Out popped a curly headed woman of about twenty-eight. Her blue eyes sparkled with life, and at the sight of her Rambo went into leaps of joy. This was Kathrina, his dog sitter.

From the drivers' side came a man in his thirties, dark hair and dark eyes. This was Patrick West, with the toned body of a martial artist, and the cool eye of an architect. Both visitors lavished love on Rambo and then greeted Jasmine.

"Load or unload?" Pat called, over the sounds of the joyous dogs.

"Come in and refresh, first," Jasmine called back. "We can unpack the van later."

"You don't have to ask us twice," said Kat.

A few hours later, Jasmine's guests were rested and refreshed, and all caught up on the news. Jasmine had explained her swollen lip, and dinner plans were already made. Brenda had called to say that Tyler was in town and asked if Jasmine would like to come by for dinner. When it was explained that it would be Jasmine plus two, Brenda was even happier.

BRRRINGGGG! An old-fashioned telephone ring came from Pat's pocket. "It's Mr. Wilkinson," he explained. "I gave him a special ringtone. Told him we'd be arriving today." Pat pulled out his phone and answered the call.

"Hear you're in town," Mr. Wilkinson shouted so everyone could hear, even through the tiny cell-phone speakers. Mr. Wilkinson was of the generation that remembered ear trumpets. "Want you to come by as soon as possible, m'boy. Bring that lady and her dog you're traveling with, I'll feed them dinner, too."

Pat gave Jasmine a *What should I do?* look. Despite their freshly made dinner plans, Jasmine knew the Wilkinson house could be a very important client for Pat. She flapped her hands at he and Kathrina; *go, go*. To Kathrina she whispered, "I'll give you a key to this place. You can let yourselves back in. We'll have lots of time to catch up tomorrow."

"Sure Mister Wilkinson, we'll be over shortly. Thanks for the invite," Gavin said.

The rest of their time was spent getting Jasmine's things out of the van and neatly stacked in a corner of the games room where she could unpack at leisure.

"Jaz! There you are!" Paula's sister Tyler stood on the porch of Brenda Carter's home, bouncing in place. "Paula's talked about you so much already, it's almost scary."

Jasmine stifled a laugh and let Rambo jump out of the back of the dented Prius. Before he could get away from her, she caught him by the collar just in time. She glanced over at Tyler. "Can I let him go?"

"Sure. Our dogs are outside, too. The chickens are penned up." She pointed vaguely in the direction of the barn, which stood a few dozen yards from the house.

"I hear them already," she replied, letting go of her completely out-of-control canine. Like lightning, he shot around the corner, toward the barking dogs. She raised an eyebrow. "Looks like he just arrived in doggie paradise."

"That's a definite. As long as you don't mind if he shows up all dirty."

"No. That's what the garden hose is for. As long as he's happy, I can live with just about anything." She turned her attention to Tyler.

"I've heard so much about you, too. I'm getting to be good friends with Paula, my neighbor. I know you're the proud owner of the studio I just leased. Thanks for that. The place is perfect."

Tyler waved it off. The grace of a dancer was in her movements, "It's great if at least some of it gets used. I'm going to be on the road for a while anyway." She kicked a rock aside with the tip of her toe. "Or maybe not, we'll see. But there's still space downstairs. So I can always come back and disrupt your meditation classes with my music," she concluded with a wink.

Tyler was very lively, very bubbly, and reminded her of a sassy leprechaun if she interpreted the twinkle in her eyes correctly. "Absolutely. Come bother me anytime. I'll just claim this is an advanced class when that happens. Mindfulness in Chaos."

Tyler blinked, then chuckled at the dig back at her. "I'm starting to see why my sister gets along so well with you. My sister was always a real tomboy. I don't think she ever had a best friend."

"Paula is great," Jasmine returned, shaking her head.

"I think so too. But not everyone feels that way. Paula usually finds others totally annoying."

"Most of them are," Jasmine replied, deadpan.

"See? That's what I meant. But now come on in. Food's coming. The men are already at the grill."

"Is the whole clan here?" Jasmine asked.

"Heavens no. We usually only make it for the holidays. Thanksgiving, Christmas, and maybe Easter if Mom tries hard enough and makes us feel guilty enough."

"Brenda? Really?"

"Yes. To be fair, she only uses her special talent on things that are really important. However, she gets to decide what's really important."

Jasmine shook her head in amusement. "Is she dying for grandchildren, too?"

"You betcha. Fortunately, she's settled on the three eldest for the time being. Since I'm the youngest, I'll be spared for the time being."

Brenda was standing in the kitchen with Paula, Nana and Nadine. Her green eyes sparkled when she spotted Jaz.

"Surprise!" Nana hollered.

"Come in," Brenda called, drying her wet hands on a dish towel. The others also called out a cheerful hello. Jasmine's heart warmed. She felt so welcome here among these people. She gave Nana and Nadine big kisses as Brenda approached and handed her a glass of iced tea. Paula was packing potatoes in aluminum foil to put on the barbecue. Everyone pointedly ignored her lip. Obviously the bush phone had been busy and they'd decided not to make much of it.

"What's the next step for the studio?" Brenda wanted to know.

Jasmine rolled her tired shoulders. "Next week I'm going to Denver, buying materials like dishes, towels, and mats."

Tyler clapped his hands enthusiastically. "Let's all ride together. Have a women's day."

Nadine and Nana exchanged a glance and then looked at Brenda. Finally, they nodded. Paula shrugged her shoulders. "Why not?"

"Great," Tyler agreed. "Maybe Jake can come with us." She disappeared through the patio door into the garden.

"What does that have to do with men? I thought we were talking about a women's day?" Jasmine was confused.

"Well, someone has to drive," Paula chimed in. "Since it's not much fun when practically half of us have to stay sober, we each convince Jake and Dad to come along, drop us off in front of a bar, and pick us up later."

"I'm impressed. And what are they doing during this time?"

"Jake usually meets up with friends from his days on the Denver Police Department. And Dad usually disappears into the library and devotes himself to his latest studies."

"By the way, speaking of Jake," Brenda announced, with a bowl of salad in her hand, "he won't be here until later."

"Where is he?" Nana blurted.

"Working," Brenda said, pointedly avoiding saying that he was working on an ongoing investigation that was directly connected with Jasmine. Brenda met Jasmine's eyes meaningfully, and an understanding communicated between them. Jaz was grateful that no more was said.

"You mentioned what Dad and Jake will do," Jasmine started, as her mind raced to remember Jake's father's name. Jake's father was Stan, she finally remembered. The abbreviation of Stanford. She had exchanged a few words with him at the diner one day. He had been very friendly, with an absent expression behind his wire-rimmed glasses. Paula had once remarked that his mind was mostly in other realms. He was an engineer and was always tinkering with new things.

"Stan will do whatever Stan usually does," Brenda added. "So, are you in?"

"Sure. After all, I'm the one who has to go to Denver. Of course, that'll be a lot more fun if you all come along." She looked around the kitchen. "Can I help a little, too?"

"I thought maybe you could make the stuffing for the mushrooms? And the vegetable skewers? I couldn't think of many more vegetarian things."

"That's wonderful," Jasmine assured her, "I see there's corn on the cob and potatoes, too." She sat down at the kitchen table with Paula and began mixing the stuffing with spices and cream cheese. Nana joined her and cut peppers, tomatoes, and mushrooms into pieces for the skewers.

"How are you doing, anyway? I didn't have time to talk to you yesterday. I had to settle for seeing that you were still breathing. The whole fender bender thing, which, by the way, I only heard from Mr. Wilkinson," she gave her granddaughter a reproachful look, "gave me quite a scare."

Jasmine winced with guilt. She could have guessed that Nana was worried. *At least she could have called*, she scolded herself silently. "I'm sorry I didn't telephone. In my defense, all I can say is that so much has happened in the last forty-eight hours that I'm still figuring things out myself."

"Starting with your date with Jake," Paula interjected meaningfully.

Jasmine gave her a big-eyed warning stare. "I don't think that's the most important thing right now."

"No? You don't? Why did I look over and find him sleeping in your driveway this morning?" she continued to tease.

"Really?" Rose allowed herself to be distracted.

"Nana. It doesn't matter now, you wanted to hear all about the car accident."

"Very elegant. Better to distract the grandmother with mayhem on the road before talking about your love life," Paula murmured, while Jaz stabbed her with looks.

Brenda gave her daughter a warning look over her shoulder. "Are you trying to scare away your first best friend right away?"

Paula rolled her eyes, but was quiet in response.

"Don't worry. You won't get rid of me that quickly," Jasmine assured her, seeing the vulnerable expression that had flitted through Paula's eyes. "But you can be sure I'll remember every little detail and get back at you someday," she added, flashing a challenging glare.

"Girls! Can we focus here and stay on topic for two minutes?" asked Nadine sternly. The two women ducked their heads guiltily. That was Nadine's school voice, which she had perfected in her years as a teacher.

"Did Jake catch the driver who hit your car?" Nana was seriously concerned.

"I don't know what the current status is. If they caught someone, I'm sure Jake would have called me."

"Who knows? Then he wouldn't have any reason to spend the night with you anymore," Paula chirped, simply unable to hold back.

Nadine raised an eyebrow.

"Any ideas on the driver's identity?" Brenda joined in the conversation.

"There's a possibility. But I can't prove it, unfortunately. It may have been Gavin."

"Gavin?" Nana roared.

"He's the only one I know who is pissed off at me. Also, he was involved in some pretty obscure business. It was part of the reason why I decided so suddenly to come to Independence." Jasmine crossed her fingers behind her back. It was the *only* reason she decided to come to Independence. But she didn't want Nana to feel bad.

"Isn't that a pretty extreme development? From getting ripped off to driven off the road?" Nadine was not convinced by the theory.

Jasmine shrugged her shoulders. "What do I know? It's just becoming more and more obvious that I didn't know him at all, even though we were a couple for a while and he lived with me. I'm just an idiot."

"Hey. Stop that right now, Jaz." Paula reached across the table for her hand. "If someone wants to fool you, they can do it."

"My friend Kathrina wasn't fooled."

"I take it she wasn't in love with him?"

"Of course not. But if I was honest, neither did I. At least not for long. Or not really." She heaved a deep sigh.

"You're always wiser afterwards," Nana comforted her.

"Yes, maybe. But don't you understand? I just don't know if I can trust my feelings anymore." She put the last stuffed mushroom on the tray. "What if I'm wrong again?" She was voicing her ultimate fear. Wide-eyed, she looked at Paula and blinked a few times. *Dang.* Why did she suddenly feel like crying?

Paula, who immediately realized what was going on, stacked the potatoes in a basket and pushed them over to the board with the mushrooms in the center of the table. "Do you need more help, Mom?"

"No. It's all ready to go, so far."

"Good. Jaz and I will go outside and see where the men are with the fire." She got up and took two bottles of beer out of the refrigerator. One of them she thrust into Jasmine's hand.

"Hey, what about me?" complained Tyler.

"Get one yourself," was Paula's curt reply.

"Once again, typical," she grumbled.

Paula ignored her, "Come on, let's go outside."

Jasmine followed her willingly, glad to escape the line of questioning. Her nerves had been more affected by the whole story than she had realized. No wonder, given the pace her life was at right now. She glanced at Paula from the side. "Wasn't that a little harsh on your sister?"

"She's used to that from me. We're sisters. We have to bicker from time to time. That's rule #5. Rule #6 is we make up too." She shrugged. "Besides, you said you wanted a moment of peace. You can forget that around my sister. I think she swallowed a pack of long-life batteries when she was a kid and nobody noticed." Paula deliberately avoided the direct route to the backyard via the patio door. She pushed open the front door.

Jasmine laughed and dropped into the wooden rocking chair that sat on the porch. Relief. She felt her stomach slowly unknotting. "Thank you for saving me. I wouldn't have lasted much longer."

"I could tell by looking at you."

For a moment they enjoyed the cool evening air and the peaceful togetherness without having to use many words. The sun was just sending the last rays over the mountain peaks. Suddenly the dogs darted around the corner, happy to find new people to beg for attention. Rambo was the first to join them, but his new canine friends followed close behind. They appeared to be two mixed breeds. The smaller one was rough-coated, with triangular tipped ears and a black patch over his left eye that stood out prominently on his white coat. Probably a terrier mix. The other was considerably larger, a shepherd-dog mix perhaps, with longer sand-colored fur and long floppy ears. "This little one looks like Snowy, but the scallywag version of it," Jasmine noted with amusement.

"This is Pirate. Food must be hidden from him. Otherwise it's gone," Paula explained. "The other is Moss, a shepherd-dog mix of unknown origin. One day he showed up at our door and stayed. They're both over ten years old—some days you can see it in Moss—but Pirate not at all."

Jasmine greeted them both enthusiastically. But soon it occurred to the four-legged friends that important things were still waiting for them, and they disappeared again in a whirl of paws, flying ears, and fur.

Paula cleared her throat. "Listen. I know I warned you about my brother in the beginning. But I can assure you of one thing. Jake will always be honest with you."

Jasmine blushed. "Was it that obvious?"

"Not for the others. Well, maybe my mom picked up on something. With five kids, she's had more than enough practice guessing things. But I can see you two circling around each other. I've never seen Jake care so much about someone who isn't family, either."

"Come on, you're exaggerating. As a cop, he helps strangers all the time…" Jasmine broke off the sentence, afraid of revealing too much about herself.

But she couldn't fool her friend. "Sure. That's his job. But all those flings with women were over in no time. And he always communicated that clearly. With you, he's different."

"You just want me to be your sister-in-law." Jasmine tried to give the conversation a lighter touch.

"That's a bonus point, of course," Paula admitted, laughing. "But for once, I wasn't thinking about me. I was thinking about you and my brother. Maybe you'll have time to talk later tonight."

Talking to him when she wanted to rip off all his clothes as soon as she was near him? Great. But then she remembered that wasn't the only thing she felt in his company. Protected. Looked after. It just felt so right when he was there. With Gavin-the-jerk, she had always been happy when he wasn't there. That alone should have told her something. "Maybe I will, actually," she said. "Come on, let's go join the others. I'm getting hungry."

CHAPTER FIFTEEN

DINNER WAS A HAPPY and lively affair. The dogs sniffed around the tables hoping that someone would be careless enough to drop something tasty and forbidden. Tyler entertained everyone with the most impossible stories from her dance company; they were currently traveling all over America.

Now they all sat around a crackling fire pit in the backyard, as evening turned to night.

"All this intrigue, it wouldn't be for me," Paula moaned, hiding her face behind her hands. She blinked through her fingers at her sister. "How can you stand it?"

"The way I stand everything." Tyler stood on her toes and pirouetted barefoot on the grass before sinking into a deep curtsy in one fluid motion. "With a double dose of humor and dancing."

Jasmine clapped spontaneously. She was very flexible from her years of exercise training. But Tyler moved with an ethereal ease that was evident in the smallest of movements.

"You're really good." Impressed, Jasmine leaned back in her chair and grabbed the last stuffed mushroom. Despite the fact that they never missed an opportunity to tease her about not eating meat, they had a good time with the vegetarian dishes.

Tyler beamed. "Thank you. That's always nice to hear. I feed off compliments like that when my muscles burn after five hours of working out and beg me to stop. Then I think of the last person I was able to bring joy to with my dancing."

"Where do you get all that discipline! There are days when I pretty much have to kick myself to even start."

"She's always been like that. At least when it comes to dancing," Stan said, the fatherly pride unmistakable in his voice.

Tyler smiled sheepishly and plopped down, less than gracefully, on the nearest chair. "All I've had on my mind is dancing. Since I was seven."

"And boys, since you were thirteen," Paula added dryly.

Her sister waved it off. "Everybody needs a bit of relaxation in between workouts."

"That's definitely more than I need to know about my daughters' love lives now," Brenda said. "As long as it doesn't give me sons-in-law and grandchildren, I don't want to hear about it."

Paula leaned toward Jasmine and whispered, clearly audible to all, "Did you notice that she made a point of mentioning the sons-in-law first? Apparently she makes a point of putting them in the right order."

Jasmine giggled, to which Nana looked at her sternly. "Go ahead and listen carefully. The same goes for you."

She rolled her eyes. Where did that come from all of a sudden? As if she could read her thoughts, her grandmother added, "Keep in mind, I'm not getting any younger!"

O-o. She certainly didn't want to delve into this topic, especially not with Jake at the same table. Time for a change of subject. "So where are the rest of the Carter family members?"

"Sam is getting ready for the field hockey season opener," Paula explained.

Tyler set down her beer bottle. "And Cole is on a secret mission."

"It sounds very James Bond-ish."

"Almost," a voice said behind them.

Jasmine looked up. It was Jake. Looking tired.

"He works for the FBI," Jake continued. "And believe me, if he were here, he'd fill you in real quick that there's nothing glamorous about his job at all."

Jasmine turned a little in his direction to see he was staring at her. The scented mosquito candles on the table cast golden shadows on his face. She held his gaze, and a smile played around the corners of her mouth. Abruptly, she averted her eyes and turned back to the others.

Jasmine rubbed her arms to get rid of the goosebumps that Jake's gaze had sent over her body. Everything about him was so distinct. His loyalty, his humor, his good looks, and even his passion. Could people change? Was he really not the player he used to be? Held by his gaze, everything else faded into background noise. He flicked his eyes away, to the pasture behind them. He obviously had something to tell her.

Jasmine touched Paula lightly on the arm. "I'm going to take a few steps around the house."

Understanding, Paula squeezed her hand. "All right. If you both haven't reappeared in twenty minutes, I'll come find you. Just in case a bear dragged you off."

Jasmine gave her a kind smile. A few steps away from the tables and the fire, there was deepest darkness. Only the stars were visible in all their glory thanks to the clear night. Giving her eyes time to adjust to the darkness, she moved further away from the house. The dogs went with her, close at her heels. She hoped that Paula's last remark had been a joke but decided to pay attention to the dogs' behavior. They would surely warn if any animal approached.

She walked past the barn and sat down on a boulder in the middle of the meadow. Tilting her head back, she took in the endless expanse of starry sky. She welcomed the feeling of utter insignificance. It somehow put her problems back into perspective. It was so easy to get lost in the difficulties of everyday life and forget about the important things. She had a great life and a choice career that challenged her and brought her joy, and good friends, old and new. In addition, she was healthy and had enough to eat.

Her heart lightened and she felt the tension she had been carrying around for weeks dissipate. She took a deep breath and let the night sounds wash over her. A light breeze carried the murmur of voices from the fire over to her. The dogs scampered almost silently through the grass, only occasionally causing the snap of a twig or a soft sniff. A shadow materialized in front of her and footsteps could be heard. She listened tensely and only breathed a sigh of relief when she recognized Jake.

"I'm glad you're not a bear."

"I'm glad I'm not a bear, too." He nudged her. "Move over a bit."

She made room for him on the rock so he could sit down next to her.

"Ready for a chinwag?"

"Is that what you call it? Yes, but not necessarily at night, alone, in the dark. Without Paula and her shotgun. Not a good combination."

"I have a gun, too."

"I know. I'm suitably impressed," she returned glibly. "What did you want to talk about?"

He seemed to steel himself. "There's no easy way to say this. I'm not a fan of coincidences. Especially not when the last hit-and-run accident was about fifteen years ago around here."

"Just say it," she said softly.

"Gavin Smith is in county jail on charges of aggravated assault with a motor vehicle. It was Gavin who tried to run you off the road." Jake put his arm around her.

After a moment's hesitation, she snuggled against his shoulder and heaved a comforting sigh.

"So the danger is over."

"Seems so. Gavin won't be any more trouble for you. He's looking at a year inside, at least, and then probation."

She hugged him tight. "Before I came here, I was a walking disaster," she said, "I just didn't know it."

He laughed softly. "I don't think so."

A smile stole onto her lips. Before she could change her mind, she asked, "What exactly do you see in me, then?"

Pressed against his chest, nothing could be heard but the sounds of the night, the murmur of voices, and his regular heartbeat. When she already thought he wouldn't answer, he said, "For the first time in my life, I find myself counting the hours until I see her again."

"You?" Jasmine was confused.

"Well, you, of course. The woman I have my eye on."

He had his eye on her? Joy filled her, closely followed by panic. Before she could say anything back, he continued.

"I wasn't expecting someone like you. And certainly not someone I was looking for. As I'm sure Paula has told you, I've never been one to turn down a good time when it comes to women. Especially not when they are as sexy as you are. But that's all it's ever been. And to be honest, I never had to make much of an effort either. Women and uniforms…" he shook his head, as if it wasn't quite clear to him what it was about them that was so appealing.

"It actually looks extremely good on you," she teased him, trying to lighten the mood a bit. Yet she was deadly serious about every word. She felt him shake his head again in amusement.

"Whatever. It doesn't matter anymore, since you came into my life." He briefly squeezed her shoulder. "Everything is different. I want to know how you are, how your day was, and most importantly, if you missed me. Just like I miss you when you're not around me."

Jasmine was speechless. She opened her mouth and closed it again. Of all the possible scenarios she had played out in her head, this had not been one of them. Which showed once again how pointless it was to worry. "So it's not just about sex then?" she said in a scratchy voice.

The corners of his mouth twitched in amusement, and he tightened his grip around her shoulders. "I'd be lying if I said that wasn't part of it. I want you. No

VIRGINIA FOX

question about it. But Jaz—sleeping with someone is easy. If it was just about that, we'd have been through this a long time ago, and we wouldn't be sitting here with each other right now."

She thought to herself that she wouldn't mind if they finally did it. They could still sit there with each other afterwards, and she told him so.

He put his head back and laughed heartily. When he had calmed down again, he took her face in both hands and kissed her so that her toes curled. The desire for more took possession of her, and she put her hand on the back of his neck to pull him closer. When they finally let go of each other, they were both breathing heavily. She rested her head on his chest and listened to his pulse beat. "Can we please, please hurry up a little with the getting to know you part? Because as much as I appreciate the thought, it's like I can't wait for the oh-so-easy part two!"

He grumbled something that sounded like, "You're poison to my good intentions," before standing up and holding out his hand to her. "Come on. We're going back to the others before Paula calls for the bear hunt."

"I'm also going to make an announcement," she said.

"What's that?"

"I'm not waiting to open the yoga studio. I'm moving ahead. I'm not letting a little thing like a bad time with Gavin slow me down."

CHAPTER SIXTEEN

THE NEXT MORNING

"There you are at last, big brother." Paula delivered a sisterly boxing punch to Jake's upper arm. They were standing in Jasmine's kitchen drinking coffee. Kathrina and Pat were just shuffling in, trying to wake up. Rocky trailed them. He waited patiently while a bowl was filled with some dry food.

"You weren't so easy to find, Jake," Paula continued. "Although I should have guessed."

He rubbed the spot where she had hit him without making a face. As a big brother, he had to fulfill certain expectations. But he was pretty sure his arm would turn blue later. Paula had always possessed impressive punching power. He assumed it was because she had grown up with three brothers. He saw that she registered his movement, the satisfied grin on her face speaking volumes, and dropped his hand.

"Too late," she teased him. "I saw it."

"Coffee?" He held the pot over her head.

She dodged, giggling wickedly.

"What are you doing here so early in the morning anyway? And in such a good mood?" he grumbled.

"I've been up for a while. And I'm always in a good mood."

Jake refrained from commenting and just snorted.

"Relax. Here, I brought you, or rather you all, breakfast. It's not warm now, though."

His expression brightened when he saw homemade buttermilk biscuits and waffles. His mother's recipe, of course. "Why didn't you say so in the first place?" he complained. Immediately he began to prepare the rest of the breakfast. Honey, apricot jam, and maple syrup appeared on the table. After pressing plates and cutlery into Paula's hands, he began to cook oatmeal.

At that moment, Jasmine shuffled down the stairs, followed by a sleepy Rambo. The bandage was off the side of her mouth and the swelling had almost disappeared. She stopped at the landing and stretched with pleasure while the big dog yawned heartily.

Jake was about to greet her when he was distracted by the narrow strip of flat belly that became visible. Yoga actually seemed to work, if Jaz's body was any guide.

Paula took a platter from his hand and pushed him aside. "I'll do the serving here. When you can tear your eyes off her, I'll give you a spoon."

He was about to protest but shut his mouth again when he realized that she had a point. Stupid.

Jasmine's blood rose to her cheeks. Great. She was already starting the day with that constant embarrassment that always seemed to start up when Jake got within twenty yards of her. Finally, she decided on a lame "Good morning. Come and sit, Kat and Pat. Please help yourselves to coffee." She sat down on a chair and peered at the crowded table. "Those waffles smell too good." Yawning and stretching, Kat and Pat got coffee and then got seated.

Will you come every morning from now on?" Jasmine fixed her blue eyes hopefully on Paula in her best poodle manner.

"I'm deeply affected," Jake interrupted. "You never say nice things like that to me."

"You don't bring me a sinfully delicious breakfast either," she shot back.

"At least I cook oatmeal."

"I know. And I'll eat it good, too, the healthy oatmeal. But the highest score goes to these sweet things here." She emptied a generous amount of maple syrup over her waffles.

"I thought you were such a health nut? Isn't sugar bad for you?" he teased.

"Not until after nine in the morning," she replied with a cheeky grin.

"Will this end today with you two lovebirds or should I come back later?" asked Paula dryly.

"As long as you leave the food here." Jaz mumbled with her mouth full. Paula rolled her eyes.

Kathrina, who was more awake than Pat, followed the conversation with bright eyes roving from face to face.

Jake leaned against the kitchen counter and crossed his arms in front of his chest. He directed his comment to Paula. "Shoot. You don't voluntarily seek my company at this hour. Did something happen?"

She ran her fingers through her spikey auburn hair. "Not really. It's time I told you about the woman who showed up at the ranch."

Jake nodded and Jaz asked, "The woman? You mean the girl I saw walk out of your barn a day ago or so?"

"Yes, she's homeless. But a decent person. She was with me in the barn when I showed up with the shotgun in my arms. Instead of getting scared, she first heroically stood in front of the horses so I wouldn't shoot them. Heroic, don't you think?"

"Admirable." Jasmine pushed a biscuit onto her plate. "Do you have shotgun incidents with everybody who shows up around here?"

"Very funny. Shortly after that, she disappeared, or rather, she successfully hid from me." Paula ran her index finger along the wood pattern of the table. "I didn't see her again until this morning, when she let the dogs into the barn. She'd swept up, too. So I left her some breakfast."

"And what are you going to do with her now?"

"Knowing my sister, she'll probably let her stay," Jake interjected. He pushed himself off the counter and began pacing around the kitchen.

"My animals like her. They run a better background check than any database."

Jake made a sour face.

"What else am I supposed to do? Have her arrested?" asked Paula defensively.

He rubbed the back of his neck. "Let me ask you this," Jake shot at her. "How do you know she's an adult?"

"She said she was eighteen," Paula shot back.

"Well, that's a great form of ID," Jake said, sarcastically. "Do you have a name?"

This time, Paula's cheeks turned red. "If she's a kid what happens?"

"Child Protective Services need to come right away. She'll be sent to Denver for processing. If we can get a name out of her, I can survey the databases."

"She can't be sent to Denver!" Paula cried. "We can't check on how she's doing that far away. She'll get lost in the system."

"Don't panic," Jake said soothingly. "Just ask her for some ID today. Maybe she is eighteen. If so, this conversation is for nothing."

Paula exhaled loudly. Relief was clearly written on her face. "Good, I was worried I was going to have to take some kind of action right away."

"Just don't lollygag," Jake zinged back.

"Good, now that that's settled, we can finally move on to the interesting stuff." Paula turned to Kathrina and Pat. "What's up with you two? Having a good visit so far? Things quiet enough for you?"

They both laughed.

"We have news from Mr. Wilkinson," Pat said.

"Dinner was nice? Do you think restoring his old place is possible?" Jasmine asked.

Kathrina nodded enthusiastically. "He wants to take us on an architectural tour of Breckenridge, and Aspen, and other places for the next couple of days to see similar houses by the same builder."

"What do you think about that, Jaz?" Pat said. "We just got here, and it means leaving you again."

"Anything for the client. And anything for the preservation of worthy Colorado architecture, I say," Jaz assured him with a laugh.

"We'll be back in time for the Indie Music Festival," Kathrina explained.

"Which is what we all wanted to do together, anyway."

"Works for me," Jasmine said. "When does he want to leave?"

"Do you have to ask? As soon as possible," Pat said.

"Time for me to go," Paula interrupted. "Jake, don't forget the shopping trip tomorrow. Kay?"

"Kay. Time for me to push off anyway. Bye all."

Pat and Kathrina excused themselves and Paula showed herself out. Jasmine cleared the dishes, went out to the porch, and lost herself in the harmonious movements of her exercises.

It was strange. Gavin-the-jerk had always made fun of her yoga-influenced habits. His comments hit hard. In the end, she had been careful not to mention anything to do with yoga. No wonder they had nothing more to say to each other. Jake was different.

Paula walked into her kitchen and thought about how to proceed with the homeless female she was pretty sure had returned to living in the barn. The fact that this female might be a child changed things, and Paula felt very protective. On the one hand, she had to obey the law and report the situation if this was a child. On the other, she wasn't about to hand a kid over to the system with no way to keep her from getting lost, or returned to her abusers as sometimes happened, or getting sent somewhere worse. Finally, Paula made sandwiches and filled them generously with meat, cheese, lettuce and tomatoes. With the sandwich in a plastic container and a bag of apples in the other, she made her way to the barn. Barns and Roo followed close behind her, as they always did when she carried edibles.

"Now all of a sudden you're the best companion dogs imaginable. Real shadows," she teased them.

In the barn, she sat down in the feed room and left the food container clearly visible on an oats barrel so mice couldn't get at it, or dogs. She put the bag of apples next to it. "I'm leaving this food here," she announced, not knowing if the girl was even there to hear or not. "I want to be friendly and let you know you can stay. Knowing your name would be nice, too." That was the closest Paula felt she should get in terms of asking about identity. She needed to establish trust first.

Through a crack in the hayloft, the girl watched what was happening. She hardly dared to breathe. Only when the woman set about mucking out the stable did she relax a little. The work made enough background noise that a rustle would not be noticed. Impatiently, she waited for Paula to leave the barn again. But she took her time, cuddling her horses and talking to them in friendly terms as she worked away.

The quiet atmosphere lulled her, so that the girl almost missed the moment when Paula finally left again. Tense, she forced herself to wait a little longer. Maybe Paula would come back again. After all, the dogs already knew her, so she didn't have to worry about them starting to bark. She hated the thought of being surprised.

She counted to three hundred, then climbed down from her hiding place. She had seen that the woman brought apples for the horses. The door to the feed room squeaked as she pushed on it, and she held her breath. But outside everything remained quiet. She spied the bag and greedily grabbed an apple. With a silent prayer of thanks to the horses, she soothed her guilty conscience. She didn't want to deprive them of their apples. But she hadn't eaten anything since she'd bolted. The last meal had been some carrots found in the tack room yesterday. She was sorry for running into Paula so rudely. Really sorry.

As she chewed the apple, her eyes fell on the plastic box. A sandwich? She peered inside. *Jackpot!* After a few minutes, she had polished them off. She quenched her thirst at the faucet on the wall and even scrubbed her face in the running water. So much for getting ready for bed. As for a toilet, she would disappear outside behind a tree later, when it had grown dark. But that could wait. She sat down with the horses in the fresh bedding and enjoyed the moment.

An image of her drug-addicted parents flashed in her mind. But she pushed away the looming sadness and concentrated on the horses who were peacefully chewing on their hay. For the moment, she was full and safe. Her eyelids fluttered and she fell asleep.

CHAPTER SEVENTEEN

THE WOMEN'S SHOPPING TRIP day arrived. It dovetailed with Jasmine's need for yoga supplies. After a long drive to Aspen, Paula's vehicle was stuffed with orange and blue mats, scented candles, incense sticks, towels, teacups, flowers, a clay Buddha, and some wooden shelves. Jasmine's feet hurt from running around, so, locking up the truck securely, they headed for the comfortable lounge chairs of the bar. The others promised to meet them there shortly. Brenda and Tyler had ridden along with Nana and Nadine. Stan and Jake were in their own vehicle, ready to take passengers who weren't up to driving.

"Does this driving service work in reverse for the men at some point?" asked Jasmine.

"Maybe after a field hockey game or something. But we don't keep a record of who drives whom and how often. The main thing is to make sure everyone gets home in one piece. It all 'works out in the wash' as Stan likes to say." Paula leaned over to a neighboring table and reached for the menu card laid out there. "I'm starving. Shopping makes me hungrier than mucking out the barn."

Jasmine looked out the bar's large window. "They're already coming," she added, waving.

The others trooped in, similarly famished, and in no time ordered a wide selection of appetizers. Spring rolls, stuffed jalapeño peppers, nachos and tacos were brought to the table, accompanied by the largest pitcher of iced strawberry margaritas Jasmine had ever seen. "Now I understand the need for the car service," she muttered.

Two margaritas and countless appetizers later, she sat back and patted her full belly with satisfaction. "Yummy, very yummy. Slowly I'm learning all your secrets. That reminds me, how come I don't know about your indie music concert-festival thing? My friends from Seattle told me about it."

Everyone looked at each other and shrugged their shoulders.

"There's every kind of music," Tyler explained, "it's not limited to one style. It's the best in new bands. I try not to miss it every year."

"It's held in a cleared field that they make into fairgrounds, so there's lots of room," Nadine said.

"Hope your friends bought their tickets," Brenda added.

The eating and drinking went on and on into the evening. Jasmine noted most everyone, including Nana and Nadine, were drinking her under the table. She preferred not to think about getting up in the morning.

"Who wants another?" Tyler made it her mission to keep all the glasses filled.

Paula waved her off. "Not for me, thanks. Unless you plan to feed my animals tomorrow."

"Let me think." Tyler glanced toward the ceiling. "Sorry, but no. I should have stopped about three margaritas earlier for that myself."

"That's what I thought," Paula grumbled.

"What happened to your drinking?" teased Jasmine, accepting a new glass.

"It only exists in competition with you." She grinned and pointed at Rose and Nadine. "If those two are involved, it's better to quit while you're ahead."

Frowning, Jaz looked at her glassy-eyed grandmother. "Have we drunk that much already? I'm not feeling it."

"That's why I'm counting," Paula said. "Maybe you'll go to the bathroom? Just to test the effects on your sense of balance?"

"I don't need to test my sense of balance. I'm a yoga instructor for something. I do practically nothing all day but stand on one leg." She grunted indignantly, and then hiccuped.

Paula stifled a laugh. "So go ahead. Get up and show us the dying swan or whatever those great exercises are called."

Jasmine could not resist this challenge. So she stood up and had to grab the table for support right away. Conveniently, a solid shoulder was nearby. A man's shoulder? She squinted her eyes and blinked. Jake and Stan had arrived.

Jake stood looking down at her, shaking his head, before turning to his sister. "Are you serious?"

"I'm not their overseer. If you want to blame someone, you need to talk to Rose, Nadine, or Tyler."

He looked to his mother for support, but she just shrugged. "I stopped interfering years ago. At your request, among others," she said.

"Let her go, Jake. She was just about to show us her latest yoga trick." Tyler couldn't wait.

"I don't think Jaz does any more yoga today," he muttered, only to get an elbow rammed into his abs. "Hey. I'm trying to help you here."

"Wrong," Jasmine slurred. "You're trying to tell me what I can and can't do. I live and breathe yoga. I can do the exercises backwards in my sleep." She said the words with more confidence than she felt. But now she couldn't go back.

"I give up," Jake said, taking a step away from Jasmine.

Suddenly robbed of human support, she staggered for a moment before regaining her composure. Whew. That was a close call. Her big mouth was going to get her killed. She took a deep breath and tried to focus. She shifted her weight to her favored standing leg and brought the rest of her body into a horizontal position. Just as she thought triumphantly "there you go!" she lost focus and tumbled belly-down to the floor. At the last moment, Jake caught her and pulled her to him. *Quite handy to have such a strong man around*, she thought dreamily.

Jake held out his hand to help her up and shook his head in amusement. "Don't you know that Jaz is an absolute lightweight when it comes to drinking?"

Paula ducked her head guiltily while the others went wide-eyed.

With one fluid motion, he lifted Jasmine up.

With Jake, it was completely different than with Gavin, she thought. The quips between them were friendly. Moreover, he had announced one morning that he would be working out with her. She had been very surprised, but happily included him. While he had been surprisingly relaxed about the individual exercises—he was clearly more flexible than she would have given him credit for—it had given her a little satisfaction when he complained the next day of muscle soreness. Any jokes about yoga were always accompanied by a self-deprecating grin, which she appreciated. Her train of thought was interrupted as the room spun and lost focus.

"Here," Paula said, handing Jake an armful of shopping bags. "You take her nonperishables. I'll take her groceries straight to the studio tomorrow."

"Do that. But better not count on her until afternoon. I have a feeling our friend here is going to feel tipsy for a while."

Everyone watched him as he carried Jasmine out. "How romantic," Rose sighed.

"True," Nadine agreed with her. "We couldn't have planned this any better."

"Too bad, she probably would have liked being awake for that exit," Paula said.

"We can tell her in detail tomorrow," Tyler replied unconcerned. She raised the pitcher. "Last call for alcohol."

Jasmine woke and tried to get her bearings. Jake's scent of soap and leather rose to her nose. She took a deep breath and snuggled closer. Her eyes flew open. Snuggled? She lifted her head. Everything began to spin. Funny, her feet didn't seem to be touching the ground.

Amused, Jake looked down at her as he carried her to her house. "Do you want me to put you down?"

She had to think about that first. "Ashually, I'm quite comferble where I am," she slurred. By now they were at the front door.

"Keys?" Jake asked.

She rummaged in her purse ineffectively until he took it and found them. "Rambo is home," she reminded him.

"Ah, yes. The bloodthirsty attack dog," he sighed, taking it upon himself to have a serious word with her about security measures when she was sober. With his shoulder, he pushed open the door and carried her inside.

He glanced at the figure in his arms. Her eyelids were heavy, but the look she gave him underneath said it all. She looked scrumptious, and showed she felt the attraction that existed between them, even in this condition. Too bad he had to keep his hands off her tonight. As if she had guessed his thoughts, she raised a hand to his face and slowly slid her fingertips down his cheek to the pulse on his neck. He took a deep breath to keep his out-of-control hormones in check. Sometimes it wasn't easy to do the right thing, he thought through clenched teeth as the delicate scent of her perfume hit his nose. Carefully, he laid her down on the sofa, where she promptly closed her eyes and fell back asleep. He removed her shoes as well as her pants and, after a long look at her shapely legs, covered her with a quilt.

After greeting Rambo, he let him out the door to do his business. Going into the kitchen for a moment, he returned with a bottle of water and a bucket, prepared for any eventuality. Jasmine hadn't moved from the spot.

Her chin-length blond hair surrounded her face like a halo. Carefully, he stroked her cheek with the back of his index finger. She curled her lips into a faint smile and snuggled closer to his hand. His heart grew tight. No question about it. The little, currently very drunk female had crept into his heart. Unbelievable. A short time ago he would have laughed out loud at this idea. But that was exactly what had happened. Now he just had to come up with a plan to convince her that he was the one for her, too. Tonight, however, it was enough for him to watch over her.

Someone was pounding on the door. Jasmine hid deeper under the covers and hoped that the person would disappear. Soon. There was a pounding behind her temples, and her mouth felt like a zombie rat had spent the night inside. Or three, for that matter. After the pounding didn't stop, she finally sat up and held her head. She groaned. Margaritas were evil. Very bad. From then on, she would stick strictly to her healthy diet and give alcohol a wide berth.

"Open up already, Jaz! I know you're in there."

Tyler? What was Tyler doing here? Jasmine was confused. She pushed herself up from the sofa and pushed the blanket aside. And froze. Why wasn't she wearing pants? Tyler pounded on the door again before she could form a clear thought. She really wished she wouldn't do that. The noise in her head didn't really need amplification, either. "I'm coming," she croaked, causing Rambo to lunge toward the doorway, tail wagging. The poor thing probably needed to get out badly, she guessed.

Her pants were lying neatly on the coffee table. She slipped them on. Who had folded them? Not her, anyway. She just slammed her clothes into a corner even when sober. And what time was it? She had no idea. In fact, quite a few of the last twelve hours had been in the dark. She yanked open the front door. "What?!"

"Top of the morning to you," Tyler trilled, floating princess-like through the door. The only thing that kept Jasmine from kicking her back out was the crackle of a bag she carried with *Miss Minnie's* printed on the side. Rambo noticed the bag, too, as she could tell by his ears tipped forward. She let her eyes wander back and forth between the bag and the dog a few times. Rambo noticed and started to pounce. She nodded imperceptibly at him. He pushed off with his hindquarters and flew through the air, straight toward the paper bag in Tyler's hand.

"What the—my muffins!" Tyler broke off, just barely managing to hold onto the front door as she watched the black dog run off triumphantly, tail held high.

"Rambo, here!" Jasmine called. If he managed to disappear outside, she could forget her share of the spoils. She reached for a can of treats sitting right beside the door for occasions like this, and rattled it loudly while letting out a loud whistle. *Ouch.* She winced. *Avoid whistling at all costs when you have a roaring headache*, she reminded herself. Miraculously, Rambo returned and placed the bag at her feet. Then he sat down and wagged expectantly. She grinned and gave him the well-deserved cookie, while snatching the muffins out of reach.

"And here I thought I was going to have to raise you from the dead. Instead, I'm getting a circus show," Tyler said.

"Tea?" Jasmine asked, like nothing had happened and headed for the kitchen. "I'm not really awake yet either. Or sane. But having already sinned with alcohol yesterday, I might as well go right ahead with the sugar today. The only thing that helps with a full-blown hangover for me." Jasmine scowled at herself as she put water on for a cup of tea.

"That's what I thought," Tyler answered. "Me, too. Which is why I brought you a serving of fat with sugar, but also this." She held out her open palm. On it were two tablets. Jasmine eyed them suspiciously. Tyler rolled her eyes. "Why don't you just cancel today and swallow this stuff, even if it doesn't fit into your diet plan?" When Jasmine still made no move, she opened the kitchen cabinets, got a glass, and filled it with tap water. "Open your mouth and swallow. Just imagine how nice the day will look without a headache," she purred.

Reluctantly, Jasmine reached for the glass and the aspirin. "Thank you." She swallowed the headache pills and poured her tea.

Wordlessly, Tyler pulled a muffin from the bag and held it out.

Jasmine snatched it up, gratefully inhaled the scent of the bran and banana muffin, but wisely set it aside until she sipped some tea. Her brain slowly got back on track. "So. Come on out with it. What are you doing here?"

"I'm the changing of the guard. Jake sent me. For some reason he blamed me for you having too much tequila yesterday." She frowned. "The logic doesn't quite make sense to me, I have to admit." She held up a hand and counted off on her fingers, "You're over twenty-one, not a former alcoholic," she glanced briefly at Jaz, who nodded affirmatively before continuing, "have known alcohol and yourself for a few years as well. Why should I be held responsible for you? I don't quite understand. But since I can empathize with how you feel the next morning when you've had one glass too many, I'm happy to play nurse and breakfast courier."

"Where is Jake, anyway?" Still a bit confused, Jasmine rubbed her forehead. The fog in her alcohol-soaked mind was slowly lifting. Only the feeling of safety and security was clear in her mind. Had Jake brought her home? She closed her eyes to trace those snatches of emotion and jerked her eyes open again, as the missing pieces of the puzzle fell into place. She propped her head in her hands and groaned.

"Did you just remember that you danced naked for my brother?" asked Tyler, who appeared to have a little devil sitting on her shoulder.

Jasmine blinked through her fingers at Jake's sister. "It's not quite that bad. But he carried me from the car into the living room. I was probably drooling all over his shirt."

Tyler raised an eyebrow. "Ugh. You think my brother is drool-worthy?"

Jasmine rolled her eyes and instantly regretted it. Even aspirin couldn't work miracles. "I do think so, but

I'm afraid it was more alcohol-induced yesterday. Not very sexy on my part." She blushed.

"I don't know," Tyler said, with a twinkle in her eye. "If you ask me, he doesn't see it that way. This morning on the phone he seemed rather, how shall I say, frustrated. You really do seem to trigger all his chivalrous instincts. Why else would he organize a breakfast for you instead of disappearing after having his fun, yesterday?"

"Can't I have both?" sighed Jasmine theatrically.

"As long as you wait for the prince in your tower like the good princess, it won't happen," Tyler replied dryly.

Surprised, Jasmine twisted and turned the statement in her head. Actually, Tyler was right, what was she waiting for? After all, she had already clearly shown she was interested in him. It didn't get much clearer than that. Unless she took matters into her own hands. Determined, she stood up and sank back into the chair with a grunt. She needed to wait to feel halfway functional again. After that, a hot shower was in order.

Smiling compassionately, Tyler handed her a light-blue glazed cupcake and poured her a refill of tea.

CHAPTER EIGHTEEN

At the ranch, the girl paced back and forth between the barn and the trees, the dogs close on her heels. She was restless and worried. The woman had been out almost all yesterday and didn't come home until late. There had been no food. Her stomach growled. Maybe the woman had grown tired of feeding an extra eater? It wouldn't be the first time something like that happened. She wasn't stupid. All the food that was constantly in the stall and eaten by her secretly, the woman put out for her. Or not so secretly. That it disappeared was obvious. And as happy as she was about the food, she could never really enjoy it for fear of being confronted. But the prospect of simply being forgotten scared her even more.

She put her hands into the jacket she had borrowed from the tack room. In the evenings and early mornings, it was chilly. Fortunately, there were countless warm work clothes lying around in the stable. Finally, she paused in her aimless worry. Maybe she should just do all the work that needed to be done. She had already done a little bit every day. If she did it all, maybe the woman would reconsider and give her some food. Nervously she looked at the house. The space in front of the house, where the pickup truck usually stood, was still empty. Paula, as the woman was called—she suddenly remembered—was often not there during the day. But at feeding times she was usually always back on time. Something was not right here. And she feared it had to do with her. Nausea rose in her throat. On the verge of tears, she pushed the fear aside with all her willpower and concentrated on her task.

First she filled up the horses' water trough. They came to the water, snuffling softly. She leaned against the heavy big barn door that led to the pasture and pushed against it with all her might until it stood open. The horses watched her efforts with trusting eyes. They had long become accustomed to her presence. One by one they left the stable and began to graze. The girl eagerly set about mucking out the stalls as well as the paved floor inside the barn. When she finished, she filled the wheelbarrow with hay, which she then stuffed into the feed trough with her skinny arms. Not knowing what else the horses were getting to eat, she preferred to leave it alone.

On one of the rare occasions in her past when she had been allowed to visit a library, she had devoured all the horse books she could find. She was aware of what delicate digestive systems these beautiful animals had, and how they easily came down with colic. When she was done with that, she let her eyes wander around the barn. Was there anything else to do? If so, she couldn't see it.

With a shrug of her shoulders to no one in particular, she left the barn and crept over to the house. Now it was the dogs' turn. The furry noses did not leave her side. Grateful for the company, she took time to stroke each one on the head before continuing on her way. She had discovered the dog's food during one of her rare forays through the house. The large bag was in the pantry adjacent to the kitchen.

On the porch, she took another look over her shoulder at the driveway. When she didn't see or hear a car, she carefully pushed open the door. Tiptoeing, she crept into the kitchen. The clack of the dog's claws on the wood floor was louder than her own footsteps and made her flinch. In the kitchen, she grabbed the first available container and filled it halfway with kibble. Barns and Roo showed their excitement by jumping in the air on the spot, spinning around. With a big smile on her face, she dodged them and made her way back to the porch where the food bowls were.

"You're real circus dogs," she giggled. Startled, she put her hand over her mouth. Barns decided he had shown enough restraint and jumped up at her. With great accuracy, the heeler's head hit the bowl and knocked it out of her hand. Horrified, she watched as the container flew through the air in a high arc. Food scattered all over the porch. She slapped her hands in front of her mouth and swallowed hard. Mistakes were always severely punished in her experience, so she ducked. When nothing happened she remembered she was here alone and managed to pull herself out of shock. On her knees, she tried to maneuver the dog food back into the bowl as fast as she could. Only when the first dog's snout got in her way did she realize that the dogs were simply gathering the food for themselves. She glanced at the bowl in her hand. She had collected a meager handful so far.

The dogs made short work of the scattered food. Fortunately, they didn't fight, they just gobbled. She wiped her hands on her pants and took the container back to the kitchen. There were bananas on the kitchen counter. Her stomach growled. With a furtive glance over her shoulder, she reached over and snarfed one down. As she devoured the sweet fruit, she looked longingly at the door to the bathroom. A hot shower would be fabulous. But she didn't dare do that today. Not when she had no idea when Paula would be home. She shoved the empty banana peel into the pocket of her much-too-big, borrowed jacket to toss on the compost heap outside. Better to let the evidence of her presence disappear inconspicuously.

Determined, she pushed herself off the kitchen counter. Cleanliness was overrated anyway. And at least she had running water, even hot, in the wash trough in the barn. Luxury, so to speak. Instead of feeling sorry for herself, better she should use the time to groom the horses, and water the flowers in front of the house.

Tyler left, and Jasmine slowly got herself together. She gathered up her to-do lists and plans, stuffed them into a cloth bag, and last but not least, grabbed her yoga mat. Her goal was to organize all the cleaning supplies and other purchases from yesterday at the studio. As for the near future, Jasmine planned to "christen" the studio by doing a gentle workout as soon as she got there, dirt or no dirt. The familiar exercises would do her good and hopefully relieve some of the tension she had inside.

Soon, she was at Main Street. Jasmine and Rambo parked and jumped out. In a better mood, thanks to Tyler's headache pills, she strolled down the street and waved at an isolated vehicle. She had no idea who was in it, but it didn't matter. People on the street were greeted, that was just how it was. She assumed she would soon be able to match most of the cars to their drivers, as well.

Lost in thought, she unlocked the door, then raised her head and listened. Knocking noises, voices and footsteps echoed through the empty rooms. She hadn't known that one of the adjacent buildings was also being renovated. That wouldn't be so bad. Maybe then they could help each other out like good neighbors, in case something was missing. Except she wouldn't be ringing the bell for a cup of sugar, but rather to borrow a handful of nails. Jasmine just hoped the remodeling work next door would be limited to a few days, too. Otherwise, she would have to postpone the start of her class. Her students needed a quiet environment to relax during yoga or meditation classes. She was surprised that the noise was so audible. But for that moment, it didn't matter.

She shouldered her bag and yoga mat and began climbing the stairs to the second floor. When she reached the top of the stairs, she stopped, stunned. Everywhere people were busily giving the old rooms a new shine. Slowly, she climbed the last few steps.

Nana held out a big thermos of tea. "Here, kiddo. I hear you had a rough night."

Nadine was also here, busily cleaning the large windows. In one corner, she spotted Paula assembling shelves with her mother, Brenda. A miniature version of the two—was that Tyler assisting? A man with loopy white hair and thick-rimmed glasses crossed the room. His eyes blinked myopically and seemed to dart from corner to corner. Finally, he stopped in front of her.

"Excuse me, miss, would you possibly have a pencil for me?"

Jake popped up behind him, reached behind his ear, and pulled out a pencil. "Here it is, Dad." With a sly grin, he waved at her and joined two other men.

She recognized Nate, one of the other few newcomers to Independence. He had moved here six months ago with his daughter Shauna and his ex-wife Nancy, and had taken over the veterinary practice from the old doc. She learned that from Miss Minnie after asking where the closest vet was located. Minnie had turned around and called his name loudly through the diner. Alarmed, Nate got up from his lunch and tried to find out about the emergency. Miss Minnie had pointed and called out to him, "A new customer for you. You can pay the cost of the ad via tip." Fellow diners stifled laughter as he sat back down with a shake of his head. Jasmine guessed he hadn't quite gotten used to the way this small town worked.

She did not know the third man. Like the other two, he was tall, his broad shoulders standing out under his shirt. There had to be something in the water the way this place teemed with good-looking, well-built men. At the moment, they were busy building the partition between the classroom and the locker room. Among the familiar faces were many who, though complete strangers to her, were helping out alongside her friends. Even some children joined in. Ellie, the daughter of Mark and Sandra Holt, who ran the stationery store on the same side of the street as the studio, was painting trim with splashes of red paint. Everywhere Jasmine looked, she met friendly stares. Individuals greeted her directly or waved. But everyone continued to work as if this were their normal Saturday activity.

Nadine marched busily back and forth between the individual work groups with a list in her hand and seemed to be directing the whole thing. When she caught sight of Jasmine, her expression brightened and she headed straight for her. "I'm glad you're here. I have a few last questions about your plans."

"My plans?"

"Yeah, you recorded how you'd like it a couple of days ago at the diner. I hope that's still current?"

Slightly overwhelmed by all the helpful activity around her, Jasmine glanced at the drawing. "Uh, yeah. Pretty much, anyway. But tell me, what's going on?"

Nadine blinked. "What do you mean by that? We're fixing up your studio. Rose told us all about your plans, which, by the way, are especially popular with the female demographic, so we came in this morning to help you get started."

Overwhelmed, Jasmine leaned against the wall. Nadine eyed her critically and gave her an affectionate pat. "There, there, who's going to cry here? That's just how we do it here. There's a special phone alarm set up for that. Usually the Disney Sisters start it. You know how it is. They're always the first to know. You wouldn't believe how proud Rose was that this time she was the one to start it."

That, on the other hand, Jasmine could well imagine. At that moment, she felt a great love for her grandmother, and gratitude for all the friends and acquaintances who willingly sacrificed their time to help her get started.

"Hey! We took a break from our tour!" a voice called out. It was Pat, with Kathrina, carrying something in a large frame.

Jasmine threw her arms wide open to embrace them. "What have you got there?"

Kathrina turned it around. "Pat painted you a logo in the studio colors. You can hang it in the window or put it on the wall."

Fighting tears again, Jasmine embraced them both as Rocky found Rambo and cavorted.

Paula sauntered over and held out a glass to her. "Here's to you, Jaz. Seems like the guardian of karma finally remembered you. Drink. You've earned it after all the stress you've been under lately."

"After last night?"

"At least toast. It's good luck."

"You're right!" Jasmine accepted the glass and took a sip after toasting with Paula. "Prosecco? At ten in the morning? Now I realize why everyone is here. Well, luckily I'm not solely responsible for the disaster, if there is one," she joked.

Before taking another sip, she noticed Pat slipping away, and Tyler appreciatively watching his fine physique go. But that juicy detail would have to wait. "Give me something to do before the work's all done," she said, to no one in particular.

Pat pulled up to the Prairie-style Wilkinson house and checked the angle of the sun over the Rockies. As part of the restoration, it was vital that the majestic outside views be preserved as design originally allowed them. That meant not blocking light at sundown, say in the dining room, as the family sat down to dinner. Mr. Wilkinson lived here pretty much alone these days, but if restored, someday the house would shelter another family.

Pat got out of the van, pulled out his phone, and began snapping. Mr. Wilkinson was out, but he'd given Pat full permission to take pictures anytime. In Pat's opinion, the house was very special and could easily be awarded special historic status by officials in Denver, with the proper application and documentation.

The Wilkinson home was designed by a colleague of Elizabeth Wright Ingraham, the granddaughter of the great architect Frank Lloyd Wright. Wright and her husband settled in nearby Colorado Springs, about two hours away, just as the 1950s were dawning. In 1970 Elizabeth formed her own architectural firm with some associates, one of whom designed the Wilkinson house with similar use of natural settings that Wright Ingraham and her famous grandfather were noted for. The house had a "low-slung" human-scale exterior, built into a rugged hill. It incorporated natural light via windows and skylights, and used organic building materials.

For Pat, it was the assignment of a lifetime, something that could make his reputation nationally as an architect. As the sun went down, and colors deepened around the 4500-square foot house, he imagined subtle lighting for the grounds that would come on just as purple dappled the rocky ridges behind it. But before he ever got to that finishing touch, the home needed structural reinforcement and repair. It had been buffeted with seasonal winds up to a hundred miles per hour ever since it was built in 1970, and the foundation needed serious work.

Pat had brought Rocky with him, Kathrina's mastiff. The big dog needed some fresh air and to "do his business." He and Rambo were a bit much to handle together, and everyone was busy at the studio, so taking Rocky was Pat's way of helping out. Rocky sniffed the bushes and trotted back and forth as Pat found the angles of the house he needed with his camera phone.

After both males had finished with their "business" they got back in the van and headed for the diner.

Main Street looked almost magical at twilight. Soft lights came on, bathing the storefronts in gentle yellow illumination. Tiny fairy lights bedecked potted shrubs and bushes. The air was fresh and cool. Tyler walked lightly along the street, toward the diner, as Independence transitioned from day to evening. Time away from the touring show to visit family was a rare treat, and allowed her to reflect on how grateful she was for her life in Las Vegas. Cirque-du-Soleil-type shows attracted the world to Las Vegas, and they demanded world-class dancers, athletes, and gymnasts. To get cast in that kind of show, commanding one hundred dollars per ticket and up, was confirmation that you were a pro.

At twenty-three, Tyler was in her prime. What would she do when the day came that she couldn't dance anymore? Dancing was her life. Always had been. For as long as she could remember, it had been her dream to become a ballerina. That goal relaxed a bit, over time, to professional dancer in a show tour—still highly desirable and respectable. Every night Tyler balanced on tiptoe on top of a silvery moon in a gossamer dress that looked as though it were made of moonbeams and quicksilver. All of it suspended one hundred feet above an adoring audience.

She could not imagine a life outside the world of dance. Was there even one? Absorbed in thought, she did not notice a man kneeling on the street in front of a dog. She crashed into him, and hit the ground hard with her backside. She was grateful it wasn't a knee. She groaned and rocked to get up. But the man and the dog circled her, concerned.

"Can't you be careful?" the man scolded her as he checked the dog's paws.

Tyler finally noticed who it was. Pat! And Rocky! "Oh, poor boy. Did I hurt you?" she asked, letting Rocky sniff her hand while she rubbed the side of her hip.

"Oh, it's you," Pat said. "Did you hurt your ummm…" He didn't want to say "butt" or "rear" or any word that would get him in trouble.

"No," she replied, "fortunately it's made of solid muscle."

Her reply surprised them both so much that Pat looked her right in the eye. When their eyes met, the whole situation changed; it felt as if they were the only two people in all of Independence. The air crackled with electrical energy. Tyler half expected to hear thunder, which would most certainly follow the feeling that had struck like lightning.

Pat refocused on the young woman with the incredibly large, sea-blue eyes who had almost stepped on Rocky's paws. Admittedly, she wasn't big enough to do any damage to the big mastiff. But that was not the point. What was the point again? Oh, yes. Walking without paying attention to surroundings. He was about to lecture her again to make his point when he paused. Joyfully, the woman patted Rocky's broad face and even indulged in a big, slobbery kiss on his chin. That was going a bit far for Pat's taste.

After days with Kathrina, first in the van, and doing the architectural tour with Mr. Wilkinson, Pat felt the need for some time off. Tomorrow he could meet up with Jasmine and Kathrina. That night, he didn't feel like having complicated conversations about architecture and what his plans were. He suddenly realized that Tyler was studying him as a smile threatened to turn up the corners of her mouth. "May I buy you and your four-legged friend some food now that I've run you over?"

He raised an eyebrow. "Do they sell dog food here at the diner, too?"

Tyler made eye contact with Rocky. "I don't think he'd mind hot dogs."

That got a grin. Pat felt his brooding face brighten with a smile. Tyler scrambled to her feet. She had stumbled across a super specimen of the male species. And he was nice to animals, too? She decided right then and there that he was just the distraction she needed on this vacay.

"So, what'll it be? Can I feed you?"

Pat was closely following the expression on her face, and bit his lower lip in concentration. So the attraction was mutual. All the better. Just the thing after these last exhausting weeks.

"Sure. I never turn down free food," he said.

"Doesn't get offered to you much, though, obviously," she murmured, letting her gaze slide over his broad shoulders and flat stomach, which showed off superbly under his shirt.

Amused, he asked, "Inspection complete?"

She met his gaze with a mischievous smile. "Not quite. But I still have time. I'll just quickly let my sister know that my plans for the evening have changed." She typed a quick message into her phone and turned it off.

He followed her example, assuring Kathrina he would take good care of her dog, and promising to be in touch tomorrow. A strand of Tyler's light-blond hair fluttered in her face. He lifted his hand and stroked it back behind her ear. The gesture felt strangely intimate.

"They have the most delicious chili dogs here," she said.

"You seem to know your way around. Do you live here?"

"No," she replied curtly, asking back, "What's your name, anyway?"

"Pardon me. Our stormy meeting made me forget my manners. I'm Pat." He held out his hand to her.

She shook it. "I'm Tyler. And your dog?"

"That's Rocky. He's not mine." He gave her a wink. "His owner and I are just visiting here."

Of course. It had to be like that. She finally met an interesting man, but he was already tied up with her family. The thought annoyed her. She recognized the name of the dog as one Jaz had mentioned. But no matter. For a few hours, she could easily avoid all questions. The next day, she'd be gone, anyway. And by the time she returned, he'd be back in Seattle. So, no reason not to enjoy this moment.

Tyler blinked. Sunlight was streaming in through wooden blinds. Strange. The sun never shone in her room in the morning. Sleepily, she turned over and encountered resistance. A large, muscular, warm resistance. A satisfied smile stole across her face as the events of the last few hours came back to her mind. At some point they had ended up at the river with a case of beer, meeting there in their own vehicles. They enjoyed a steamy evening in this RV, and a mutual decision was made that each other was the perfect distraction for an evening out. It was always pleasant when they both had the same expectations.

She looked around the mobile home. The Carter family had kept it as a shelter on the river during fishing season, for years. The bed she was lying in, as well as the couch on the other side and the tiny shower, were already very familiar to her. Thanks to Pat's creativity in bed she now knew more ways each location could be used pleasurably. She stroked his back lightly, but was careful not to wake him. It was better not to delay the inevitable for long. Tyler hated long goodbyes. She'd rather get it over with quickly, much like ripping off a Band-Aid. Tiptoeing, she gathered up her scattered clothes. Rocky raised his head briefly, but immediately lowered it again when he noticed that she made no effort to take him with her. At the door, she hesitated and took one last look at the wonderful man in the bed. Determined, she shook her head and slipped out.

Pat heard the door close with a soft click. He sighed and pushed his long legs out of bed, pulled on boxers, and shuffled into the RV's small kitchen to put on some coffee. He almost gave himself away when she stroked his back. Only too gladly he would have picked up where they left off last night. But he had already sensed yesterday that she didn't plan to stay. Yesterday, that had been just fine with him. And today? Today he wasn't so sure.

Aside from the fantastic night, the rest of the time he spent with her had been wonderful. She had a dry sense of humor, was good at laughing at herself, and had no problem with slobbering dogs. She'd already told him how to lock the place up, just by turning a button in the door handle. He sighed. And she was gone.

With steaming coffee in hand, he sat down at the tiny kitchen table and fished his cell phone out of the pocket of his cargo pants. They happened to be lying on the kitchen counter. When he turned the phone on, it beeped like crazy. Someone had left message after message. Kathrina and Jasmine had both left messages that Mr. Wilkinson was looking for him. And Mr. Wilkinson had left his own message. Two minutes later, Pat was behind the wheel of his own rental van, a confused Rocky beside him, enjoying the drive back to Independence.

CHAPTER NINETEEN

"WHERE HAVE YOU BEEN all this time?" Kathrina wanted to know as she jumped in Pat's van. He noticed that her face was pale with dark circles under her eyes. She gathered her long dark hair into a careless knot and wrapped herself deeper into her jacket as if she were freezing.

Pat hugged her tightly. "I'm sorry. My cell phone was off. I just turned it back on."

"Rocky?"

"He was a good boy and enjoyed our outing."

Kathrina sighed with relief and seemed to let go of some annoyance.

"Shall we take a look at beautiful Independence?" asked Pat.

"I'd rather have something to eat. And Mr. Wilkinson was asking about where you were, too."

"Sounds good."

Kathrina seemed strangely distracted. But Pat figured that probably the same could be said about him. In his case, it was compounded by the fact that he just couldn't get his Friday night acquaintance out of his mind. His usual procedure of enjoying a night out and then going about business as usual with no problems didn't seem to be working this time.

Kathrina stared out the window and took in the unfamiliar landscape. "Would you pack up your things in Seattle and move here? At least for a while?"

Pat thought for a moment and shrugged. "Honestly, right now I couldn't think of anything better. In Seattle, it's constant conflict with my business partner. Here, with the right project, maybe I'd find my way back to my old love, restoration architecture. I've missed that a lot in recent years. The separation from my business partner was painful but turned out to be quite good in the end. It forced me to get back to why I chose this job in the first place."

Kathrina looked at him in surprise. "I didn't expect such philosophical insight first thing in the morning. Makes me feel kind of superficial right now. Deep thoughts about life and work; maybe they don't go with dog grooming and dog sitting." She looked a little mournful.

Pat reached for her hand across the car's center console and gave it a quick squeeze. "Now stop it. Maybe you lead a simpler life and you're already in touch on deeper level."

A laugh bubbled out of her.

"Now that we're on the topic," he said with a grin, "are you planning any profound changes in your life?"

"I don't know." She plucked invisible lint from her sweater. "With me, it's more like you two are my two closest friends. My family is in Poland. Which I never visit. For good reason. "If you and Jasmine are suddenly sitting here in the middle of nowhere, what am I going to do in Seattle?"

Pat considered. He didn't want to dismiss her concerns with a flippant remark. "I never thought about it that way. Does that make me a bad friend?"

"Course not," she said simply.

"Let's see if Mr. Wilkinson buys my proposal before we make plans for me to move here."

"You're making it dependent on a project?" Kathrina frowned. "Surely there would be other projects around here you could apply for?"

"Probably. But things like that always take time. The decision would come next year at the earliest. In addition, I'm not fixed on this area. I'm more focused on the project than the place at this point. It's not like I would want to move here because of Jaz."

Kathrina watched him from the side.

"What is it?"

"Were you ever, you know…"

He raised an eyebrow questioningly and shook his head in denial. "Uh, no, I don't. What are we supposed to have been?" He reached for his water bottle.

"Well, a couple."

He gurgled and almost choked. Coughing, he passed the bottle to Kathrina. "No. Definitely not. There was never anything more between us."

They stopped in the parking lot behind the diner and made their way inside. "Now we're about to see if the diner lives up to its reputation as Independence's gossip central," Kathrina said with a grin, as Pat held the door open for her.

Miss Minnie, standing at a table just around the corner, eyed Kathrina narrowly. "Welcome to the information center."

Kathrina and Pat exchanged looks and grinned.

"Can I finally bring you some real food instead of pouring coffee?"

Pat laughed and called after her as she stepped up to the counter. "That's what we were just talking about. You know your guests well, Miss Minnie."

She straightened up and stretched her enormous bosom forward. "That's my profession. I hope you can actually restore houses, too, and not just repaint them."

Kathrina bit her lower lip. Miss Minnie didn't pussyfoot around, she always got straight to the point.

"The food will be here in a few minutes. I'll bring you water. Do you need anything else?" When they both shook their heads, she added, "Mr. Wilkinson is sitting over there if you want to talk to him, Pat."

With his mouth open, Pat stared at her.

"What? Did you expect me not to know what's going on in my town?" With these words, she placed the Denver daily newspaper in front of Kathrina. "Here. To give you something to do in the meantime, child." With those words, she rushed away. The ribbons of her apron flew behind her.

"Your town," Kathrina repeated, impressed, as Pat left the table and headed for Mr. Wilkinson.

A man dining at the next table smirked and folded up his newspaper. "Are you aware that around here Mr. Wilkinson is considered the unofficial mayor?"

"Oh? Why unofficial? Is there an official mayor?" she asked with interest, while keeping her eyes fastened on the revolving door Miss Minnie had disappeared through.

"Sure. A female mayor. But there's also a community council that consists of seven people. The Disney Sisters are part of that, as well as Mr. Wilkinson. The power players of Independence, if you will."

"Miss Minnie is a force of nature," Kathrina mused, turning to face the stranger. She almost fell off her stool. She held on at the last moment and squirmed inwardly when she saw his amused look. The man looked like a true Viking; reddish-blond hair, an angular face, and bright green eyes. Broad shoulders, and if she interpreted the contours under the long-sleeved T-shirt correctly, sinewy muscles. Finally, she found her voice again and croaked, "You wouldn't happen to be related to Paula, would you?"

His mouth curved into a broad smile. "You know my sister? And survived the encounter?"

"Hey, don't say that about your sister!"

At least he shrugged guiltily. "You're right. But she didn't exactly invent the term *social skills*."

"So far, she's made a better first impression than you," Kathrina replied flippantly. She had no idea which little devil was sitting on her shoulder right now. But it was getting on her nerves that this guy was sitting here, talking about his sister to strangers and acting as if he had the whole world at his feet. Which was probably true if you looked like him.

He seemed more amused by her outburst, which only annoyed her more. "And yes, I met her recently. We have a mutual friend," Kathrina added.

Immediately his expression became serious. "Jaz. The new yoga studio owner." It was a statement, not a question. So he knew.

Kathrina squirmed uncomfortably in her seat. She didn't quite know what to do with this suddenly very human side of the Viking. Did it have to be like this? she thought, still annoyed, but also fascinated against her will. And when a sympathetic side was added to masculine good looks, a man was practically unstoppable. She consoled herself with the thought that this would not be a problem for her anyway. After all, she wasn't interested in him and he certainly wasn't interested in her. Her hormones, which were doing a dance of joy in her belly and cheering her on to throw herself at him on the spot, were not interested in her rational considerations. Distance was the order of the day.

She felt uncomfortable. Her face felt hot. She desperately needed distance from this hunk of testosterone that was suddenly showing emotion, too. Time to back off. "Well then, it was nice to meet you, brother of Paula."

"Sam."

"What?" He was completely throwing her for a loop. Now, to make matters worse, he was smiling.

"My name is Sam," he repeated patiently. "And you are?"

"Kathrina. Friend of Jaz's, and passing through." She added the last almost defiantly as she got up from her chair. In doing so, she nearly tripped over the chair leg.

In a flash, his hand shot forward and steadied her at the hip. All the nerve endings in her body seemed to short-circuit. Hastily, she took a big step back to break the contact. That time, fortunately, without almost falling down. One had to be grateful for small gifts from the universe or whoever was in charge at the time.

Sam watched Kathrina walk over to Mr. Wilkinson's table. The unofficial mayor was deep in conversation with the man she'd come in with—a tall man—and he briefly put his hand on her back. Her boyfriend? Surprised, he realized that he didn't like this idea at all. She was an impressive woman, with her height, long dark brown curls, and blue eyes the color of a glacial lake. Not to mention her very, very appealing curves.

As the star player on the Colorado Blizzard team, Sam had his pick of women. But most of the fans were model-thin. Always on the verge of starvation and still on a diet. As interesting as a glass of water in his opinion. He longed for a woman who didn't immediately stab him with a hip bone. Or burst into tears just for raising his voice. He wasn't violent or anything, for heaven's sake. His peaceful father would turn his head around single-handedly if he showed a tendency that way.

True, his quick temper was well known. It was just too bad that most women assumed they could tame him. Otherwise his days in the NHL would be numbered. You didn't stay at that level for long if you suddenly mutated into a wimp. He snorted. How had he even come up with this absurd train of thought? Oh, right. Curves. And what curves, he thought, as his gaze retraced the room to Kathrina. She had pepper in her butt as well as a deep loyalty to her friends, and even her friends' friends, the way she'd put him straight. He usually only got disapproving looks like that from his coach. It would be interesting to see where this tension between them led.

Sam winced inwardly as he reviewed his comments regarding Paula. It wasn't his usual approach when it came to charming pretty women. But Kathrina had literally upset him. The teasing between him and his sister was legendary, and old habits were hard to break. So he had resorted to flippant remarks. Too bad Kathrina was just passing through. Otherwise he might have had a chance to revise her first impression of him.

Like many of the people now trickling into the town, he tried to come back every year for the Indie Music Festival and spend time with his family. He glanced over at Kathrina again. And promptly caught her eyeing him. Embarrassed, she averted her eyes. Interesting. He put some bills on the table to pay for his food, and left the diner.

Kathrina, who was watching him out of the corner of her eye, breathed a sigh of relief. At last he was gone. Mr. Wilkinson had filled them in on the fact that Sam was one of the local celebrities. A hockey player in the NHL. That explained his Viking-god body. Her mouth watered when she thought of his muscles. That was also where his obvious arrogance came from. She shook her head imperceptibly. It was always the same. She knew from bitter experience that good-looking men thought they could get away with anything. She would keep her hands off. No matter what her hormones said about it. Fortunately, she didn't have to deal with him. Tonight he was playing with his team in Denver. A home game. There was no way she was going to watch that on TV, she swore to herself.

CHAPTER TWENTY

The morning of her opening, Jasmine was a bundle of nerves. Today would be the first official classes. For the past few days, she had been handing out flyers and posting them everywhere. So far, thankfully, no one had complained. Even her personal sheriff hadn't said a peep.

Jake. Heat rose in her face. The last few days Jake had been on night shift, so she'd barely gotten to see him. If this were Seattle, and she'd been single, she would have pounced on him at the first available opportunity. But the scarce time spent together wasn't the only reason, if she was honest. She didn't really know what was holding her back. Probably she was simply too cowardly to make the first move.

In any case, it had meant that while they still ate together every night, they circled each other as the air crackled with unquenched sexual desire. At least on her part. Frustrated, she rolled her tense shoulders. After all, Jake still seemed concerned for her safety.

"Ready for the big day, Rambo?"

He looked at her expectantly. Were there going to be cookies?

Jasmine, correctly interpreting his look, shook her head in amusement. "No. No cookies. Lots of attention, though, for sure." At least she hoped so. Of course, if no one showed up, she'd have to actually comfort Rambo with a treat. Resolutely, she stopped the pointless speculation and headed for her studio.

Halfway down the street, she stopped as if rooted to the spot. People were forming a line that ran along the stores on her side of the street. Was the bakery having a two-for-one coffee promotion today, of all days? As she slowly approached, she saw that people were standing together in groups, waiting. Waiting for what? She greeted the friendly faces. Some she already knew from recent renovations when so many wonderful people pitched in. Others she had seen at the diner, and others she knew because they were friends with Rose or someone else in her circle of friends.

Overwhelmed, she gulped and pushed her way through the crowd to the door. Unlocking it, she casually asked a bystander, "What's going on here today?" She didn't dare believe they were here for her opening. It couldn't be that at all.

The man's eyebrows shot up. "You don't know? You single-handedly papered the town with your flyers. And by now you should know how this works. At least half the people are here so they can have their say at the diner today. But who knows, maybe you'll convince a few of them to come back regularly."

Puzzled, she glanced around. "You mean to say you're all here to take a trial yoga class?" A good portion of the crowd nodded. She had expected all sorts of results, just not what she saw here before her. Overwhelmed, she chewed on her lower lip and thought quickly. There was no way she could accommodate all of them together.

Finally, she said to the crowd, "I'm so glad you all came. But there are just too many of you. Maybe you could split up into groups? Those who have to go to work right away come first, okay?"

Some nodded in agreement, while someone from further back scolded. "And the rest of us? Are we supposed to stand in front of the door for ages?"

"Of course not. The others can go to the diner or the bakery for a coffee. Even better, a tea during that time. The bill is on me." She hoped her monthly budget, which she had stretched to the limit anyway with all the purchases for her center, could stand it.

"Just make sure you don't draw a crowd like this every morning. That could easily happen to you if they expect free coffee," someone warned.

"I'll take care of that when the time comes. Right now, I have to give these twenty potential students a great yoga lesson so they'll all come back," Jasmine mumbled and went into the building.

Her new students followed, chattering and laughing. As expected, the majority were female. But she was surprised to see that there were also a few men among them. And not twenty-somethings. They were more likely to be around sixty, if she didn't completely misjudge.

As soon as she stepped into the studio she had so lovingly decorated and prepared over the past few days, she felt the rooms welcome her. Practicing yoga was great. Teaching it, however, filled her with a deep satisfaction. Working with people, showing them how they could improve their flexibility and in turn, their health, was her calling. An exercise resort was not her calling, she realized with sudden clarity. She would be happy to lead the classes there, but someone else had to create it. Someone with a passion for the hotel business and all its ups and downs.

A stone she hadn't been aware of fell from her heart, and she suddenly felt light. She had made the right decision. And even though there might not be forty people waiting outside her studio every day, she would make it. While she was still thinking about it and people were slowly coming out of the locker room area, heavy footsteps sounded on the stairs.

Jake's head appeared on the landing. Joy filled her. What was he doing here? Behind him, his colleague Toby followed with a scowl on his face. He had a gym bag slung over his shoulder. At the top, Jake stopped, hands on his hips. "Well, well, well," he said, nodding appreciatively. "The police department has decided to express its support and show up for your opening. But I see that's not even necessary."

Toby's face brightened. "Does that mean I don't have to roll around on the floor?"

Jake gave him a stern look.

Jasmine bit the insides of her cheeks to keep from laughing out loud. Toby's relief was unmistakable. She hoped Jake would take the pressure off of him soon. It was obvious he'd rather be anywhere right now than here, of all places.

"Well done, Jaz," Jake said to her. His eyes lit up.

With a jolt, Jasmine realized that Gavin-the-jerk had never had a positive word about when it came to her job. When she looked at it closely, all her exes, few as they were, had only ever made fun of her profession. As soon as the initial fascination over her agile body wore off, respect for her job dissipated, as well. She pushed aside the unpleasant memories and concentrated on the men in front of her.

"I'm sorry, but the group is full. If I had known that you wanted to join, I would have reserved a place for you. There will be different groups at different times each day." Toby, who had just looked delighted, stepped back in horror. She stifled a laugh. Jake poked Toby in the side with his elbow.

"That's all right. I'm glad the opening is such a success."

"Maybe the sheriff can book a private lesson?" added Toby helpfully, trying to get one over on Jake.

"Maybe," she replied, letting Jake know with her gaze that she would definitely be interested in a private meeting soon. But then she tore herself away; she had new students to teach. "Class is about to start. Please go to the change rooms if you need to," she said.

She waved goodbye to Toby and Jake. Toby saluted and Jake squeezed her hand briefly. A tingle made her nerve endings dance.

"Too bad those two gorgeous guys didn't stay," Miss Daisy said, beside her. "At least then we would have had an entertainment program."

"Don't worry, Miss Daisy. I'll make sure there's enough variety."

Miss Daisy shuddered. "I do have to beg. Even though these gentlemen are quite all right, I'd rather not see them without their shirts on for an hour. The sheriff, on the other hand…"

Jasmine laughed. "It's okay. I get it. We can ask the mayor if he'll make his police officers available to us for this." Her remark was meant jokingly but Miss Daisy didn't seem to think the idea was far-fetched.

She suppressed the urge to laugh out loud, and walked forward. As she clapped her hands, the murmur of voices died down and people looked expectantly in her direction. A broad smile lit up her face. This was what she had missed. Yoga. For the first time in her professional life, in her own studio. And it felt great.

In brief, Jasmine explained the planned flow of the class. "There are mats over there against the wall. We're about to do a few moves on them." She gestured with her hand to the shelf in a corner where materials were neatly stacked. "They will be cleaned daily. You can bring your own, of course. If anyone wants to buy one, I'll be happy to help you after class."

"I told you, it's just a sales gimmick," came a muffled voice from the third row.

She laughed. "Sure. And a good one, too," she returned with a wink, which drew renewed laughter. She felt fine about it. Laughter relaxed people, broke down defenses, and generally put people in a good mood. "So. Back to the real reason we're here. Yoga. I'm going to give you a brief summary of what yoga is, and why it's useful for all of us, and then we'll get started. Some of you are here because you've heard something about yoga and are excited to finally practice it." She paused, letting her gaze slowly roam over the crowd, making personal contact with each one. "And others are here because they want to know what kind of foreign stuff the newcomer is offering," she added dryly. "My goal is to give you a class that will sweep you away and turn a skeptic or two into a fan. Are you ready?"

"Show them," her grandmother called from the back row, jabbing her elbow challengingly into the sides of her neighbors.

"Yoga is not only a theory of movement, but rather a philosophy of life. I have some books about it that I'd be happy to lend if anyone wants to look into it in more depth. In simple terms, the concept involves keeping the body and mind healthy through a combination of exercise, diet and meditation. In the various classes, we focus on improving our flexibility, strengthening our muscles, and consciously using our breathing. If you would like to take a closer look at nutrition, you are welcome to sign up for one of the nutrition classes. However, these will take place at the diner in collaboration with Disney Sisters. For more information, see the flyer on the door."

These classes had come about at the last minute when she had been brooding aloud in the diner over the problem of how to make nutrition classes interesting with no kitchen to cook in. Miss Minnie had been polishing glasses unobtrusively, but eavesdropping on the conversation. Minutes later she offered Jasmine her kitchen for a small fee. Every other Monday night, when business was bad anyway, the diner's kitchen was now Jasmine's. She survived one of Miss Minnie's bear hugs before being gently warned not to make people read her mind for what she wanted. "Just ask, girl. The only thing that can happen is that people will say no."

Jasmine had to admit that was true. Her self-confidence still had potential for development. That was probably why she was skirting around Jake like a cat around a bush instead of just asking him directly what exactly it was between them. Or unceremoniously jumping all over him. She concentrated again on her students, who thankfully hadn't noticed her brief mental vacation.

"Before I started yoga, I had the idea that it involved impossible contortions that I wouldn't be able to do anyway. I'm sure many of you feel the same way." A few people looked to the side, embarrassed. "For your peace of mind, I can assure you that's not the case. You wouldn't believe how many of the exercises I recognized from gym class."

"As if that would make it better," someone grumbled. "I always sucked at sports."

She ignored the interjection for the moment, but made a mental note to pay special attention to the person later during the exercises. "Simple stretches, alternating between tensing and relaxing the muscles, and breathing, which is so vital."

"Who needs air?" quipped another new visitor. She hadn't taken a mat, but leaned against the wall next to the window, walking stick firmly in hand. Jasmine suspected she wasn't sure the lady could get up from the floor without help. A proud and dignified woman. She made a mental note of that, too, with the intention of mentioning the possibility of private lessons later. Many found it easier to master their first attempts in a private setting, until they were sure they would not be laughed at by others. The need to maintain dignity Jasmine understood well, even if it failed her personally, lately. Her car crash of the last week came to mind.

After a short demonstration of five simple exercises, she went from participant to participant, assisting and motivating wherever needed. Everyone was warm and most had satisfied smiles on their faces. Goal achieved. Now she only had to repeat the trick four more times.

An hour later she jumped down the stairs, elated. After locking up, Jasmine made her way to the car with an exuberant Rambo. He'd spent the day enjoying admiring glances and petting from students. Then she'd taken him for a run over the lunch hour. Rambo was having a very good day. She looked up and spotted Jake leaning against her car, waiting for her. A broad laugh bubbled out of her and she started running. Rambo kept pace. She ignored the dog, her focus only on Jake. His face reflected the same joy she felt at seeing him. As she literally fell around his neck, he caught her with his strong arms and spun her around. After a quick kiss on her mouth, he murmured in her ear, "Your first day was a success?"

Warm breath on her skin sent a shiver down her spine. Almost giddy with pleasure, she leaned against him, enjoying the feel of his muscles under the cotton fabric of his shirt. "You guess right. I've actually had five full classes. Right now I'm only teaching three days, and probably some of today's participants won't come back after their curiosity is satisfied. But I'm pretty sure I'll be able to hold all the lessons. The other two days I'm working with the school," she gushed. She was tingling with pent-up energy.

Jake grasped her hips and pulled her against him. "So, what now? My shift doesn't start for a few hours."

She nodded and held his gaze with her eyes.

He felt the heat spreading furiously inside him and swallowed to clear his head. "At the diner?" he asked, struggling to keep his voice nonchalant.

She shook her head, a mysterious smile on her lips.

"You're going to drive me out of my mind, woman. Tell me where already. If we stay standing here so close together much longer, I can't guarantee my next actions." To make sure she knew what she was doing with him, he pulled her in tight.

"I got the power, huh?" she teased. Not that it bothered her, quite the opposite. It was a heady feeling, knowing she had the same effect on him as he had on her. "Come." Impulsively, she pulled him by his hand toward the SUV.

"Where to?" he asked, perplexed.

"Home."

She didn't have to tell him twice. He kissed her hard on the mouth and covered the distance to his vehicle with a few big steps. She put both hands to her burning cheeks. What had she gotten herself into? It wasn't a very well thought out decision and she hoped she could handle the consequences. A honk snapped her out of her thoughts. Jake was driving already, sticking his head out the window. "Changed your mind after all?" he asked, his eyes drinking her in.

Was the look a promise of things to come? To hell with reason. There was time enough to be reasonable tomorrow, she decided. She jumped into the car, barely remembering to invite Rambo.

At the house, Jake was already waiting for her. Second thoughts fled when she saw him standing there like that, with his faded jeans and long-sleeved Broncos shirt showing off sinewy muscles underneath. She got out of the car and left the door open so the dog could jump out. Suddenly shy, she stopped as if rooted to the spot.

Jake's eyes narrowed.

"It's too late to change your mind now," he growled, pulling her into his arms.

An hour later, Jasmine lay completely spent.

With his fingertips, Jake was drawing lazy circles over her velvety skin. He appeared fascinated with her, everything about her. She was determined to prove his fear wrong—that the allure would be lost once they made love. He looked as though he preferred not to let her out of bed at all. He groaned.

"What?" she grumbled sleepily.

"Nothing," he reassured her, brushing her hair out of her face.

She was too tired to follow up and preferred to snuggle closer to him.

"I have to leave for work. I'm sorry." He shook his head and gave her a playful pat on the butt.

"Hey!" she exclaimed, but had to bite her lips to keep from laughing out loud.

After he left, she turned on her back and stared at the ceiling. Now, alone, her mind kicked in again and the doubts about the correctness of her decision returned with full force. Her last attempt with a man had definitely ended in disaster. Restless, she rolled from side to side. If she was honest, she had to admit that the two men couldn't have been more different.

Gavin-the-jerk had been a charmer. When she'd first met him, she'd even teased him that all the things he told her couldn't be true. But somehow she had let herself be convinced that he was serious, and before she knew it, he had moved in with her. Against the warning bells she had heard ringing. They rang not only within herself, but for friends as well. She hadn't listened to her intuition, and not to Pat or Kathrina. Only a few weeks later, Gavin dropped his facade and showed his true colors. The fact that she had stayed with him for so long was mostly to do with her stubbornness and, if she were honest, also with comfort.

Jasmine sighed and turned and turned the thoughts in her head. She had drawn the wrong conclusions completely. She hadn't ended up in this crappy relationship because of her poor people skills, but because of ignoring the warnings of her intuition. If that were really true there was nothing standing in the way of things between her and Jake. Except maybe his reputation as a womanizer. But even Paula, who had initially warned about her own brother, was now admitting that he had been acting one hundred and eighty degrees different than usual over the past few weeks. Jasmine listened within herself. Her own feelings about Jake were good. Admittedly pretty hormone-soaked at the moment, but still.

She flipped back the covers and buried Rambo under them. He had sneaked back into her bedroom unnoticed. He burrowed out from under the coverlet and licked her neck. "Yeah, big guy. Me too," she murmured, cuddling his ever-lengthening curls. "About time Kathrina got back to give you a haircut, isn't it?" He looked at her with a hopeful expression as he panted, making it almost look like he was smiling. She could relate to that. After her post-coital epiphany, she felt like smiling, too.

CHAPTER TWENTY-ONE

AFTER A SHOWER, Jasmine sat on the porch snuggled in a wool blanket. At sundown, the sky was streaked with gold, and the craggy Rockies grew shadows like old men grew beards.

Her cell phone chimed musically. The screen said *Paula*.

"What's up? I missed you in class today," she said instead of a greeting.

Paula snorted on the other end of the line. "This is going to take some convincing before I make a public fool of myself while trying to fold my body into a pretzel. Besides, I've got other things to worry about right now."

"What?"

"My homeless woman-child we-don't-know-yet has reappeared."

"That's what you were hoping, right?"

"It is. Yes. No. I don't know."

"Whether she's a woman or a child you just want to help, right?"

"Yes, of course. My horses shine like they were groomed at night, the barn is practically clean when I show up in the morning to feed them. The tack is greased. And believe me, I didn't do it."

"So your stable roomie is making herself useful. I would find that remarkable in a child."

"It's an argument to believe she's an adult, yes." Paula sounded frustrated. "I just need to talk through a plan of action with someone. She spooks easily, and I don't want her running away because I pushed too far, too fast. Are you up for some dinner at the diner?"

"I still have a ton of stuff to do. But I could pick us up dinner to go and you could join me at the studio."

"If this is a cheap way to get me to help you, it's working."

"Great, see you there."

After Jasmine had hung up, Paula stared out into the falling twilight. What was she going to do with Leslie? Maybe it wasn't her name, maybe it was just a stencil on a backpack. But it felt better to call her something. Paula couldn't close both eyes much longer and keep leaving food in the stable. Soon it would get too cold to let her sleep there. She had to hand it to the girl, she really hid thoroughly and left no trace of her presence. No handkerchief, no clothes, nothing. If she hadn't happened to see it with her own eyes that one night, Paula would probably attribute the missing food to mice. Very voracious mice, but still. It spoke to the fact that the girl had practice at being on the run. How sad it was to lead such a life.

While Paula complained more often than not about her large family, she was well aware of how blessed she was with relatives. She pushed herself off the windowsill.

VIRGINIA FOX

Maybe Jaz would have some ideas for an action plan. Maybe she would know what to do. Anything except abandon Leslie in at the nearest child welfare office.

Inside the diner, Jasmine waited for her takeout order for two. Miss Minnie had baked a Provençal vegetable cake to celebrate, topped with a variety of grilled vegetables and spiced up with Italian ricotta and Greek feta. She could hardly wait for it.

"Good of you to drop by, girl," Miss Daisy said, patting her hand. "My sister's been in the kitchen all afternoon preparing this delicacy for you. It's our thanks to you for enriching Independence with a new recreation. Since my workout this morning I've been feeling muscles I didn't even know existed."

Jasmine grinned. Miss Daisy had also been in one of her classes today and had bravely joined in the gymnastics. And had been pleasantly surprised to find that at over seventy years old, she could still touch her toes.

"I didn't know I could still do that," she said, dumbfounded. "I haven't tried that in at least twenty years."

"Now you see what you could do if you did yoga regularly."

A calculating expression crept onto her face. "I wonder what Kurt will say when he realizes that this old girl has a few new tricks up her sleeve."

Jasmine had almost choked on a laugh while trying not to imagine what Miss Daisy and her widowed lover

Kurt were up to in their free time. Instead, she said, "Keep at it. If you get in regular workouts, your muscles will get used to them. Just wait it out."

At that moment, Miss Minnie came through the swinging doors that separated the kitchen from the bar area, balancing a cardboard box. "Here. You and Paula enjoy the meal. On the house."

Jasmine looked from one sister to the other. "Are you sure? I mean, you're going to pay for your lessons, too. The free trial lesson was just today."

"And you pay for your next meal again. Then it fits," said Miss Daisy. "There, now go and enjoy your evening with your hot sheriff's sister."

Jasmine blushed. "He's not 'my' hot sheriff." Her face got even hotter when she thought about how she'd already partied with Jake in private.

Miss Minnie watched her warily. "Was it good?"

O-o. Could the ground please open up and swallow her? She hadn't experienced anything so embarrassing since she'd been caught kissing Bobby Junior in kindergarten.

Miss Daisy interjected. "I think we can resolve at least some of the bets. It's obvious you've grown closer. Today?"

Incredulous, Jasmine stared at her. "You actually expect an answer to that?"

Miss Daisy just nodded, and Jasmine realized with horror that the rest of the diner was waiting for a response as well. "Spit it out already. One way or another we'll find out anyway." Daisy's eyes sparkled with amusement.

Jasmine gave up. Even though she didn't know how these people were going to figure it out unless they took Jake or Rambo into interrogation, she didn't doubt for a moment that they were serious. "All right. Yes, Jake and I have already…" she searched for the right word, "…celebrated. Privately. And just to get it out of the way, yes, it was great. And he more than lives up to all the rumors surrounding his reputation." When she looked up defiantly after this confession, she saw only astonished faces. Everyone's mouth was literally open.

Miss Minnie managed to speak. "I don't think anyone expected that much information, but thank you, my dear. That will keep the gossip mongers busy for a while."

Jasmine grabbed her vegetable pie and fled the diner, while behind her money was already being diligently exchanged from one hand to the other and Miss Minnie was keeping accurate records. What had she done? She only hoped Jake would understand that she had been completely overwhelmed by the pack.

Inside the studio, Jasmine set dinner down on a little break table and went to get two folding chairs. Dragging them back to the table, she noticed that the overhead light had a cobweb on it. There were still a few spots the cleaning team had missed, and this one was evident now that the sun was going down. Opening the folding chair, Jasmine hopped up and batted at the web with her hand. That did nothing. She got a paper napkin from the takeout bag and tried the same move.

Still couldn't reach.

With one foot on the folding chair, she placed the other foot on the table and gave a good swing at the web. She wiped the light clean. And kept going.

"Eeeeeek!"

The table wobbled, the folding chair snapped shut. *CRASH!* Jasmine tumbled to the floor. And that's where Paula found her a little while later.

THE NEXT DAY

Leaning on a cane, Jasmine hobbled up the steps to her studio. She didn't know what to expect. All she knew was that the minute Paula heard of the accident, she had contacted Tyler and persuaded her to extend her vacation from the show a few more days. Tyler had kindly agreed and said she would step in as temp instructor at the studio. Jasmine was supremely grateful especially since Tyler was supposed to be back with her dance troupe by now.

Limping up to the second floor, Jasmine peered through the staircase railing. She was amazed to see that the class was almost full. Now she could hear Tyler's words, too, and she went wide-eyed. "Stretch, stretch, stretch. Pull it. Don't give up. Yeah, that's it. And what are you doing over there? You think this is a day at the beach? The rule here is one hundred percent commitment or go home."

Apparently, Tyler followed the approach of a drill sergeant. This gave Jasmine a glimpse into the hard dance training Tyler went through on a daily basis. Jasmine stifled a smirk and tackled the final steps up to the second floor. At least it hadn't stopped people from coming. That was something, after all. When she emerged at the top, all heads turned toward her.

"Thank God," someone muttered. "Hopefully things will loosen up a bit around here."

Tyler stared grimly at the back row where the comment had come from. "Don't get too excited. It'll be a while before Jaz can take over here again."

Unfortunately, Tyler had hit the nail on the head. At first Jasmine imagined she would be back on her feet in no time. A few bruises wouldn't stop her. But she had definitely underestimated the extent of her fall. What worried her the most was her hip. As hard as she tried to mobilize it, it just wasn't getting any looser. Her impatience wasn't helping either. And heck, as glad as she was that Jake's sister was helping out, the yoga studio was her own personal project.

Tyler saw the conflicting emotions flash across Jasmine's face because she said, "But Jasmine will lead the nutrition classes and the meditation classes as planned. You'll be rid of me soon. After all, I have to enchant humanity with my dance." She pirouetted on the spot.

Jasmine felt bad right then and there. Here was Tyler, helping her out when she had important things to do, and she was trying hard not to hurt her feelings at the same time. *Sometimes I can be a really selfish jerk,* she thought. To everyone else in the room, she smiled, this time from the heart, and said, "For me, this is great. By the time Tyler is through with you guys, you'll already know how it goes. And don't think I'm going to continue with you as innocently as I started. That was lulling you into a false sense of security. Now I know you can touch your toes."

Loud laughter from the other side of the group.

"Laugh quietly. I also expect a perfect sun salutation. You have learned it now!"

She turned to Tyler. "I'll make some tea and sit on the sideline, if I may."

"Sure. It's your studio. You're welcome to fill in on my dance lessons if I ever move back to Independence."

"I'd think twice about that if I were you. Now if you'll please excuse me, I need to call Paula. We're overdue for a conversation."

Leaving Tyler to her teaching, Jasmine went straight back to Paula's house. After telling the latest news, and downplaying the ache in her hip, she said, "All right, then. Let's go in and talk about your house ghost. That's what we were going to do before I decided to practice flying yoga on a folding chair and a table."

They went into the house where Jasmine sank down on the couch.

Paula got two bottles of light beer from the refrigerator and handed one to her. "Or would you rather have tea and pain pills?" she asked.

"But it's before noon," Jasmine protested.

"I know, but it's five o'clock somewhere, and we're about to have a serious talk."

"Thank you, I'm fine. I wanted to get through today without painkillers. That's where a little alcohol comes in handy. And if 'a little' proves insufficient, there's always whiskey."

"Sounds like a plan." Paula raised a bottle. "Cheers. Here's to you getting better as soon as possible."

"I hope so." Jasmine took a sip of the cold drink. "So tell me. What's your runaway been up to lately?"

"Eating everything I put out for her. And keeping the barn spick and span. Weeding the flower beds around the house. Neatly rolling up the water hose. Grooming the dogs and the horses."

"Everything, so to speak. Wow."

"While I think it's all great and admirable, I also have a guilty conscience. I'm not exactly sure how old she is anymore."

"You think she's still a child?"

"Could be. But if I press for the information, she may bolt again. I need to figure out a way to make her trust me."

"You can't make anybody trust anything. It has to happen naturally."

"If she's a child, this situation is bordering on child labor. Besides, a child belongs in school."

Jasmine frowned. "Where does she wash?"

"I think partly in the barn. But I suspect she's also showered here in the house once or twice. There were towels hung differently than I had hung them. Another time, the shower head in the guest bath was still dripping."

"And nothing else was missing or stolen?"

"No."

"Maybe you could offer her a room in the house?"

"I was doing a little research. If I get in direct contact with her, which I would be if she came into my house, then I sort of officially know that she's here. That means I'd have to make an official report. Then she'll be picked up by Child Protective Services immediately, and that's it."

"What about a temporary foster situation thing?" Jasmine asked, groping for words. She searched her brain for what she knew about foster children. It wasn't much. "Couldn't you apply for some kind of temporary permit?"

Paula stood up and began pacing the living room, as she always did when something was bothering her strongly. "What if she turns out to be a total idiot kid?"

"Paula, you might be overthinking this," Jasmine soothed. "Do idiot kids always clean up and behave responsibly without anyone telling them to?"

"You're beginning to sound like my brother."

"Could you even imagine taking in a foster child?" Jasmine said gently.

Paula paused her pacing and looked out the window. "Surprisingly, yes. No idea why. I don't hear my biological clock ticking." She snorted. "Usually I'm lucky if I get along with adults. But this girl has kind of done it to me. One thing's for sure, giving up is a foreign word to this one. And that impresses me immensely." She leaned over further to get a better look out the window. "Jaz, look. The girl is making friends with Rambo right now. Quick."

"I'm having a hard time with quick right now," Jasmine grunted as she hoisted herself up from the sofa.

"So it's okay that I leave Rambo with you tonight while the rest of us go to the concert?"

"Absolutely."

"You don't mind missing it?"

"I'll go tomorrow. Somebody's got to watch the fort."

Jasmine finally made it over to the window. By the barn, a girl sat in the grass, besieged by all three dogs and a couple of playful goats. "That's her?"

"That's her," Paula confirmed.

Jasmine studied the girl. Shaggy, shoulder-length hair, a long-sleeved, threadbare T-shirt and torn jeans. Worn sneakers on her feet completed the picture of neglect. But her face was radiant as she greeted the newest member of her dog pack. She evenly distributed strokes and made sure that no one came up short.

"No wonder the dogs keep tight," Paula grumbled, her nose close to the windowpane. "They don't usually get petted this much in a whole month."

"Roo seems to enjoy it, if his exposed belly is any indicator."

"Like your dog is any better," Paula said, alluding to the fact that Rambo had possessively placed a paw on the girl's arm.

"I'm not denying that at all."

The girl stood up and disappeared into the barn. "What is she doing now?"

Moments later she returned, a rake in her hand. She began sweeping up the leaves, loose straw, and hay in front of the barn. Laughing, she fought off Roo and Barns, who jumped up at her, and shooed Barns away a bit when he tried to grab the handle of the rake.

"She's quite something, I have to admit."

"Now do you see why I'm having such a hard time taking the next step?"

Jasmine nodded. "Go get your laptop. You do have a laptop, right? And Internet?"

"Hey. Independence may be in the middle of nowhere, but technology has arrived here, too. Sure, I have Internet. It's just not the fastest connection."

"Then get it and let's find out what it has to say about the rules and regulations of foster care in Colorado."

CHAPTER TWENTY-TWO

Two HOURS LATER, Jasmine walked sloooowly back to her own house. Paula had offered to drive her, but Jasmine wanted to try her hip. The walk wasn't too bad. Inside Nana's place, she lay down on the sofa and closed her eyes. *Just for a moment*, she thought.

When she awoke it was one-thirty p.m. and Jake was sitting next to her on the sofa. Her feet were in his lap. "Did I actually fall asleep?"

He smiled at her. "Looks like it. Do you need anything?" He kept his eyes fixed on the TV, where a football game was playing silently.

"I might be tempted to take advantage of that offer a little bit. Doesn't happen every day that someone serves me from morning to night."

He let out a sound like a growl as he leaned over and lightly bit her where the shoulder merged into the neck. "Be glad you're not fully fit yet. Otherwise I'd show you right now who's serving who."

The air crackled between them. A tugging in her stomach reminded Jasmine of the hours she had spent with Jake yesterday, just before the fall. Naked. In her bed. She took a deep breath. To ease the situation a bit, she said lightly, "As much as I'd like to find out, it's unfortunate that I'm, what's the word Nana uses for it, *indisposed* at the moment."

Jake raised an eyebrow and grinned knowingly. "Don't worry. The offer doesn't have an expiration date. But for now, I'll fix you something to eat, and then we need to talk."

That sounded serious. She decided to keep him company while he cooked, and hobbled on her healthy leg into the kitchen where she sat down on top of the kitchen counter and let her legs dangle.

As she had agreed with Paula, she let him in on the results of their Internet research. Jake listened intently as he chopped vegetables and cooked rice. He was cooking a veggie-rice dish. Her mouth watered.

He tossed one vegetable after another into the wok pan, sautéing with a little vinegar and soy sauce. "A child is not the same as one of Paula's strays that she keeps taking in," he said abruptly.

"Strays?"

"Didn't you know? Barns and Roo are orphans. She found them abandoned in a box on the side of the road."

"What about the Shetland pony?"

"Dolly? I think she saved her at a fair. And this time it seems to be this girl. So I want to make sure she's aware of what she's getting into."

"Hmm. She's done pretty well with the animals so far, hasn't she?"

"Sure. But a child is a little more complicated, don't you think?"

"What do I know about raising kids?" She frowned. "On the other hand, I think you learn a lot about a person by seeing how they treat animals. And your sister is unbeatable at that."

"Says you."

Jasmine playfully kicked his butt with her healthy leg.

"Hey," he laughed. "I see you're doing much better today." After mixing the rice with the vegetables and mushrooms, he covered the pan with a lid and turned off the stove.

"I'm drinking as a substitute medication. Want me to set the table?" She made an effort to slide off the kitchen counter with a little elegance.

He stopped her by stepping between her legs and putting his hands on her hips. "You're not supposed to do anything today. I'll take care of it in a minute."

"I'm not comfortable with you doing everything and me just sitting."

"Don't worry, I'll make it all up to you. In bed."

Blood rushed to her face and she averted her eyes. Jake gently put his hand to her cheek, forcing her to look at him. "Hey. Are you okay? With you? With us?"

After a brief inner debate, she mustered all her courage to ask him all the questions burning on her tongue since their evening together. "Is there an us?" she blurted out, fiddling nervously with the waistband of her yoga pants.

His blue eyes looked at her with concern. "Of course. I thought that was clear. What did you think? That it was just about sex?"

"What do I know?" She went on the defensive. "I'm not the one with a reputation as a lady-killer."

As tired as he was of discussions about his past behavior, his expression said she had a point. So he hugged her tightly and tried to make it clear once and for all. "Don't you know that everything is different since you? I haven't exactly lived like a monk. But I've always communicated what's going on openly and honestly."

He let go of her and took a step back so he could look into her eyes. He took her hands and stroked with his thumbs as light as a feather. "You are the one for me, as corny as that may sound now. But it's true. When I'm with you, I feel more alive. Completed. I didn't even realize before that something was missing. But since you've been in my life, I feel it very clearly." Frustration showed in his face. "Mom and Dad have been together for almost forty years. They've been through good times and bad. Bottom line is that they've been through it all together and come out stronger. Because I grew up with it, I took it for granted. But in the course of my work, I stumbled across so many dysfunctional families that the risk always seemed too high. I preferred to keep female relationships superficial, and then nothing could happen to me."

The kitchen was so silent, Jasmine could hear her own breathing. His clear gaze met hers again. "But with you I can't keep my distance. I don't want to. Not even from the first time we met." When she still said nothing, he asked, "Still not convinced?"

Why did she suddenly have a lump in her throat? "Yes, convinced," she said, in a clear voice. "I feel the same way. You don't seem to have any problems with it, but I find these feelings pretty scary. My past relationships pale in comparison to how I feel about you."

He closed his eyes and lowered his forehead to hers, "You wouldn't believe how happy I am to hear that."

"Is the great heartbreaker insecure?"

She felt his lips twist into a smile. "So far, it's never been about my heart, either." He straightened up again and looked at her. "Let's eat. Then, let's spend the afternoon fishin' with Jimmy before I have to work."

After one night in the single-cell Independence jail, Gavin had been sent up to Breckenridge to wait for arraignment. Like all inmates at the county lockup, Gavin was allowed a small number of phone calls. He waited his turn in a cold, grey holding cell, and when given the order, approached the "call box" which was a simple receiver on a cord that connected to a general operator when picked up.

"Hello, I'd like to make a collect call." Gavin recited the phone number and held his breath while the phone rang. After a week, at least, the other party picked up.

Skinky's voice said, "Yeah?"

"I have a collect call for you from county jail," said the operator. "Will you accept the charges?"

"Uh, yeah."

"Skinky! It's Gavin."

"Dude, what took you so long? We've been waiting for you to call."

"Wha—?"

"Cuz we showed your paper to some of Aldo's friends. You remember Aldo's friends?"

Gavin figured the meaning of "Aldo's friends" meant they were Italian, which also meant they were mob-connected. "Uh huh," he grunted.

"And they thought the, uh, *artwork* was bitchin'. They want *more*."

"How can I do that from in here?" Gavin snapped.

"You can't. But you can tell me *how*. Like, give instructions."

Gavin didn't say anything. He leaned back as far as the telephone cord would let him and rolled his neck to relieve tension. So, his quality improvements to the funny money had been noticed. "Sure, sure, I could do that," he said, finally. "In that case, I'm going to need a favor."

A cool breeze on her bare skin woke Jasmine. Jake had talked her into spending the lazy afternoon on another fishing trip with Jimmy. The Blue River was a riot of color under the midday sun. The deep blue water edged green river grass, as trout jumped and flashed their white bellies and rainbow-speckled scales, before plunging back into the water.

After splashing in the river, Jake and Jasmine spread their clothes out on rocks to dry, and wrapped themselves in thick towels. After that, they pounced on each other. Jake had been very interested when she showed him what could be done with a woolen blanket in the open air. In the process, they must have lost the towels. An hour or more later, they had dozed off, nestled together under the mild sunshine.

Now, a big cloud had pushed itself in front of the sun, and the air cooled. Despite Jimmy's warm fur on her belly, Jaz shivered. The cat had joined them, fat and happy from the many small fish he'd caught. She carefully pushed him aside and went to the stones where her clothes were spread out. She knew Jake was enjoying the sight of her from half-closed lids. At the last moment he was able to catch the jeans Jaz threw at him.

"Hey!"

"What?" she asked with an innocent look in her eyes. "I just wanted to wake you up. At first I thought of cold water, but we've already had that today."

Jake reached out and tickled her lightly until she gasped and begged for mercy. He stopped, but kept her on his lap. "Will you go to the second day of the music festival as my date?"

"Sure. I'd love to. I've already made arrangements with Paula and Tyler to meet up before the opening concert tonight. We heard there are going to be some pretty great food trucks there."

He kissed the tip of her nose. "No problem. I'm on duty there tonight. But I'll look for you."

Touched by his concern, she kissed him. Fortunately, before the kiss got out of hand, Jimmy spoke up. He wiggled between them for pats and chin scratches.

Jake gave Jimmy the attention he was yowling for. "Is Rambo with Paula?"

"Yes, with all the tourists loose in town. I thought it made the most sense to take him to your sister's. He's had fun at her place all day."

"So you're going to be home all alone now?"

"Yes. But it's only for a few hours. Then I go to meet up with the others. Pat and Kathrina are going to wait for me by the popcorn concession."

Jake had no idea why, but he had an uneasy feeling in his stomach. "I can wait for you, too."

"Jake. I don't want you to be late for work because of me. And I don't feel like rushing insanely right now either. I'm looking forward to the concert tonight, I'd like to take a shower at my leisure now and get dressed up a little. For you." She looked him straight in the eye and kissed him briefly on the mouth. "Now go, take your fish-catching hangover home, throw on your snazzy uniform, and keep order among the festival-goers. I'll be fine."

He gave up. Because of the car accident, he was probably just a little paranoid. It would subside, given time. It was very difficult to decide exactly what his intuition was trying to tell him. Now, for example, it was probably laughing its head off because of his worries.

They dressed and headed back to her place.

When he said goodbye and drove away, Jasmine breathed a sigh of relief. As much as she had enjoyed the afternoon with Jake and was looking forward to seeing him again in just a few hours, she was relieved to finally have some time to herself. Because of her accident, she'd spent a lot of time in the company of others. Paula and Jake, also her grandmother, and people at the diner, and at the studio. She was "peopled out" for now. Everyone had a tip on how bruises healed best. She enjoyed the attention and care of others very much, but enough was enough.

CHAPTER TWENTY-THREE

THE FLIGHT WAS FULL. The airplane engines droned under the heavy load. Skinky and Aldo fit right in with other music lovers converging on Independence and surrounding areas for the Indie Music Festival. This year thousands of fans were expected. But Skinky and Aldo weren't on their way for the music. Gavin was super-pissed at the Jasmine chick they had chased down the stairs a few weeks ago. Gavin had tried to get her back by running her off the road but she still hadn't come to see him in jail. Hadn't posted his bail, nothing. So, she really needed a big scare, and Skinky and Aldo were the right guys for the job. After they scared Jasmine back to Gavin, he promised he would tell them his secrets for making that great counterfeit loot. They were very motivated to make Gavin happy.

"Please fasten your seatbelts in preparation for landing in Denver," the pilot said, over the loudspeakers. Neither of the two made a move to click their belts. They would wait until the airline attendant stood over them and made them do it.

The pair weren't traveling with guns, but Aldo's friends had arranged to have a couple of pieces left in an airport locker, and they already had the key. He'd left plenty of ammo, too.

Tonight was the opening concert of the festival and everybody in Independence was bound to be there.

Tyler locked up the studio and made her way to the diner. It had been a great day of teaching and she'd truly enjoyed reconnecting with the people of Independence. The diner was a hubbub of conversation and the air was thick with the smells of comfort food. There wasn't a spare table, but Pat and Kathrina gave a wave and beckoned her over. On the way over to the table, she couldn't help but admire Pat's dark hair and eyes, his fine physique.

"Are you coming tonight, too?" Not at all dance-like, Tyler plopped down on a chair beside them. She guessed that she and Pat would just play it cool. She didn't know how much Kathrina knew, and it seemed she had her poker face on, anyway.

"You mean to the opening concert of the Indie Music Festival?" Pat asked.

Tyler grinned and raised a thumb appreciatively.

"Yes, Mr. Wilkinson has given us the evening off."

The table burst into laughter. Everybody in town knew *the mayor* was squeezing every ounce of attention he could from the visiting architect. But that was okay, because it was ninety-nine percent sure the exercise would result in a paying assignment for Pat.

"I'm just along for the ride," Kathrina said. "But after the concert, I've got to get back to Seattle. I have a business to run."

"You're leaving right after this?" Pat asked Tyler.

"Jasmine's boo-boo will be all gone in a day I expect. By Monday she should be teaching classes by herself.

She can't manage advanced exercises yet, but neither can most of her students. So that shouldn't be a problem. Tomorrow morning I'm bound for the Denver airport."

"Too bad. I hope you come back soon."

"I don't really know yet." Tyler winked. "I'll have to see where my next engagement takes me. I'll show up for the obligatory Carter family reunions, count on that." The wink revealed that she enjoyed family visits, and grumbling about it was more theater than anything else.

"Christmas it is," Kathrina said.

"Will you have dinner with us?" Pat asked.

Tyler let herself slide off her chair. "I'd love to. But too many things to do, people to see, mother to visit."

"We'll catch you at the concert a little later?"

"Natch."

Pat watched her go with a certain longing in his eyes. Kathrina noticed, but she didn't comment. Just tucked it away for future reference.

The entrance to the Indie Music Festival was colorful and teeming with concert-goers. It had artwork, blow-up sculptures to admire, and was a cakewalk in terms of security. Skinky and Aldo breezed through after a half-hearted, amateur pat down performed by temporary employees who failed to find any guns. No metal detectors made it easy.

The tough guys roamed through the crowd, scrutinizing each face they passed. Music boomed from the main stage and the air was perfumed with hot dogs, candy corn and whiffs of marijuana.

Skinky nudged Aldo with his elbow. "Remember what she looks like?"

Aldo shrugged his shoulders. "Short, on the skinny side, blond."

"Great. That's about a quarter of the people here."

"We're supposed to look for that plus yoga pants and sneakers."

Jasmine was running late. Somehow, she'd lost track of time in the bathtub. The fact that she had changed her clothes three times hadn't helped her time management either. In the end, she had settled on a khaki balloon skirt, a white long-sleeved T-shirt, and comfortable ballet flats. She hoped Jake would appreciate her efforts. It was a whole new experience, too. She was still overwhelmed by all the new feelings that were crashing in on her just thinking about him. But by not pressuring her, just proving to her in his calm and determined way every day how important she was to him, she was slowly getting used to the idea of being a couple. *I like this*, she thought with a satisfied grin, as she grabbed her scarf and a light jacket.

Pat and Kathrina said they planned to meet her inside the festival entrance at the popcorn concession. They would all go to the main stage together. Jasmine couldn't wait to see her friends again. If she played her cards right, maybe at least one of them would come here permanently. That desire was probably a bit selfish. But it didn't change the fact that she would be glad to see them. Rambo had already been dropped next door at Paula's, who had agreed to pet-sit for the evening. Mr. Wilkinson had begged to sit Rocky, explaining he was terrific company.

Fifteen minutes later, Jasmine parked her car in the field that served as a parking lot during the festival. Luckily it hadn't rained in days, or this could have turned into a mud lake, she mused, carefully making her way through the stubble of the harvested field in her ballet flats. When she reached the first food stalls and booths, she stopped. She would never find her friends in this throng. She'd better call them.

After the first ring, Kathrina answered. Unfortunately, the connection was poor and her surroundings were filled with murmuring voices, the sound check of the opening act, and many other noises. Jasmine almost didn't hear her friend. She put her cell phone on speaker, hoping to hear better that way.

"Hi Kathrina, this is Jaz. Hold on a second."

"Jaz, where are you? Somehow everyone stood me up today."

"I've been running late. That's why I'm calling you. I wasn't sure where I would find you. But what about Pat?"

"He's right here. Stuffing his face with funnel cake."

"What about Tyler? Has she made it yet?"

"She'll show up for the concert at the latest. From what she said, she knows the band and is excited about them."

"Right." Kathrina muffled the phone for a moment as she discussed something with someone in the background, then she was back. "Rose and Nadine just showed up. Meet me at the popcorn stand in ten minutes? There's an Indian curry cart right next to it that also sells vegetarian specialties. Miss Daisy told me about it this afternoon."

Jasmine said goodbye and glanced at the time display on her phone. Ten minutes. That gave her plenty of time to explore. She set off, first walking along the periphery of the booths to get an idea of the size of the festival and what it had to offer. She didn't notice the men who started moving close behind her.

"DUDE!" Skinky gave Aldo a nudge with his elbow as concert-goers streamed around them. They were passing by a ten-foot-high blow-up sculpture of a rainbow trout with a lascivious grin on its face.

A little blonde marched right in front of them, headed to the popcorn seller. She wasn't wearing yoga pants, but she was still easy to recognize. Even with the cane and slight limp.

"Do you want to get it done here?"

The other shook his head. "I don't have my silencer with me. You?"

He patted his jacket pocket. "Me neither."

"Over there."

"Where?"

He pointed away from the bobbing, twisting trout. "Behind the porta potties. Nobody's using them right now."

Jasmine paused. Hadn't she just heard familiar voices behind her? Why did the hairs on the back of her neck stand up? Uncertainly, she turned around when she was grabbed by the arm and yanked behind a concession stall. She let out a sharp yelp which the music from the main field covered. Immediately, a hand pressed roughly on her mouth, another grabbed her hair and pulled at it. A face shifted into her field of vision, then a second. Her eyes widened in horror. Strange voice number one and number two! But how could that be? She groaned. Apparently Gavin-the-jerk was still stalking her, using his slimy friends.

Her brain switched back on and she bit her captor's hand hard while aiming the ball of her foot at the other's knee. That hurt her foot. Ballet flats weren't great protection for that. The element of surprise belonged to the other side but she managed to loosen their grip. Jasmine took a leap forward. Her foot had taken more damage than she thought. On her second step, it buckled painfully. Before she could recover, Stranger Voice No. 2 yanked her back. "We were going to make this short and sweet. But every time we try to do you a favor, you act like a pain in the ass."

Jasmine shuddered as she spotted the eerie gleam in their eyes. Where was her personal sheriff when she needed him? She regretted making fun of his protection concerns.

Flanking her on both sides, Gavin's thugs half-carried her between two concession tents and back to the porta potties. As the festival had only been open a short while, there was no one using them. They squeezed between two potties and into an alley that was closed off due to a line of generator trucks. It was the perfect no-man's-land for an abduction. The guys pulled their guns and, one on each side, rested the barrels against Jasmine's temples.

She just stared at them, unflinching.

"She ain't scared," Stranger Voice No. 1 said.

"She's going to be," Stranger Voice No. 2 said. "She's going to learn a good lesson. Know why?"

"No. Why?"

"Because Gavin told me she got a dog. A big poodle." He tapped Jasmine's skull with the gun. "We're not here to shoot you, yoga witch."

"That's a relief," she said, sarcastically.

He tightened his grip on her. "We're here to shoot your dog."

CHAPTER TWENTY-FOUR

Just a few hundred yards from the spot, Jake roamed through the crowd of visitors. At the corner of the curry cart, he spotted Tyler looking around, in search of someone. She was accompanied by Pat and Kathrina. He strained to catch a glimpse of Jasmine. She was nowhere to be seen. His uneasy feeling came back with a vengeance. In a few long steps, he reached his sister.

"What's wrong?" he asked brusquely.

"Jasmine is late. We were supposed to meet here ten minutes ago."

"Have you called her?"

"Yes, she's not picking up."

Jake topped his hat back in contemplation. "Maybe she's just late."

"Somehow I think it's more than that."

Jake didn't know Jasmine was running late, either. Especially not in combination with what his intuition had been trying to tell him for hours. He pulled the comm out of his pocket. "Jaz is missing," he informed his deputies. "I want everyone on post in five minutes, whether you're on duty or not. BOLO."

"I forget what BOLO means, Jake."

"Be On The Lookout."

Paula made a face. "But I thought the guy who was bothering Jasmine was in jail?"

"He is. But maybe he's got a friend on the outside. If she really just lost track of time over a bag of popcorn, I'll buy you dinner."

At that moment Toby appeared. "What's your gut say, boss?"

"That we better hurry up. We're looking for Jasmine. She shouldn't be hard to spot with that cane she's using."

"All right. I'll alert the fire department guys. I'm sure they'll help out. The more of us, the better."

Jake turned back to Tyler, who had gone pale at his radio-comm conversation. "I've got to go. Can you organize everyone?"

She nodded, along with Kathrina and Pat.

"Keep your eyes open, assign areas, search, and if you suspect anything, call me on my cell. Tyler, can you please give them my number?" He raised his thumb and sprinted off.

Jake's mind was racing as his eyes systematically scanned the area. The way Tyler and company had described the sequence of events, Jasmine had just arrived at the festival when they spoke on the phone. Without further ado, he turned toward the parking lot. When he found her car, he forced himself to slow down to try to retrace her steps. It wasn't easy. His gut was screaming at him to hurry but running around blindly served no one.

He reached the first tents and stalls, and stopped. Who knew what direction she had taken in that half hour between her conversation with Kathrina and the agreed-upon appointment at the meeting place? A wave of fear came over him, but before it got a complete grip, he resolutely pushed it back and gritted his teeth. Fear was not an option. Methodically, he worked his way counterclockwise along the edge of the festival.

"Sheriff, do you have a second?"

Jake turned to see Martha, a woman who was running the stand selling local honey products. He gave her a glance before going back to scan the crowd with a laser gaze. Right now, he couldn't care less if someone stole her bee products.

"I'm in a hurry right now, maybe later?" he said. "My girlfriend is missing. And with everything that's happened lately, I have a very bad feeling."

"That's what I wanted to talk to you about."

Jake wheeled around. "Did you see her?"

"Yes. I was about to greet her when she turned and walked away from me. It was sudden and kind of weird. Two bull-necked men with tattoos were on either side of her."

"Did they threaten her?"

"I couldn't see that clearly. But I know they're not from around here. That's what made me wonder. Her friends who are here on a visit, aren't they a man and a woman? Right?"

On such days, Jake felt an immense affection for Independence and its residents, where everyone took an interest in each other's lives. "Yes. That's not them. Did you see which way Jasmine and her party went?"

Martha frowned. "I'm not sure. Toward the main road, probably. To be honest, I was a little annoyed that she didn't greet me. So I didn't pay any further attention. Now I wish I had been more attentive."

Jake knew exactly how she felt. Still, he reassured her. "You've already been a big help to me, Martha."

"Good, then go and save your princess."

Although he felt anything but heroic, he nodded and sprinted off. Over the radio, he let the others know which trail he was following before he started running.

He ran down the concession row, slowing his steps only when he got nearer the concert-field.

"HELLO INDEEEEEPENDENCE," an announcer brayed. "HOW YOU ALL FEELIN'?"

A new band took over the main stage and fresh music started up with a blast of volume. Jake could hardly hear himself think. He wanted to dash off again but a hand on his upper arm stopped him. "What the—" Annoyed, he was about to break away when he realized who was detaining him: Ace, a member of the fire department.

"Take it easy. I heard about your girlfriend over my comm. You okay?" Ace asked.

"Fine. Glad you're here to back me up."

"Where have you searched?"

"I was just about to stake out behind the porta potties."

"There's an alley there between the backs of the porta potties and the lineup of generator trucks. So loud back there, you'd never hear anything."

"You take one end, I'll take the other."

A soon as Jake peered around the side of the last pottie, he saw two men fleeing the scene. There was no sense yelling, *Stop or I'll shoot!* They'd never hear him. He took off in hot pursuit.

The two men took off across the cleared field beyond. If they made it to the woods at the edge of the field, he would probably lose them. Jake poured on the gas and pounded after them. He was catching up! The man he was closest to took advantage of the moment and gave him a hard blow with his elbow. Then they were locked in a struggle. Jake felt a punch land against his ribs and then against his nose. Tears welled up in his eyes. Furious, he lunged blindly at his attacker, got him in a headlock, and squeezed. Over the man's shoulder, Jake could see the other one pull a gun from the waistband of his pants. Meanwhile, his stranglehold was starting to slip. He took another elbow to the side of his head. White stars exploded behind his eyelids. It was difficult to breathe.

A gun roared.

Moments later, Jake came to. He was lying face down in the dirt, and when he lifted his head, he saw two figures disappear into the woods. He tried wiggling his fingers and toes. They worked. He pushed himself into a sitting position. His shoulder was bleeding. The cap of his shoulder had been grazed by a bullet. But he was alive, and not mortally wounded. He got up and struggled back the way he came.

Behind the porta potties, he found Jasmine. She was unconscious, lying on her side in the dirt. Her cane had fallen at an angle beside her. The shock of seeing her like that stopped him cold. Then, Ace was by his side.

"Your deputies and the ambulance will be here in a minute. I've instructed them to go without a siren and come in like it's a routine visit."

Gratefully, Jake nodded to him. He picked himself up and walked over to the woman who had been the only one to touch his heart. And now it looked like he was about to lose her again. Her condition was shocking. He crouched down and gently stroked the hair from her face. Immediately, he wished he'd left it alone. She looked terrible. Her cheek was split open, there was a bump forming on her temple. Her left arm lay twisted beneath her and he prayed it wasn't broken. Naked fear gripped him. She could not be allowed to die. With trembling fingers, he felt at her neck for a pulse. After a few seconds that seemed like an eternity, he finally felt a flutter. Her pulse was still strong. Thank God.

Relieved, he sank down and remained sitting next to her. As if in a trance, he barely felt Ace take him by the arm and lead him aside to make way for the paramedics. Only when they placed her on the gurney and hoisted her into the ambulance did he awaken from his stupor. "I'm going with you," he informed the paramedics. His voice sounded raspy. Apparently they could tell by the look on his face that any argument was futile, and they let him in.

Ace came to the door. "I'm going to stay and help your guys."

Jake nodded.

When Ace just looked at him with a serious expression, he knew it was bad. Nausea rose up in him. Rubbing his face, he asked, "How do you want to proceed?" He had no problem following Ace's strategy, because Jake knew he was very familiar with situations like this. Although he never spoke of his time in the Navy, it was an open secret that Ace had been on several sensitive missions and returned successfully. Dark shadows in his eyes spoke of unspeakable things and contradicted the casual demeanor he displayed for most people. Right now, the shadows were plain to see, at least to Jake. And he knew Ace would have his back one hundred percent.

"Tell Toby those gunmen disappeared into the woods. They should be able to track them with the dogs. Also, call my sister Paula. She can activate the bush phone with a Be-On-The-Lookout for all citizens."

"Roger that," Ace replied.

"Those perps are armed," Jake added. "We have to get close to them quickly and take them out. Promise me one thing? Until those two are zip-tied and on the ground, you won't quit."

At the hospital, Rose and Nadine sat side by side on the cheap plastic chairs in the waiting area, holding each other's hands. Paula had left Leslie at home with the animals and she wandered restlessly back and forth in the hallway. She hoped the doctors would soon be finished with their examination and kept glancing impatiently at the clock.

"Paula, why don't you join us?" called Rose in a hushed voice, patting the seat next to her.

Silently, Paula shook her head. If Rose knew why Jaz was lying in there, she wouldn't be so kind. She bit her lips and took a deep breath in a desperate attempt not to cry. Completely lost in thought, she didn't even notice Rose stepping up behind her to give her a hug. That was all that was needed to make Paula, who never cried, cry. "It's my fault," she sobbed.

"What's your fault?" Rose scowled, and held her away a little.

"If Jasmine hadn't fallen at the studio and hurt her hip, maybe she wouldn't be here."

"What are you talking about?"

"I was the reason she was there. And if she hadn't been hurt, maybe she could have gotten away from these bad guys who hurt her."

Rose gave Paula a little shake. "Did you push her off the chair?"

"No! I didn't push her off the chair—" Paula said, shaking her head.

When Paula shook her head, she said sternly, "Exactly. So it's not your fault at all, you hear!"

"You don't understand. If I hadn't insisted on meeting her for takeout, she wouldn't have been setting up the table at all."

"She probably would have still gone to the diner anyway. And probably gotten takeout."

"You think?"

Rose snorted.

What Rose said actually made sense, Paula had to admit. She blew her nose and wiped the tears from her face as a female doctor approached.

"Mrs. McArthy?"

Rose stepped forward and pulled Paula with her. Nadine rose from her chair and put her arm around both their shoulders.

"How bad is it?" asked Rose, her grip on Paula's hand almost painful.

"Nothing is broken, but because she's had two injuries in a week—she fell off a table, you said—we're keeping her here for observation. She's also on some pretty good pain meds, so we want to watch her."

"When can she go home?"

"This isn't a big city hospital where you are pushed out according to an amount of hours printed in a policy manual. She'll be discharged when the doctor thinks it's right. It would be good if she weren't alone for the next few days."

"Can I see her?"

The doctor nodded. "Absolutely. I'm sure she'll be asleep soon, though. She's been given painkillers."

While Rose and Nadine followed the doctor, Paula said she would be there in a moment and stepped out. She turned on her cell phone. One bar. She hoped the weak signal was at least stable, and dialed Tyler's number. In brief words, she explained the situation.

"Now, of all times," Tyler said, shocked. "That's really nasty."

"That's why I'm calling you. I know this seems premature, but I'm thinking ahead. I was hoping maybe you could fill in at the studio for a few more days?"

"Me? I'm not a yoga teacher. I was okay for one day but—"

"I know that. But, professional dancer, you know enough about working out and stretching to keep Jasmine's show on the road. I'm guessing you've taken a yoga class, too."

"Sure. Still…"

"Maybe we can get someone from Denver to fill in if she needs it. If you could just hold the place open for a few days. Please."

"Hmm. I'll see what my tour calendar looks like. Maybe I can push something, after all, the understudy is always happy for a chance to push me aside. I wanted to stay for the festival anyway." She managed a small smile.

"You are the best sister. Thank you."

"Would you like me to have that printed on a T-shirt for you to remember the next time we have a sisterly dispute?"

"For once, I'd love to. I have to get back to Jasmine's room with Rose and Nadine. I'll keep you posted."

CHAPTER TWENTY-FIVE

JASMINE DIDN'T KNOW what had woken her up. It was dark and she couldn't see anything. The feeling of floating on a cloud felt delicious. The more awake she became, the more a thousand needles prickled her head and lungs. She wanted to get back to her cloud as quickly as possible. She was drifting away again when heard a voice.

"How are you feeling, darling?"

Nana sat beside the bed holding Jasmine's hand. Nadine was beside Nana, a comforting hand on her shoulder.

Jasmine started to speak but her throat was so dry, all that came out was a croak.

"Where's Jake?" was all she could manage.

"He's resting in the next room," Nana said. "They're waiting for x-rays to come back. If no ribs are broken he can be released." Nadine leaned in closer. "What happened, Jasmine? Did those men beat you?"

"No," she answered. "They pulled me and threatened me, but didn't hit me. I think I fainted."

Nadine looked at Rose meaningfully. "She must have hit her head when she fell."

Jasmine racked her brain to remember. She had fainted. What caused her to faint? Then it came back. *Rambo. They said they were going to kill Rambo.* But before she got a chance to tell Nana out loud, the pain meds took her consciousness away.

The nurse bustled in and marked a note on the chart at the end of Jake's bed. "Good news, Sheriff Carter, you are being discharged. That gunshot only grazed your shoulder."

Jake swung his legs out over the hospital bed. "Can I see Jasmine?"

"For a short time, yes."

Jasmine's attackers had gotten away, but Toby said they wouldn't stay free men long. Unfortunately, the festival had called on all their law enforcement reserves, and there wasn't a full force to conduct a manhunt.

"Don't come back until you have good news," were Jake's parting words. Jake hoped to have it in a few hours at the latest. He got up, tore off the hospital gown, and dressed himself. Painfully. Moving the grazed shoulder made it burn like Hades. They'd offered pain meds, but he didn't want his faculties dulled.

He hurried out of the room and went next door. Jaz was lying, pale and unconscious, against the white sheets. Nadine and Rose made room so he could sit by her side. He reached for her hand and stroked the back of it with his thumb.

"Jaz, can you hear me? I hope so. It's me, Jake."

Her eyelids fluttered. As though she were fighting to regain consciousness.

"I'm here with you, Jasmine. I need you. I've only just found you. Do you know how rare it is to find your soul mate? I'm sure you'd laugh if you could hear me. I know you're still skeptical about us. And yet you must have sensed it too. Otherwise, you wouldn't have gotten involved at all. Because you can be pretty stubborn, sweetheart."

Nadine and Rose exchanged looks.

Stubborn? Granted, the rest that Jake had said was very romantic. But stubborn? Jasmine tried once again to open her heavy eyelids, and croaked slowly and barely audibly, "Stubborn? Is that the best you can come up with at my bedside?"

"You're awake? How are you feeling?"

It was clear to her by now that this place was a hospital. She felt pain in various spots but no idea how she'd ended up here. If this was the receipt for all her karmic efforts, she had to seriously rethink the concept. If only she wasn't so tired! Her eyes fell closed again. "Was it a bus that hit me this time?" she asked.

"Jaz! No, you did a free fall onto hard-packed dirt. Really did a number." Panicked, Jake reached for the button to call the nurse.

Only seconds ticked by before a nurse came by and checked Jasmine's vitals. "She's doing fine. She woke up on schedule."

"Are you sure?" The panic was evident in his voice.

"She's sleeping. That's the best thing for her right now anyway." She eyed him sharply. "And for you, too, the way I see it."

A little reassured, he lowered his tense shoulders. "Thank you. But if you're sure everything is all right, I'll go to the station house now."

She studied him for a moment and then nodded. "I'm sure of it. She should be awake longer later on. Come back." With that, she turned and left the room.

Jake stroked her left cheek with his fingertips. Her lower jaw was bruising up. "I'll see you in a bit. Now I have to get rid of the bad guys first."

At the words "bad guys" Jasmine's eye flew open. Her mouth worked to form words.

"What is it?!" Jake, Nana, and Nadine all said at once.

"It's Rambo. It's Rambo they're after," she whispered.

"What?"

"She's delirious," Nana said.

"No I'm not," Jasmine said in a louder voice. "To teach me a lesson. Said they'd kill Rambo."

Jake looked wildly at Nadine and Nana. "Where's Paula?" he said urgently.

"She went out to use her phone," they said.

Jake jumped up and bolted out of the room.

Paula was halfway home when she realized her cell phone had died. She made a mental note to put it in the charger as soon as she got home. The nights were black out here, and a cell phone was a must for safety. With the crazy events of the day, she'd forgotten the car charger, and a bunch of other things too. She didn't want to leave

Leslie alone and responsible for the animals too long, but felt that everything was probably safe for the short while she'd been at the hospital. Gripping the wheel, she kept her eyes on the road and stayed alert. All they needed was another accident, and she was determined not to have it.

Finally outside the house, she sat behind the wheel for a moment. Tilting her head back against the neck rest, she closed her eyes. She was so exhausted that she could have fallen asleep on the spot. It wasn't just the all-nighter that was getting to her. She could feel the fear for Jasmine eating away at her, and she didn't even want to imagine how her brother Jake was feeling right now.

She opened her eyes again. It was no use resting. Leslie and the dogs were in the warm barn, and the girl deserved a hot meal. She got out and made her way to the house. She frowned. The porch steps were wet in places. But before she could make sense of it, something else caught her eye. The yard was swept and tidy. The dogs weren't coming out to greet her because Leslie was likely feeding them right now inside the barn.

Paula kept going into the house to change her clothes. First, she plopped her cell phone into the charger. Then, dressed in jeans and a flannel shirt, she slipped into her work boots. Western boots with thick rubber soles. Best suited for stable work and comfortable as slippers. Which, in Paula's mind, gave them a clear point advantage over any other footwear.

A smile stole onto her lips. It seemed her stable fairy had been busy, and she immediately felt remorse. In her anticipation of the festival, she had forgotten to put some food out for the little girl. That was a nice way to thank her. Kicking herself, Paula trudged back to the kitchen. As if on cue, the phone in the charger sprang to life, gibbering with half a dozen texts and phone messages. One from Jake made her blood run cold.

"Get you and Leslie inside the house and lock up. Keep the shotgun handy. Armed and dangerous men headed your way. Do not flee in the truck. You are safer inside. Stay off the phone. Keep this line clear. Deputies will be there as soon as they can."

On the other side of the woods bordering the festival grounds, Toby and Ace took the statement of a disgruntled music lover. The young man was dressed in a lime-green T-shirt that said, *I survived the Indie Music Festival.* He also had a green wristband that showed he was a paid concert-goer.

"I parked it right here," the young man complained. "Now my truck's gone. A black four-by-four. Almost brand new."

Toby raised an eyebrow at Ace. "Why are you parked all the way over here and not in the concert lot?"

"You think I'm made of money, dude? Over here's free."

Toby turned to Ace. "Think it's our guys?"

"They're the types that know how to hotwire," Ace replied.

"Aww, what does that mean?" the festival-goer moaned.

"It means we'll find your truck eventually. But your insurance is probably going to have to do the rest."

Toby and Ace strode away, leaving the young man standing there with his mouth open.

⛰️

"*Woof?*" Rambo was the first of the dogs to hear a sound.

"What is it, Rambo?" Leslie asked. "Is something outside?"

The barn door slid back and a dark figure was silhouetted against the sensor lights coming on outside.

"Leslie?" a voice said.

The dogs bounded over.

"I'm here, Paula," Leslie called.

"Come inside the house. I have a hot dinner put on for you. In fact, gather up your things. I'd like it if you and the dogs spent the night with me. Would you like that?"

⛰️

In the kitchen of the main house, Paula's heart contracted painfully as she watched Leslie shovel the warm meal into herself. The dogs had already been fed so they sat at Leslie's feet, waiting in the off-chance that she dropped some food.

"I have a proposition for you," Paula said. "Why don't you finish your dinner while I tell you about my proposal?"

The runaway held her breath. Should she dare to listen to the proposal? Or would she rather run away while she still had the chance? Again, her eyes fell on the food. That was the clincher. She would listen until the spaghetti ran out.

"Surely you know by now that I won't hurt you or let anybody take you away." Paula paused to give the girl a chance to speak up. "I have to tell you the truth. There are some bad men who might be on the way here. But the police are looking out for them, and I have my shotgun."

Leslie stopped eating. "Why don't you run away in the truck?"

"Because the police specifically said not to do that. They have guns and they might shoot us on the road. We're safer inside my house."

"Did you tell the police I was here?"

"No. But I told my brother. And he said to get you inside. So, it may get crazy here tonight, but I'm going to do everything I can to keep you safe. Okay?"

Leslie looked like she only half believed.

Paula didn't want to do it, but it looked like she was going to have to offer proof. The upside was getting Leslie to believe her. The downside was panicking her. She made a quick decision. "Here, I can play you the phone message." Paula put the phone on speaker and played Jake's message.

"Get you and Leslie inside the house and lock up. Keep the shotgun handy. Armed and dangerous men headed your way. Do not flee in the truck. You are safer inside. Stay off the phone. Keep this line clear. Deputies will be there as soon as they can."

Leslie listened with a wide-eyed expression. "He knows my name?"

"He's my brother, I told him about you."

"It sounds real. I don't think you could make that up yourself."

"You're right. So all the usual rules are off tonight. We have to work together. And take care of each other. Are you ready to do that?"

Leslie nodded. "Is that why your shotgun is leaning against the kitchen counter?"

Paula nodded. She opened a low cupboard, dug in the back, and pulled out a box of shotgun shells. As she filled her pockets with them, she said, "The bad men might not come. They might not come at all." She felt like crossing all her fingers and toes. "And in that case we'll remember this night for the rest of our lives. We'll toast marshmallows and tell the story around a campfire."

Leslie giggled. "Was that your proposal?" she asked.

"Only part of it." Paula knew that if she talked about foster mothering and all that system-talk, it might panic Leslie. So she decided to appeal to her finely honed work ethic. Instead of a place in the family, which was nothing positive in Leslie's world, Paula decided to offer her a job.

"It's like this. The work here is actually too much for me." Which, of course, wasn't true. Except for emergencies like that day, she had her little homestead well in hand. But that didn't matter here. "I've noticed you're always helping me out. Like a Girl Scout. You do your job very well. And since I happen to be looking for an extra worker, I thought I'd ask if you'd be interested in a job." She held her breath.

Leslie's eyes narrowed suspiciously. Like it sounded too good to be true.

"I've done some homework. And I got in touch with Roger White, an attorney who specializes in children's law. I have a meeting next week. Plus, I have strong ties to this community and a lot of people will pull strings for me. And that means they'll pull strings for you. After all, your right to shelter and an education is law."

"So, what's the catch?"

"There are certain conditions attached to the job."

"Conditions?" *There was nothing for free in life*, Leslie thought bitterly.

"Wait," Paula said quickly, sensing she had almost lost the girl. "Why don't you listen to the terms first? Okay?"

Leslie put aside the bowl of food and crossed her arms.

"I can only pay you an allowance, but in return you get room and board."

"In the house?" came the surprised answer. Almost as if the words had slipped out against her will.

Paula stifled a smile. Yep, there was definitely interest there.

"Sure. I don't have an extra place to live. But the house is big. I'm sure we can get by each other. You'd have your own room, of course," she added.

A room of her own. Leslie had never had that before. At first she shared a room with her mother and her respective lover, and later, with the various foster families. There had been at least three.

"Sure. There's breakfast and dinner, too."

"What about lunch?"

Then came the difficult part. Paula wrestled inwardly with herself whether she should actually lay all her cards on the table. But finally she decided to do so. In her opinion, honesty really was the best policy. She took a deep breath. "At school, of course. Where else?"

Silence. It seemed like half an eternity to Paula. In reality, it was probably more like thirty seconds.

"You want me to go to school?" Leslie didn't quite know what to make of it. She had always enjoyed going to school when she'd had the opportunity. The other students were another matter entirely. She looked down at herself, saw the ripped jeans and broken sneakers, and shook her head. "Sorry. I'll work whatever you want. But no school."

Paula stumbled when she heard the answer. Why didn't Leslie want to go to school? It didn't make sense, especially after the first question about school had sounded very hopeful. She decided to postpone this discussion. For now, it was important to coax the girl out of her hiding place in the barn. "All right, then. No school. For now."

BRINNNGGGG! The cell phone went off. Leslie and Paula's heads jerked around to look at it. Paula could see it was Jake. She forced herself to remain calm. She picked up the phone.

"Hello, brother."

"Paula. The perps are a couple miles away, moving slowly like they're looking the terrain over. Toby and Ace are following them. So far, undetected."

"Are you sure they're coming here? Why here?"

"They're coming to Jasmine's house. They already know she's not there."

"What are they looking for, then?"

"Rambo."

Paula thought for a moment. "And when they don't find him there, they'll move on to the next house. Which is me."

"My thoughts, too."

"What should I do?"

"For now, nothing."

"Are you sure we can't run?"

"No. For now, you're safer in the house. Got your shotgun loaded?"

"Yes."

"Where is Rambo?"

"He's right here."

"Is there a way you can lock him downstairs in the root cellar?"

"Why would I do that? He'll bark his head off."

"Never mind then."

"What's this got to do with Rambo?" Paula could hear Jake's mind clicking away. *Should I tell her, should I not tell her?* Then she felt him shut down like a steel door.

"Nothing. I'll be in touch again soon." He disconnected.

Paula set the phone back in the charger. "Did you hear that?"

"Every word."

"Would you like to see your room?"

"Sure."

Paula picked up the shotgun and noticed that her hands remained miraculously still. As she led the way out of the kitchen and to the stairs that would take them to the second floor, she said a quiet prayer of thanks that, so far, no sounds outside were disturbing the dogs. They were following their humans, unconcerned. *Maybe,* Paula thought, *we can get through this. Maybe the gunmen won't make it this far.*

On the second floor of the house, Paula stopped and pushed the door open. "Here. This would be your room."

Cautiously, Leslie ventured a look. The room was not very large, perhaps twelve square feet. Two windows offered views of the horse pasture. Good. That way she would always know when someone approached. The walls were painted a pale sky blue. In one corner was a simple desk with a chair, and on the other side was the bed. Both were made of light pine wood and gave the whole room a friendly atmosphere. Above the bed hung a framed picture. She took a step closer to get a better look at the details. Barns and Roo, trotting along behind a herd of goats.

She spun around once to take in her surroundings. Then stopped and looked at Paula. "It's so beautiful. Way too beautiful for me. I can sleep in the barn, too. I'll still do the work, but the barn is fine."

The wide eyes and the fear that could be read in them almost broke Paula's heart. But she tried to keep a neutral expression on her face. She suspected Leslie would not respond well to pity. "This room is reserved for staff. You see for yourself, it's very simply furnished. I must be able to rely on you being well enough to do your work. Sleeping in the stable is out of the question."

Abruptly she turned, without giving Leslie a chance to say anything in reply. "Come on. There's still a lot to do."

She showed her the bathroom. "Here are towels, you'll find soap there. Paula pointed to a shelf. "You can deposit your personal things there."

What personal things? Leslie asked herself, but said nothing.

They went downstairs and Paula continued her tour. She pointed to the room across from the kitchen. "That's the living room. I have dibs on the remote control," she remarked, raising an eyebrow.

Leslie, still not trusting her voice, just nodded.

"When I'm not around, you can watch TV. Tomorrow we'll go shopping, then you can tell me some things you like to eat. While we're at it, we might as well go shopping for work clothes." Her eyes fell on the bundle in Leslie's hands. She was almost proud of herself that she had thought of the work clothes. Otherwise, the girl probably wouldn't have accepted a wardrobe. On they went through the kitchen. At the sight of the bananas, Leslie felt some remorse. She opened her mouth to confess her banana theft to Paula. But then she closed it again. Probably it didn't matter. As it was, she could soon eat as many bananas as she wanted. All sorts of feelings suddenly rose up inside her. It was all so much outside her world of experience that she didn't even know what to feel.

Paula nudged her and she flinched in such a way that Paula jumped backwards, startled. "Don't touch me," Leslie hissed.

Paula raised both hands. "I'm sorry. I didn't mean to scare you. Just explaining the washing machine here. Maybe you want to wash some of your clothes? That's your own responsibility. Your laundry, I mean."

Leslie just nodded. Opening her backpack, she separated the few clothes in there from the tattered paperback book, and stuffed them into the washing machine.

"Wait," Paula interrupted her, "I'll get you some of my clothes. Then you can wash what you're wearing while you're at it."

Leslie looked down at herself. This was probably a good idea. "But your clothes are way too big for me."

"I don't think it matters. I just want you to have something to wear while your clothes are in the machine. You're not going to a fashion show."

That got a smile from Leslie. "Do you think I could take a shower, too?"

Glad that she felt safe enough to ask for something, Paula gave her a friendly smile. Her facial muscles already felt quite strange. Constant smiling was not in her standard program. Hopefully, the situation would return to normal soon. But when she saw the distrust in Leslie's gaze turn into something that almost looked like hope, she was sure the right thing had been done. "Sure. I'll put the clothes in front of the bathroom for you. You'll find me in the living room."

Leslie nodded, gave her a shy smile that disappeared in a moment, and started upstairs to the bathroom.

The cell phone rang in the kitchen.

Leslie reversed back down the stairs.

With icy calm, Paula went to get the phone. Leslie and the dogs followed, very closely.

It was Jake.

Without an introduction, he jumped in. "Toby and Ace are tailing them. They're a quarter mile from your place. We have backup coming from the other direction so we can surround them, but officers are coming all the way from Breckenridge. As of right now, they're ten minutes away."

"Should Leslie and I get in the truck? What about getting away on the horses?"

"The problem is there's only one road and you'll be the only moving targets on it. That's always been the problem."

"The horses can go across the fields."

"Are you going to start jumping them over fences?"

"N-No."

"You need to go with Leslie and the dogs down into the root cellar and lock yourself in."

"Sure," Paula said. "Anything else?"

"No. Still got your shotgun?"

"Absolutely."

"Don't do anything stupid."

"No, of course not."

"Why don't I feel like you're listen—"

This time, Paula was the one to hang up.

She put the cell phone in her pocket and turned to Leslie. "I want you to go down into the root cellar with Rambo and lock yourself in. Keep him quiet."

"What about Barns and Roo?"

"They're going to stay on the main floor. They're your second line of defense."

"What about you?"

"Me? I'm your first line." Paula picked up her shotgun and doublechecked that it was loaded. She patted her pockets and made sure they were filled with shells. Then she picked up the gun and said, "Go now." She waited until Leslie and Rambo had disappeared down the stairs. Then Paula pushed the kitchen table in front of the door.

Shooing Barns and Roo away from the main entry, she let herself out and heard the lock click securely. Then she walked out to the road. A glimmer of headlights flickered in the distance. She took out the cell phone and speed-dialed Jake. He picked up on the first ring.

"Paula?"

"Those gunmen still headed my way?" she asked.

Yes, where are—?"

"The bad guys are still out front? Toby and his guy are tailing behind them?"

"Yes but—"

Paula hung up the phone again. She thought of her innocent animals in the barn. She thought of Barns and Roo, inside the house. And Leslie and Rambo, downstairs.

The headlights heading her way got bigger and brighter.

Paula shouldered the shotgun and clicked the safety off.

She counted to ten before she started blasting.

CHAPTER TWENTY-SIX

WHEN JASMINE AWOKE the next morning, she didn't know where she was. She raised an arm to shield her eyes from the glare of the morning sun that fell through the window. And instantly regretted it as a pain rippled through her shoulder, down to the tips of her toes. "Was I hit by a train?" she groaned aloud.

"No," replied a sleepy voice.

Carefully, she turned her head towards the window. Jake was sitting in an armchair and looked pretty battered himself.

On the spot, the experiences leading up to this came crashing down on her. She had to close her eyes for a moment while she pushed all the impressions, especially the terrible ones, to the back of her brain. "What are you doing here?" she croaked.

"Watching over you," he said.

"Watching me," she repeated dumbly. "May I ask why?"

His expression changed from concerned to serious. "Do you remember getting abducted at the concert?"

"Apparently, I hit my head pretty hard, if that's got anything to do with the jackhammer throbbing in my skull. "Don't you need to talk to those guys, make them pay, or press charges? Whatever you sexy lawmen do?" she tried to joke.

"Paula stood in for me," he said.

She gingerly lifted one hand an inch—*ow!*—and let it fall. "What are you talking about?"

"She went out in the road with her shotgun and drove the gunmen straight back to Ace and Toby. The bad guys are in jail already."

"Tell me all the details!"

"They thought it was the Breckenridge police shooting at them. When they found out it was one woman with a shotgun, they were pissed."

"Tell me from the start."

He stood up and sat carefully on the edge of her bed. "You don't have to worry about details anymore. Just get well."

She stared at him, anger clear in her gaze. "We were in bed together once."

"Twice, when you get right down to it," he interrupted her, smugly.

She ignored him. "And already you're going all Neanderthal? The poor mistress hit her head and now we'd rather not bother her with the hard facts of life? You can forget it. My head hurts like hell, and my mood matches." Exhausted from her outburst, she let herself sink back into the bed.

A nurse came in. "Sir? You seem to be upsetting the patient. I don't want to have to ask you to leave."

"No!" they both said, as if from the same mouth.

Astonished, the nurse looked from one to the other. "All right. But I'll be back in five minutes."

When she left, Jake cleared his throat. "I'm sorry. That was condescending of me. But I was just trying to protect you."

"Jake…"

"No, let me finish. It almost kills me to think how easily I could have lost you yesterday. Now that I've finally found you." Forcefully, he looked at her. "On top of that, I'm a cop, and I'm sworn to protect the people of my small town. That may sound arrogant when I talk about *my town*, but that's how I feel. And my instinct is to protect what belongs to me." Frustrated, he ran a hand through his hair and looked out the window. "You're the only one I seem to fail at. This is the second time in a few weeks that I've failed to look out for you."

Jasmine was touched by his words and also a little surprised. She would not have thought that he had such deep feelings for her. *You're no different*, whispered a voice in the back of her mind. *Be glad*. Still, she frowned at the last sentence. "It's not your fault. You were at work. You'd have to chain me to you to guarantee my safety every second."

"I've thought about that, believe me," he murmured.

She rolled her eyes and immediately regretted it as pain shot behind her eyes.

Concerned, he leaned over her. "Why don't you try to stay calm? And before you get all worked up again, here's the quick summary of last night. Gavin's friends who held you up in Seattle came back here to pay you a visit. They were arrested last night."

Cold fear gripped her. "Rambo? Is he okay?"

He nodded. "He's fine. He's still with Paula. Now maybe you'll understand why, after the arrest, I sat by your side all night. And why I didn't want to worry you about it as soon as you woke up." He pressed a gentle kiss to her temple. She nestled her face against his hand. That got a smile from him. "I have to go. I have reports to file. I'm sure your grandmother and Nadine will stop by later."

"Wait. When can I get out of here?"

"I'm not sure."

"Just when I had my studio opening. My business will go down the toilet." She clenched the hand that didn't hurt into a fist.

"This isn't Seattle, you keep forgetting. Paula is already working on a plan. Ask her when she gets in later. By the way, she feels bad about the accident, too. She imagines none of this would have happened if she hadn't called to meet you for takeout dinner."

"Seems like the god complex is in the Carter family." Jaz blew him a kiss and drifted away.

After dealing with the nonstop paperwork that crime generated, Jake headed home for another shower, and to feed his cat. Jimmy was already waiting for him, meowing to break the heart of anyone within earshot. His owner bent down to take off his shoes and scratched him behind the ears with his other hand. The cat let him for a moment, then ran to the door, where he stood on his hind legs and scratched at the wood. Scratches in the varnish testified to the fact that he often tried to attract the attention of his food master in this way.

Inside, Jake put his shoes behind the door and went to the kitchen, where he filled the water bowl with fresh water and put dry food down. Greedily, the cat dove in.

"Better now, huh Jimmy?" Jake grabbed a beer from the fridge and plopped down on one of the chairs at the kitchen table. With the cold bottle pressed to his forehead, he watched his starving cat fill his belly.

What a mess.

Maybe it was time to seriously consider a career change. Teacher. Maybe he should become a teacher. Or work in construction. Hopefully, he could still manage to mix cement. Disgusted with himself, he got up and took a shower.

Five hours later, he woke up on the sofa. Disoriented, he looked around. He was wearing only the sweatpants he'd slipped into after showering. Gently, he repositioned Jimmy, who had snuggled up to him, and stood up. The cat didn't even twitch an ear.

Jaz! He wanted to visit Jaz after all. He frantically searched for his jeans and a sweatshirt, when it occurred to him that no one would probably let him see her in the intensive care unit after eleven o'clock at night. Slowly it dawned: he wasn't good as a boyfriend, either.

His cell phone vibrated. He pulled it out of his pocket. It was a text message from Tyler.

Glad u slept. Jaz better 2-nite. Awake briefly, spoke two sentences. Wants 2 c u tomorrow. Now go back to bed!

Against his will, a smile flitted across his face. Siblings were a wonderful thing. Tyler knew him like no one else. Except perhaps his mother. As ordered, his phone rang, his parents' number on the display.

"Hi, Mom."

"Jake. How are you? I've tried to reach you a couple of times. But you were probably asleep." Without waiting for a response, she continued in one breath, "I heard about the new trouble. Even though I personally welcome the fact that two more violent criminals are off the streets."

"Mom," he admonished her, but with little conviction in his voice.

"It's true, isn't it? In any case, I assume you had sense enough to actually sleep for once today. I put lasagna in the fridge for you. Put it in the oven for ten minutes and it's warm."

Food. He hadn't thought about that at all. He couldn't even remember his last meal. Yes he did; donuts at noon. His stomach growled, as if to let him know that the donuts were but a distant memory.

On the other end of the line, he heard his mother audibly inhale and exhale. "Are you feeling guilty about what happened? Am I right?"

"Yep," he admitted. He paused, then continued in a choked voice, "If I had done my job right, Jasmine wouldn't be in the hospital at all."

"So, you're all-powerful now? Omniscient?" she asked sharply.

"What? No!"

"How could you have foreseen the events? Unless you were hiding something from me, like possessing a crystal ball. Otherwise, you had no reason to believe that another attack on Jasmine was planned. Your attacker, that ex-boyfriend, was behind bars. It was safe to assume she was out of danger. We all agreed on that."

"But I should have insisted on staying with her and taking her to the festival. I had a bad feeling all along."

"It's certainly reasonable to trust your intuition next time. But even that's no guarantee. Jake, She's a grown independent woman with a clear idea of what she wants and what she doesn't want. That night, she did what she felt was right. And short of you having her secretly shadowed, there was nothing you could have said to change her mind."

Jake swallowed. Rationally, he knew that. If only the message would reach his feelings, too.

"Eat something and go to bed, Jake. It's getting late. Your friend is doing well, considering the circumstances. She's asleep, and there'll be time enough tomorrow to work through problems."

After the conversation, Jake felt relieved. It was strange how, even now that he was an adult, his mother still managed to make him feel better. Or worse, depending on what he had just done. He shrugged and went to the kitchen to heat up his lasagna.

Jasmine awoke to the light coming on. A nurse was entering readings into the chart hanging at the foot of her bed. She opened one eye and blinked against the glare.

Pain coursed through her head and she quickly closed her eye again. *Oh great.* She had to be in the hospital, unable to work, and would still not be allowed to sleep in.

"How are you today?" the nurse asked good-humoredly. When she only mumbled something back, the nurse continued, "Don't worry. You'll be rid of me in no time. I just have to take your blood pressure, and then you can go back to sleep."

Jasmine doubted she would fall asleep again so soon. She briefly considered trying meditation. But if she was honest, even this effort seemed too great. On a trial basis and to keep herself busy at least a little, she wiggled her toes. On the left, it worked wonderfully, even if she felt the tiny movement up to the top of her skull. On the right, nothing happened at all, except that her foot started throbbing harder.

A hard skull had its good points, she thought, recalling Jake's first words yesterday. She longed for his presence. He gave her a sense of security and safety. She blinked hard to get rid of the tears that were threatening. Now was not the time to have a nervous breakdown. Her goal was to get better in record time and finally get on with her life. She didn't know if the universe had planned a long break for her, but surely less drastic measures would have been taken. By now, she was grumbling half aloud to herself.

"Are you talking to yourself?" She heard Jake's voice from the door.

She opened the one eye again and looked over at him, a wry smile on her bruised face.

He came closer and gently clasped her hand.

"I'm wrestling with the gods of fate right now. My argument is that they could have arranged for me to slow down in a less spectacular way. By winning a contest, for example. Three weeks in the Bahamas for two people or something like that."

Her voice sounded pretty upset. Not that he could blame her. He could imagine how she felt. "At least your head is already working amazingly well again," he encouraged.

"It works. Half the time I forget where I hurt."

"It's not that easy to keep track of, either."

"That's true again."

For quite a while both said nothing and simply enjoyed each other. She, lying in bed, and he sat on the chair next to it, her smaller hand in his large one. She turned her head and nestled her unbruised cheek against his hand. "I'm glad you're here."

He smiled, but his expression remained tense and guilt flashed in his eyes. "If I had paid more attention, you wouldn't be here at all."

"That's the biggest lie I've ever heard. No one could have known that someone else was after me. I just hope those guys stew in jail as long as possible and you find out who was the mastermind behind the whole thing. Because I'm getting tired of staying in this particular hotel." She screwed up her face. She wasn't really fit enough for much talking and emotional outbursts yet. But some things just had to be said and couldn't wait.

"But don't you see—" he continued.

"No. I don't." She snapped, cutting him off. "And if you have nothing positive to say to me, and you're only here to protest your guilt and wallow in self-pity, then please leave." She closed her eyes and turned her head away. She didn't have the energy, didn't he understand that? The tears she had so successfully repressed earlier were back in her eyes.

Hurt by her harsh words, Jake stood up. "I'm sorry you feel that way. I'll come back in the evening." When she didn't reply, he turned and left.

When he was gone, Jasmine immediately felt sorry. She loved this wonderful man. She was sure of that by now. But she knew she would have gone crazy if she had to listen to him any longer. She hoped he would figure out by evening what she had been trying to tell him. She cursed softly to herself, and fell asleep again.

CHAPTER TWENTY-SEVEN

SIX WEEKS LATER

Jasmine was sitting on a mat in her living room, pushing herself through a rehab program. She was already feeling much better. The doctors were also pleasantly surprised by the speed of recovery. Physically, she had nothing to complain about, except for a few aches and pains. Her mental health she was not so sure about.

Jake had moved back in after Pat and Kathrina left to go back to Seattle. Once they got past her emotional outburst at the hospital, he apologized the next day and promised to let the guilt issue rest. Of course, she was glad for his help. Annoyed by idle thoughts she couldn't do anything about, she let her mind wander to her friends.

Pat had struck a deal with Mr. Wilkinson and his plan to renovate the old house was slated to go forward. He was basically returning the van to Seattle with Kathrina and then flying back to Colorado. Kathrina had hinted that she could possibly see herself moving to Independence, too, but she had been pretty hush-hush about specific plans. Jaz hadn't followed up either. After all, she knew firsthand what it was like to get a small business off the ground. Kathrina would be giving up a well-run business that she had built in Seattle to start over out here.

In terms of the yoga studio, Jasmine taught exactly one lesson before Tyler took over for a week and then she had to go back on the road. After that, the studio sat empty for six weeks. A real success story.

Jasmine sighed and carefully pushed herself up into the cobra position. Only yesterday she had received confirmation from the doctor that she was completely healed. Unfortunately, no one had communicated that to the appropriate parts of her body and they refused to cooperate at the moment. At least the way she would like them to—as they had before the accident. Which, as she knew, was illusory after such a short time. Nevertheless, it annoyed her.

As well, Jake annoyed her. Since the accident, he watched over her every step, worse than any mother hen. And there was no one out to get her anymore. She couldn't say she was sorry, even though she felt it good to *try* to feel sorry for her attackers. Her path to enlightenment was even further away than previously thought, she noted self-deprecatingly. Primarily, she was relieved to know her life was no longer in danger. Only Jake refused to accept that as fact.

This morning she had kicked him out of the house. Nana's house. Told him he wouldn't have to come back unless he finally stopped guarding her all the time. To make it clear she was serious about it, she stuffed all his things into a large gym bag and left it outside the door. Now all that was left was his cat, Jimmy, stalking Rambo. The poor dog already didn't know where to hide. She could well relate to the feeling.

Slowly exhaling, she lowered herself back onto her stomach. She repeated the exercise twice more, careful not to overdo it. Too much did not always help much.

She often found herself explaining that to the overzealous among her students.

To relieve the strain on her hip, she moved into the child's position and rounded her back as she stretched her hands away from her palms, facing downward. As she relaxed, her thoughts returned to Jake. She remembered what he had said to her when she awakened from her coma. *Stubborn.* Imagine, that was like one jackass calling another long-eared. Jake gave a whole new dimension to the word stubborn. She loved this man. That had become clear to her in the terrible moments when she was in the grip of her attackers. After the horrific event, the only thing that prevented her from going crazy were the memories of him; his kindness, his strong body, and the loving gaze from his blue eyes.

In the midst of the attack, she had only felt the irrepressible will to survive, to finally be able to tell him that she loved him. Life-threatening situations had the effect of reducing life to what was really important. Despite this, or perhaps because of it, she was not ready to be treated as if she were a fragile doll for the next fifty years.

She may not have been a cop, she didn't know much about self-defense or guns, but she could confidently take care of herself. That had already worked out quite well for twenty-five years. She wasn't going to let one horrible situation define her entire life.

Winding up her workout, she rolled into *Savasana*, the dead position. She looked through the window into the blue sky and watched white clouds chase one another on the wind. She could even see a mountain peak in the window's left corner. Despite the beautiful view, she was still gloomy. Apparently she couldn't make her love life work anyway. First, because she was afraid of the emotions that this particular man aroused in her, and now because he was too afraid that something would happen to her again.

"Hello, Jaz? Are you home?" Paula's voice snapped her out of her thoughts.

She straightened up. *What was Paula doing here?*

"Here I am, in the living room."

The door opened and Paula came in. Followed by Nana, Nadine, the Disney Sisters, Brenda, Holly and Sandra, the two mothers who had helped with the yoga-studio renovation. Jasmine gulped. "What are you all doing in my living room?"

"We heard what a jerk my brother is. We've known that for a while, but today it seemed like you finally got into action. Wonderful, is all I'm saying. But we all know that the right thing isn't always the easiest thing to do." Paula made a sweeping gesture. "That's why we're all here, with rich gifts."

"Rich gifts?" asked Jaz, as she wiped away a few tears.

Nana stepped behind her and patted her back. "Well, sure. Good company, delicious food, and plenty of alcohol. Just the right combination for a situation like this."

Jasmine's heart warmed up. She liked the plan. In fact, she was already starting to feel better. Nadine introduced her to the rest of the women: Nancy was the ex-wife of the new vet.

Miss Minnie handed out pigs in blankets and samosas—Indian dumplings filled with peas, peppers and potatoes. Miss Daisy provided a choice of beer, strawberry margaritas, or soda. By the time the dreaded Q&A session began, Jasmine was already on her second margarita. So she didn't even mind when asked how "she and the hot sheriff" were going to get on now. The question didn't bother her but the term *hot sheriff* definitely did. The jealousy that flashed through her at the question made her gasp. At the last moment, she held back. Or rather, Paula held her back, while a knowing smile danced in her eyes. The attack had left more of a mark than she had thought. A greater propensity for violence, it seemed. Not good, she noted, and firmly resolved to return to regular meditation and visualizing peace. Even though she had briefly doubted the whole karma theory after the attack, she still had a hunch it was basically correct.

She slumped back onto the sofa. "I have no idea what's going to happen next." She gestured wildly with her hands. "I mean, I can probably go to Independence by myself. No need for an escort for that," she enthused. "Or go see Paula at dusk. Alone, accompanied only by Rambo. Without a human Rambo in tow. I'm also perfectly capable of carrying things heavier than a kilogram by myself. I don't need someone to permanently take everything out of my hands. Not that I wasn't grateful for the help when I actually couldn't do anything. But now?"

Holly interrupted, "I wouldn't mind if Andrew took the laundry or the vacuum cleaner out of my hand." The rest burst out laughing.

Jasmine raised her voice a little to make herself understood. "Trust me, this is going to get old really fast. I just want my old life back. Have fun, do things. Have sex."

Astonished faces and raised eyebrows gazed back at her. *Oops.* Had she said that last part out loud, too? As if in confirmation, the others nodded.

"Yep. We all heard that. Now we want to know the details."

She moaned and hid her face behind her hands. "Embarrassing, embarrassing. Moreover, I have to disappoint you. As I said, there's nothing to tell. That's just the problem. All I have to do is look at the man and my mouth waters." She narrowed her eyes and fixed on Sandra, who was looking pointedly off to the side. "If anyone else feels the same way, I don't want to know."

Sandra grinned mischievously. "Don't worry. I got it. Hands off. But it was just a statement of fact," she concluded, emphatically innocent. That comment made everyone laugh again, even Jasmine couldn't help herself.

"Maybe you should do something with him, have an adventure. That will show him that you're fit again."

"Exactly. This is Colorado, after all, the perfect place to snap your neck while you're having fun."

"How about a helicopter tour?"

"Or a white-water raft ride?"

"Climbing? There are these cliffs over the Colorado River."

"Have you all gone insane?" interjected Paula. "She wants to experience something. That doesn't mean she has a secret death wish."

The rest of the group fell silent. Paula sometimes had that effect. Jasmine secretly chuckled.

"The suggestions are good. However, I'd like to do something that I don't have to spend half a year learning first. And Paula, sometimes you do sound like your brother."

She frowned. "I do not. I just don't feel like fishing you out of the next rapid."

"What you want," Nana insisted, "is something that gets the blood pumping, releases enough adrenaline to knock out a bear, you don't have to learn it, and it's relatively safe." She cast a furtive glance at Nadine. The latter smiled back. A mysterious, intimate smile. Jasmine was happy for the two of them. She still had no clear idea of the extent of their relationship. Only that they were very happy together.

While the others discussed pros and cons of adventuresome activities, Jasmine let her mind wander. Would she even dare to do it? Her eyes fell on the empty margarita glass in her hand. Probably not the best time to make such decisions. As if on cue, Miss Daisy appeared, the large pitcher in her hand.

"Margaritas, beer? Who wants anything else?" she asked the crowd. All hands except Paula's went up.

"Are they all getting picked up or are they sleeping in my living room tonight?" Jasmine wondered aloud.

Paula reassured her. "Holly's husband and Sandra's husband have taken over driving duties. They're taking everyone home, including Nadine and Rose. I just had a beer and walked here."

"I had wondered about your unusual near-abstinence."

"Times are changing. Especially when you have an impressionable teenager at home," she muttered.

"Is she alone with you on the farm now?"

"Yes. She's been that way for the last few weeks. If there's one thing she knows how to do, it's how to get along in the company of animals." Paula's voice was affectionate.

"How's the paperwork moving?"

"This is all very new to me. But back to your question. Yes, Leslie is home alone. At least she's sitting in the warm house now, she's had dinner, and, flanked by Barns and Roo, can decide the TV program. But shush. All the paperwork is not permanent yet. We have so many things to decide, including school."

"It's just as important that she has time to settle in," Nadine said wisely. "I can't imagine what that little girl has already been through in her life."

"That's why I've decided to let the subject rest a while."

"And then?"

"Then we'll see," Paula replied with a shrug and a contented smile. It's nice having her around."

Jasmine turned her attention back to the others and was soon involved in a lively discussion about fear of heights. *What have I gotten myself into?* she wondered. But as she looked around the room at the women present, she realized there was nowhere else she'd rather be than with friends.

For the next few days, the thought of adventure kept haunting Jasmine's mind. There had to be just one more thing they could do that would provide high drama and thrills, but be physically closer than climbing or rafting would allow. There had to be something else.

It wasn't as if she had nothing else to do. She had reopened her studio two days ago, and thanks to the infamous bush phone, all of Independence knew that the classes were back. In a typical fit of small-town solidarity, more people had shown up the first day than she could accommodate. Thankfully, things had returned to normal.

To her surprise, a rehab group had formed. It all started when Rebecca Mirren approached her. Rebecca was a nationally known barrel racer; the sport involved racing a horse around barrels at breakneck speed. Rebecca was in the rebuilding phase after a bad fall herself, and had been looking for ways to add variety to her workouts. Yoga was the answer, Jasmine convincingly explained to her. The new, famous student brought more attention and publicity to the little studio. Jasmine was already teaching an hour more than she had initially planned.

Overall, she had come through the whole series of events relatively unscathed. Rambo was healthy and happy. Her business was thriving, thanks in no small part to Tyler's help. Now it was just a matter of getting her love life in order. She sighed and stuffed laundry into her little car. Easier said than done. Jake hadn't shown his face since she'd kicked him out. She couldn't even blame him. In his place, she'd be pissed, too. Nonetheless, she wished he would at least try to understand her point of view. It didn't seem like he would. She slammed the car door and walked around to the driver's side. he would pick up Rambo at Paula's. She had gotten into the habit of taking him over to her place in the morning before she went into the studio.

Paula was already waiting for her on the porch, a glass of freshly squeezed orange juice in her hand. Jasmine gratefully accepted the glass. After emptying half of it in one go, she pressed the cool glass to her hot forehead.

"Had a rough day?"

"I guess you could say that. But I'm just not used to effort anymore either," she admitted. "Thanks to the support of all the residents of Independence, the cash register is ringing and my classes are full."

"Really? All of them?"

"At least all of them, it feels like," she grumbled.

"But that's great."

"True. Exhausting, but great."

"There must be something else that's bothering you. Work itself hasn't bothered you so far."

Jasmine set the now-empty glass down on the porch railing and sank into the cushions of the wooden bench. "You just know me too well already."

"Right. So what is it?"

"Your brother, if you want to know for sure. He ignores me completely. There's total radio silence between us. Not that I expected anything different after I put him out the door with bag and baggage," she added self-critically.

"Hmm. Does it help if I tell you he looks like he hasn't slept in two weeks? All the deputies give him a wide berth. His mood is worse than a bear with sore paws. So you can be sure he's not going to be cold about the whole thing."

"But it's not enough that he would try to talk to me about it."

"I'm guessing, knowing my brother, he's just trying to give you the breathing room you insisted on."

"I never wanted a breather in the first place, dang it! I wanted Jake back. The Jake who would surprise me with trips, argue with me, and kiss me."

"What can I say, he's a man. Nothing works without precise instructions in clear words," Paula replied, an amused smile on her face.

She frowned. "What do you want me to do? Write him a list?"

"You could also kidnap him and tie him up, then he has to listen to you. He won't be released until he understands," a voice said behind her. She turned and spotted Leslie, who had snuck up with the dogs in tow and was obviously listening.

Astonished, Paula raised an eyebrow. "Are you speaking from experience there?"

Leslie blushed. "No, but when you were visiting Jaz a few days ago, I was watching this movie. A love story. That's where it worked." The teenager's eyes sparkled with new confidence, and the dark shadows under her eyes were gone. She'd also had a hair trim and filled out a few pounds.

Paula was about to explain that life rarely plays out like in the movies when Jasmine spoke up again. "It's really not a bad idea at all. If I can manage to get him into my car, I can take him bungee jumping. Once we get there, he won't have any choice but to join in. And since most places are a two-hour drive away, he'll have to listen to me the whole way."

Paula's look was still skeptical. Leslie, on the other hand, grinned, proud to have contributed something to the solution.

"It sounds like you've done quite a bit of research."

"Well, uh, what can I say?" Jaz trailed off, and looked at her fingernails before coming up with a sly grin. "After failing to banish your brother from my mind, let alone my heart, I had to think about alternatives."

"And the first thing that comes to mind is bungee jumping," Paula muttered.

Jaz shrugged her shoulders. "Why not? The idea came from my grandmother. It can't be that bad."

"You'd really dare to do that?" Paula shuddered at the very idea of throwing herself over a cliff on the end of an elastic rope.

"I don't know. But if Nana could do it, I can do it," she replied, with more confidence than she actually felt.

"And how are you going to get him to come along?"

"It's simple. You're going to help me with this."

CHAPTER TWENTY-EIGHT

ONE WEEK LATER

Jasmine checked the contents of the truck again: filled picnic basket, two bottles of water, a blanket, money, her ID, and a warm jacket in case it got any colder. She just hoped she could drive this behemoth of a vehicle, too. For the plan to work, she had to switch cars with Paula today. The plan was pretty simple. Paula had called Jake over to her house and hinted at something of a surprise. He grumbled at first that he wasn't in the mood for surprises, but in the end had agreed to come.

As soon as he was in the car, the plan was for Paula to blindfold him. She hoped he would go along with it. Otherwise, the whole beautiful plan was ruined. Under the pretext of having forgotten something, Paula would leave the vehicle once again, only for Jasmine to take her place. And then they would be off, headed for Glenwood Springs, ninety-eight miles west on I-70. That was more than enough time to clear up any misunderstandings. And if not, she hoped the plunge would work its magic. As a precaution, she had made a phone call yesterday to the doctor who had treated Jake's wound. From a medical point of view, nothing spoke against her plan.

A sharp whistle sounded. The agreed signal that she should hide. They had parked their car out of sight of the house behind the barn. Leslie had gone for a walk with the dogs. She was all excited about being part of the grand conspiracy. So there was nothing to give away Jasmine's presence. She slammed the door and slipped into the house, where she hid by the window so she could see outside.

As soon as Jake got out, Paula went to meet him. Jasmine hoped she would manage to stay serious. When they had rehearsed the whole thing with Leslie, she had burst out laughing all the time. But now, everything remained quiet, except for a murmur of voices. Finally, Paula came back into the house.

"You owe me. I'll be hearing for years to come that I blindfolded him."

"Yes, yes," Jasmine answered distractedly. She was so nervous that she could hardly breathe. Her stomach was rebelling, too. Whether because of Jake or the upcoming jump, she didn't know.

"Go on now, get going. My brother isn't the patient type."

Jasmine took a deep breath and went outside to slip into the big truck.

Jake heard the sounds, and although he knew it had to be Paula, he was irritated. Something wasn't right here. The engine started and the vehicle drove off. He was still puzzling over what was suddenly different. Suddenly he froze and sniffed a few times like a predator scenting its prey. The scent! Instead of horses, the whole driver's cabin suddenly smelled like orange blossoms. It was Jasmine. Angry at the deception, and yes, that her scent could still throw him off like that, he tore the scarf from his head.

"Is this a bad joke?" he demanded to know.

She glanced at him out of the corner of her eye and focused on the road, happy to have an excuse not to look him in the eye.

"I wanted to do something with you and I wasn't sure if you would agree."

"Why didn't you just ask?" He sounded genuinely surprised.

"If I remember correctly, there was radio silence between us all the time," she replied.

"That's what you wanted, isn't it? You made your opinion clear when you threw me out the door." When she dared another glance in his direction, she saw the vulnerability in his eyes.

"But only until you realize that I don't need round-the-clock security, seven days a week."

He clenched his jaw. "I'm sorry I'm worried about you. But I understand. This is no longer wanted…"

"Now you're just acting impossible." He was really starting to make her angry.

For quite a while they said nothing more. Jasmine concentrated on the road while Jake stared out the window. The awkward silence continued for over an hour. Finally, Jasmine sighed and started to talk just as his cell phone beeped. He pulled it out. It was his sister.

"Stop being such a jerk and listen for a change!" Paula said, into his ear.

He rolled his eyes, shook his head, and pocketed the phone again.

"Bad news?"

"No. Just Paula, who thinks we need her help." He sounded rather annoyed.

Jasmine had to bite back a laugh. "Look, I know you mean well. I also understand that you think you need to look out for me."

Jake continued to look out the window, but at least he didn't interrupt her and seemed to be listening. Encouraged, she continued, "But I can't live like this."

He turned to her. "What do you mean, you can't live like this? With me?"

"No. Yes." Frustrated, she broke off. Further ahead, she spotted a parking lot. She put on her blinker and took the exit.

Irritated, he looked around. "What are we doing here?"

"Talking to each other," she said, between clenched teeth. "Since this conversation seems to be more difficult than I thought, it's safer to pull over. Before I run another driver off the road."

He didn't know how to respond to that. At least he was looking at her, his gaze no longer quite as closed as before. Secretly, he had decided to try to understand his girlfriend. It had nothing at all to do with his sister's comment.

"So, what did you mean when you said earlier that you couldn't live like this?"

Jasmine closed her eyes, hoping the words would flow more easily. "I would like nothing more than to spend my life with you. To see where it takes us." She looked at him again. She needed to see his reaction with her own eyes.

Jake's face lit up hopefully. "Really? You kicked me out anyway?" His voice took on that hard unyielding tone again.

"Because if this is going to work out between us, you have to give me air to breathe. To live, darn it! My own life. The way I want it. Not the way you think it should be." She raised a hand as he moved to retort. "Wait. Let me finish talking. I'm not helpless. I'm not careless, either. The attacks on me were bad, no question. Maybe even more so for you than for me. But I can't and won't live the rest of my life according to those terrible events. Don't you understand? Then Gavin wins. And I would be a victim all my life. I refuse to be that. I survived. Life goes on. And I hope you'll be a part of it."

Jake had turned his gaze back outside and swallowed hard at her last words, visibly struggling for composure. Finally, he turned back to her and grabbed her hand. "Okay. You're right."

Jasmine couldn't believe her ears and held her breath. Suddenly it was supposed to be so easy?

"But please try to understand me, too. Call me a Neanderthal, but I grew up knowing that men will do anything to protect their family. That's not to say that Paula or even Tyler can't do that themselves. They can. Sometimes better than a man. That doesn't change my feeling that this is my responsibility. The fact that I'm a police officer only reinforces that. In that job, you are responsible for all citizens entrusted to your care. And with you, I…" His voice dropped. "I failed."

She raised her hand and stroked his cheek. "You didn't. You were there when I needed you."

He closed his eyes. "But too late. When I saw you lying there, I thought you were dead. It was bad enough when I lost my partner a few years ago. When I was working for the Denver Police Department. Seeing you like that, that was a thousand times worse. I couldn't bear to lose you."

"Then meet me halfway," she whispered, "Trust me not to take any unnecessary risks. I promise I'll listen if you're worried about anything. But I need to be able to live a normal life. To get away, to go to work, to take walks by myself."

Fear still had a firm grip on Jake's heart. But he forced himself to let her words sink in, and suddenly Paula's words made sense. He really was an idiot. He almost let the best thing in his life go. Just because he couldn't manage to let go. So much for self-fulfilling prophecies.

He smiled. "Okay. I'll try. Be patient with me." Then he leaned down and kissed her again, and again. The attraction between them was as strong as ever. She had never felt so close to him. Her passion mingled with his and she felt as if they had finally arrived where she'd always wanted to be. Then the fire flaring in her veins displaced rational thoughts. When they broke away from each other after several minutes, they were both breathing heavily.

Jasmine leaned back in her seat, her eyes half closed. If she were a cat, she would have purred. Loudly. Jake was back at last. The man she had fallen in love with.

Jake gave her a feather-light kiss on the lips before snapping her out of her daydream by asking, "What about my surprise?" A teasing twinkle in his eyes, he added, "For all I care, we can go home and celebrate."

She squinted at the clock on the dashboard. "So late already! We'll have to hurry. Otherwise we'll miss our surprise." She slid the ignition key forward and started the pickup. From narrowed eyes she glanced at him. "I'll remind you of your promise shortly. Trust me."

What have I gotten myself into? Jake asked himself, following Jasmine into the large adventure park, known far and wide for specializing in breathtaking adrenaline kicks. He hoped she had no intention of dragging him on the X-treme Thrills roller coaster that roared menacingly along the edge of the breathtaking canyon. Screams were coming from it right now. Jake had enough excitement from his day-to-day job; this he didn't need. He swallowed, his mouth suddenly dry.

Ten minutes later, he wished the surprise had been the roller coaster. They stood in a locker room and had to hold still while two park employees fastened safety harnesses around them. The fact that the man in charge constantly had his paws on Jaz's body didn't exactly help to lift Jake's spirits.

"What were you thinking? If this is supposed to increase my confidence in your decisions, think again," he rumbled. "I'm sure your doctor would wring his hands if he knew what you were up to."

VIRGINIA FOX

"I asked a doctor and she gave me the green light. Do you think I would have jumped into this adventure irresponsibly?"

Jake grudgingly swallowed the answer that was on the tip of his tongue and shook his head. Jasmine smiled knowingly. When they finally finished harnessing, they trooped out of the locker room and followed an instructor who led them to a platform. Below the platform, a mighty river flowed and splashed and swept around rocks.

The instructor attached their harnesses to a rope structure. Jake ventured a shy glance to the edge of the platform, but preferred to look away quickly. Relieved, he saw that they would be jumping in pairs. Yes, jumping. As in *bungee jumping*. Suddenly, the sun seemed very intense, the splashing river seemed very loud, and the rocks in it, very big. Birds called loudly. All of nature seemed intensely real and alive all around them.

"Did you think I would abandon you?" asked Jasmine, her arms wrapped tightly around his body. She focused all her attention on him. Otherwise, the courage to jump would leave her. She only hoped it wouldn't be her last idea.

Jake did the same and put his strong arms around her waist. Nose to nose they stood there, losing themselves in the depths of each other's eyes. "No. You would never do that. Thank you. For believing in us and fighting for us when I couldn't."

"Always," she replied, biting his lower lip lightly as they plunged in free fall toward the roaring waters of the Colorado River.

PREVIEW

*Don't miss the next book
in the Rocky Mountain Romances series!*

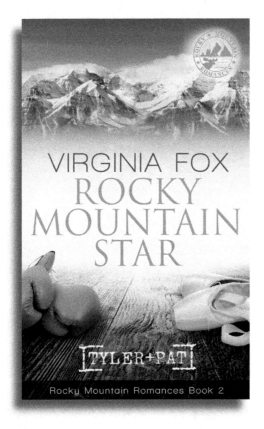

CHAPTER ONE

CENTER STAGE IN THE SPOTLIGHT, Tyler twirled and spun to *Blackbird,* played by a 15-piece orchestral rock band. She wore a black, figure-skimming sheathe sewn with thousands of crystals that flashed like midnight diamonds under the stage lights. The sheathe ended at her knees, right where the satin ribbons of her ballet shoes twisted up her calves and met the hem. A cascade of shimmering material fell all the way down her back to the floor until she raised her arms and it unfolded on the sides like a nightbird's wings.

The moment was a *prima ballerina* turn in the show and something Tyler had worked for all her life. Not bad for someone born in small-town Colorado with no connections, only talent. It had taken incredible sacrifice and dedication to master such caliber of dance while making it look effortless to the most demanding audience in the world—Las Vegas. Show producers had decided, over time, that she was worth the risk. Difficult, diva-esque performers were the stuff of nightmares for the enormous hotels that offered blockbuster live shows to vacationers. Those million-dollar shows needed stars who arrived on time and delivered spell-binding performances night after night. No matter the personal cost. And Tyler had shown she could deliver.

The live orchestra intensified, and the music swelled. Tyler leaped into the air and took flight, like a real bird. Invisible wires lifted her so she flew across the stage and landed on the tiptoes of her satin shoes. More blackbirds swooped onto the stage, the music soared, and soon they were all whirling in the air to the music, as the audience watched, breathless.

Tyler walked slowly into arrivals, her limp more noticeable after sitting in a cramped seat for the flight. Under her pants, she wore an elastic sleeve around her knee to support the ligaments. Her blond hair hung limp, and instead of walking briskly with energy, she dragged a bit. She looked small, even frail. Dancers were not large people, although she looked six feet tall onstage in a feather headdress, balanced on the tips of her toe shoes.

She was sore, very sore, and instead of being filled with anticipation at seeing her family again, as she usually was, she felt only dread. In fact, she hadn't told them she was coming—just decided to hop a plane on a whim.

For now, it was the knee that occupied her mind, much as she tried to ignore it. A little slip coming offstage, the last show before a two-week hiatus, and here she was limping around like a wimp. A little ice, a good night's sleep, and it would fix itself. Right? The three-hour plane ride in a cramped seat had simply put a little more pressure on it, temporarily. Nothing worth stressing about.

Las Vegas was bursting with Cirque du Soleil-style shows like the one Tyler starred in, but only his had a ballerina character who danced as a blackbird before coming back in an array of costumes opposite different characters. There were many dancers in the show, but only one ballerina. Only one *Tyler Carter*.

Landing a place as the prima ballerina in a Las Vegas show was the culmination of a lifetime of dedication to ballet since childhood. Ballerinas only looked ethereal and delicate. In reality, they withstood rigid physical training and discipline. *A ballerina*, the show's choreographer was fond of saying, *requires the determination of a third-world dictator and the stamina of a polo pony.*

It was one thing for Tyler to fly from Vegas to Colorado and visit with her parents between show engagements. It was always nice to be pampered for a few weeks. It was another thing to limp back to their house at the age of twenty-three when they were already under the impression that her career was fleeting and unstable. Tyler always wanted to put on a good front. And her sore knee wasn't a good front. No matter that it was just a slight tweak at the end of months of grueling performances. Wasn't she deserving of a few post-show aches and pains? Not to people outside show business, she wasn't.

Her parents might show support and understanding on the outside, but on the inside they'd be saying for the millionth time, *If she'd only chosen something practical.* But her plans and dreams included her own show in Vegas, one that would make her a household singing and dancing name, like Madonna, Beyoncé , or like Liza Minnelli in her Broadway days. Or even Britney Spears. Tyler hadn't got started on the singing part of it yet, but that would come. She was already taking lessons.

She made her way to the baggage carousel. While waiting for her wheeled suitcase to appear, she let her gaze wander. Her October visit coincided with Denver's first snow and the airport was teeming with winter sports enthusiasts. Skis, poles, boots, snowboards—even a toboggan—circled on the carousel, waiting to be claimed. The occasional western hat and boots could be seen on a few people. This was the West, after all.

Tyler spotted her suitcase. She bent over to lift it, shifting her weight to her leg, and got jostled from the side. She stifled a groan and grumbled something unintelligible. If she had to stay around these rowdy people a moment longer, one of them would end up trussed up like a turkey on the baggage carousel, destination Timbuktu.

Rolling her suitcase carefully toward the exit, she felt for her cell phone and stopped to tap the Uber app. She could have called Paula for a ride, but her sister was bossy, and as soon as she discovered that Tyler was not one hundred percent, a ton of good advice would follow. If there was one thing Tyler wanted to avoid, it was good advice. She didn't need that on the ride from Denver to Independence Junction, the small town where she had grown up. Called Independence for short, it was high in the Rocky Mountains near the famous ski resorts like Aspen and Breckenridge. But not so near that million-dollar price tags applied to the land. Independence was home to generational Coloradans, many of whom grew up and moved away. But everything changes; everything has a season. Sons and daughters were returning to settle.

It was beautiful. Clear air, a magnificent mountain panorama, beautiful trees, and warm, if nosy, fellow citizens. For a place with less than fifteen hundred people, it seemed to have everything.

Before going outside, she unzipped the suitcase and dug out a puffy parka and a pair of Ugg boots lined in fleece. No way could she board a plane in Vegas dressed in such clothing, but October in Colorado required them. The Uber arrived and she settled in for the drive. It was eighty miles to Breckenridge. Independence was beyond that.

She must have slept, because the motion of the Uber vehicle slowing down woke her. Independence was in darkness but Main Street glowed with lights. The Uber's tires crunched on the layer of snow on the road. Wooden storefronts had gentle yellow illumination in the windows, even though they were closed. The buildings mostly had peaked roofs, and some were painted different colors with contrasting trim. A green storefront had red trim, and a yellow one had blue trim. Tiny fairy lights bedecked potted shrubs and bushes.

Only the diner bustled with people at this hour of six in the evening. Tyler was hungry but knew that if she went to the diner, everyone would know she was home. She wasn't ready for that. Mostly she wasn't ready for the questions.

"Up there," she said to the driver, pointing away from the diner.

The Uber squeaked through the snow for a few hundred yards.

"Here," Tyler said, indicating a sign that read 'Yoga Studio' with an arrow pointing to the second floor. Tyler tapped in a generous tip for the driver on her cell phone. "Thanks, have a nice night." She got out with her suitcase and fumbled for keys.

Years ago, this old wooden building housed the dance school of Madame DuPont, a famous *professeur de dance* who hosted seasonal retreats for renowned dancers the world over. This was where they came to rest, get back to perfecting dance basics, and recuperate from grueling tours. As a favor to the local community, the renowned Mme DuPont taught a dance class for local children. Tyler had been one of them. When Madame DuPont passed on, she left the building to Tyler in her will.

The old key slipped effortlessly into the lock of the dark studio. She wanted to stretch a bit at the *barre*, going easy on the leg, but still releasing stress. She was going to need a chill mood before facing the family. She pushed the door open and stepped inside, inhaling the scent of wooden floorboards and the dust of an old place.

She loved everything about it. Memories of hours spent in sweaty leotards, of the strict instructions of her teacher, and the happy atmosphere of the local girls came back. It had been Madame Dupont's wish that the dance retreats continue after her death. Busy with her career, Tyler had been unable to organize the right teacher or the accommodations for dance professionals the way Madame had. Tyler wasn't sure how she felt about resurrecting the school, anyway. No idea if she could even teach. Patience wasn't exactly her strong suit. Perfectionism, on the other hand, was. But the future of that wasn't clear.

Lost in thought, she flipped on the lights. She blinked. Was she hallucinating? Over in the back corner hung a red punching bag. Gloves lay on the floor beneath it. She looked around, but it seemed she was alone. Hesitantly, she walked over and touched the sandbag. Yes, it was real. Her eyes were not playing tricks on her. The second floor of the building was rented out right now. Perhaps those people had hung the bag here.

She'd heard about working off frustrations on a boxing bag, and the idea appealed right now. She slipped off her Uggs. Barefoot, she circled the bag a few times, then bent down and slipped on the gloves. How difficult could it be? She hopped on the spot like a boxer once or twice, only to pause with her face contorted in pain. Footwork was out, it seemed. But there was nothing wrong with her arms. Gingerly at first, she tapped a few blows on the bag. Then faster and faster, she let punches patter on the red dummy. She was so concentrated that she didn't even notice someone had entered the room behind her.

Panting, Tyler braced herself, waiting to catch her breath. She hadn't known it would be so strenuous. And she was used to quite a bit from her own training. Slowly, she lowered her arms. She could barely lift them. Thirst. She needed something to drink. There was a sink in the small locker room. She could drink there. As she turned, her eyes fell on someone. An image of muscular arms around her waist and intertwined legs flashed before her inner eye. Heat shot through her body. Oh great. She was suddenly aware of scattered strands of hair that had come loose from her braid sticking to her sweaty face.

"You!" she gasped.

"I was thinking the same thing," he answered.

Funny, she remembered the way he smelled, the sensation of his touch, but she couldn't remember his name.

"Pat," he said, as though reading her mind. "Patrick West."

"Tyler—"

"Carter. I remember."

They looked at each other, memories from the summer flooding back. Along with the dark good looks and toned body, Tyler remembered he was an architect. He was planning the restoration of an historic house in the area. Which explained why he was still in town. He took off his jacket and sat on the floor.

"I didn't know dancers could work the bag," he said.

"I didn't know either, but it's great for working off frustrations."

He nodded. He looked more amused than annoyed that she was holding him up, and using his property. But if she was annoyed, he should be, too. Fair is fair, right? No, life wasn't fair, she remembered. She should have learned that much in the last few days. Turning away, she went to the sink. She needed an intervention, something, anything, to give a moment to think how to handle this. She drank water greedily from the tap and then held her whole head under the water. She squeezed out her hair, shook it out, and with a corner of her T-shirt, dried her face and walked back to the bag. Slooowly. The slower the better, to hide any hint of favoring the leg. She thought the wet hair would be a distraction, kind of a sleight-of-hand like a magician's trick, but his gaze fell to her leg anyway. She waited for a comment but he said nothing, just waited until she slid down beside him, leaning back against the wall.

"You a boxer?" she asked out of the blue.

"A little martial arts," he answered but didn't offer anything else.

She watched him out of the corner of her eye. Seems she'd found a topic he didn't want to talk about. They both had things they didn't want to talk about. Touché.

"So my dance studio is turning into a dojo?"

"You know the Japanese word for it." He looked impressed.

"I work in Vegas with dancers, stunt people, and every kind of physical entertainment professional from all over the world. Of course, I know the term."

The slight, amused smile fell from his face. "If you need the space, I'll find another place."

She ducked the invitation. "I take it Jasmine said this was okay?" Jasmine was the yoga studio owner who rented the space upstairs. She was also a friend, and likely to be a member of the Carter family if and when she married Tyler's brother, Jake. Without waiting for an answer, she said, "I guess I can't be mad at her. Jaz is the reason we met in the first place."

"You remembered." Air went out of him in a sigh, like he'd been holding his breath.

They were silent for a moment. Each thinking back to a night last summer, at a music festival, when they'd decided to leave early and spend private hours of pleasure, never expecting to see one another again.

She was tempted to rattle him a little, but couldn't bring herself to do it. "It's okay. As long as you don't interfere with my training, you can stay. I don't know exactly how my plans will turn out yet."

"Thanks. I wasn't expecting that."

"Just because I'm having a bad day doesn't mean you can't talk to me."

"Now you sound more like the woman I met at the festival."

"That's good, cause I sure don't look like her." She tossed her damp hair.

"You look exactly like her. I'd know those blue eyes anywhere. Sea-blue."

She could hear heat in his voice. He was waiting for her to say something else. Maybe to give some clue to her sudden appearance in town. But she said nothing.

"I see you have a suitcase," he said. "Need a lift anywhere? If you're finished working out, that is. No rush."

Tyler had so much to say, but a thousand words couldn't explain it all, and one word felt like too many.

He spoke slowly and gently. "Should I take you to your family?"

She coughed lightly. "No, they don't know I'm here yet."

"What do you want to do then? You're not going to stay here at the studio, are you?"

"Maybe..." She searched his face. "Maybe just take me to your place?"

He saw the look in her eye. She didn't have to ask twice.

On a snowmobile across the street, a man watched as Tyler and Pat locked up and left the studio. From the looks of it, the Vegas Twirly Girl and Mr. Fix-It were into each other. That suited him just fine. He rubbed his hands together. It had been more comfortable in the diner. But after people had tried to engage him in conversation, the situation became unsafe. It was important he keep his distance from others. Normally, it was no problem for him to remain invisible. Nothing about him was noticeable. But that didn't seem to do him any good in the place. The curse of a small town. On the other hand, for the same reason, he learned many details of his victims that he would have otherwise had to painstakingly research. Maybe he had to adapt his plan to the local conditions. But he would deal with that later.

The couple entered Pat's vehicle and started off, down Main street. The watcher shifted the snowmobile into drive, pulled a black full-face ski mask down so only eye slits were visible, and followed at a safe distance, keeping the lights off. The couple wound up a hilly road that ended at a magnificent old house. It must have been five thousand square feet. At least a third of it was covered with scaffolding and plastic tarps—tied down against the winds that blew in over the mountains. The couple got out of the ancient Cadillac Mr. Fix-It was driving, an odd choice of vehicle for a young guy, the man thought, and crunched over the snow to the dark house. A sensor light went on to illuminate the way to a side entrance.

The man made a mental note of that. No dog either. He watched as they entered the house and disappeared.

Satisfied with tonight's results, he shifted the snow-mobile into drive and drove back the way they'd come—to his temporary residence to contemplate dark plans.

Tyler blinked. Weak winter sunlight streamed in through wooden blinds. Strange. The sun never shone in her room in the morning. Sleepily, she turned over and encountered resistance with her hand. A large, muscular, warm resistance. Her eyes jolted open. *Déjà vu.* That was how the morning started the last time with Pat, after the music festival. Only then she wasn't sleeping down by the river, she was in an old house. The owner, Mr. Wilkinson, who was almost as old as the town, was staying in the bed and breakfast attached to the diner while Pat handled restoration.

She slipped out of bed, gathered her clothes, and grabbed her suitcase. The knee didn't feel too badly that morning. This room was located in the back quarter of the five-thousand square foot house. It had its own bathroom. But she didn't want to wake Pat. She silently backed out of the room. There had to be more bathrooms down the hall.

Walking along, she ran one hand down the smooth white wall. Even there, in the back of the house, the floor was made of burnished, black-walnut wood. The wood continued in the baseboards and ceiling trim. Brass sconces lit the hallway. It was a sixty-year-old house, built with the best materials of its day. The house was cold. She hoped the heating system was first on the list for renovation.

She tried the handle of a door that looked like it might be a bathroom. Score. It hadn't been used in a while, but it was clean and even had a dried-up bar of soap on the sink. That was lucky because Tyler hadn't bothered to pack shampoo. She planned on using whatever was in the house she bunked at, either her mother's or Paula's, and hadn't figured on staying overnight at a place like old-man Wilkinson's. The bath had an elegant old tub on cast iron feet and a handheld shower. She grabbed the soap and opted for a shower. The water needed to run, but it got plenty hot after a minute. It would have been nice to blame how wretched she felt due to on the time change, but no such luck. Independence was only one hour later than Vegas.

Her next dilemma was how to get into town without having to ask Pat for a lift. Rinsing off, she used yesterday's t-shirt to dry off, zipping it in into a plastic-lined outside pocket of her suitcase, and put on fresh clothes. Back out in the hall, she found her way to the main living space of the house.

The living room, or great room, as Mr. Wilkinson might have called it, was dominated by a huge stone fireplace. Everything inside seemed made of wood, brick or stone. The windows were large with deep casements and in this room, with its stuffed leather furniture and wooden chairs, the views of outside were spectacular. That morning, the world was white after a snowfall overnight.

A snowmobile buzzed past, the driver disguised by a heavy down jacket and ski-mask pulled over his face. If he noticed Tyler at the window, he didn't wave. Shoot, that guy could have been her ride into town.

Her puffy parka and Ugg boots were in the entryway, where they'd been left the night before. If she went outside and waited a bit maybe the snowmobiler would come by again. She dragged her suitcase out the front door and walked across the spacious front yard to the road. Birds were singing in the snow-covered trees. The chances of another vehicle coming by seemed remote. There was likely a toboggan somewhere around the old place. Maybe she could toboggan down the hill. It was downhill almost all the way. She could tip the suitcase on its side and hold it with both arms wrapped around. Who was she kidding? That was the fantasy of a ten-year-old. She'd could capsize and catapult herself off the road headlong into a tree.

The thought nagged that she was going to an awful lot of trouble not to wake Pat up when the theme song from her show sounded in the pocket of her parka. What a miracle there was a signal. It was her cell phone, and that ringtone was Sarah, her agent.

"Hello?"

"Sweetheart, how are you? It's Sarah? Are you in Colorado?"

"Hi! Yes, I'm home." *Not exactly*, her conscience whispered guiltily.

"Everything okay?"

"Of course."

"Just calling to make sure. Yuri said you had a little slip backstage after the last show."

Yuri! That backstabbing choreographer. Tyler wanted to growl but gave a silvery laugh instead. "Sorry to disappoint Yuri's handpicked understudy, but I'm fine."

"Good sweetheart, you know the producers worry at the drop of a hat."

"Maybe if Yuri kept his mouth sh—"

Sarah blew that off with her own airy giggle. "Good to check in, sweetheart. Ta ta for now."

She hung up and Tyler brought up the show's Facebook page to see if Yuri had made the story public. There was nothing in the comments. She clicked over to her professional page. Fans were moaning about the two-week hiatus, nothing much else. She clicked into the Facebook feed with Instagram stories. Same thing. lots of publicity pics of Tyler in her blackbird costume, and in her silver dress dancing on the moon. But nothing about her teensy slip and fall.

Forget dancing on the moon, I'm living in a fishbowl, she thought. An unpleasant and unfamiliar sinking feeling threatened to settle over her as a pickup truck with a snowplow on the front rumbled into view. The side was painted with *Joe's Snow Removal.* Tyler threw up both arms in the universal 'Please, stop!' gesture. The plow grunted to a halt.

In the light of day, with a fresh layer of snow, Main Street's colorful storefronts looked like a winter wonderland. Tyler got out of the plow-pickup and handed the driver a bill. He wouldn't take it. "Say hello to your mother for me," he explained. "It's always nice to have young people come back." He pulled away.

Then Tyler heard the truck stop and back up. The driver rolled the window down and held out a card. "You need another ride. Here's my number. I'm on call."

Tyler smiled and said thank you. As though her feet were making the decision, she strolled away from the diner and enjoyed the pretty little street. It was kept in the Breckenridge-Aspen style of one and two-story clapboard buildings, nothing larger. There were still empty storefronts, room for growth, but the trend was clearly pointing upward.

Just about to walk into the diner, she pulled out her cell phone and texted her mother, Brenda Carter. *Hi Mom. In town 4 a few days. Be home in time for supper.* There, now Momma knew first. If any news escaped from the diner, her mother would already be up to speed. Being the first to know was currency in Independence.

She pulled open the big door with *Miss Minnie's* etched in the glass. The place was bustling. Red, padded booths lined the walls while four-top tables with wooden chairs filled in the center. A big counter had padded red stools that swiveled. For the breakfast traffic, steaming hot breakfasts piled with pancakes and eggs, toast and hash browns, sausages and bacon, came out on plates almost the size of Thanksgiving platters.

The place was run by two sisters and Miss Minnie and Miss Daisy. A bed and breakfast, located right behind the restaurant, was also theirs. They shared the work and were among the best-informed residents of the small town. No nugget of news escaped their ears, no gossip went unrecorded in their busy memory banks. The diner was the only restaurant in town. No one dared compete with the Disney Sisters, as they were affectionately known.

"Come here, Tyler," Miss Minnie called, hugging her tightly. She was pressed against her enormous bosom, and no sooner had Miss Minnie finished with her than she was passed on to her sister, Miss Daisy. She was shooed off to one of the red, padded booths with a menu where Tyler spotted Jasmine McArthy. Jaz had returned to Independence from Seattle after trouble with a boyfriend-gone-bad. With the help of her grandmother, she opened a yoga studio on the second floor of the dance school. Tyler slipped into the red-leather booth as elegantly as her leg would allow and took a seat across from Jaz.

"What a surprise!"

To Tyler's eyes, Jasmine had never looked better. And why not? She'd stepped up from yoga instructor to business owner. In fact, she was probably on her way to the studio, although it was too early for the place to open. Jaz had established herself as the town's leading alternative health guru. She also was in love with a good man who was crazy about her. *Of course* Jasmine looked good.

"How are you feeling?" Tyler asked. Truthfully, getting settled here hadn't been all sunshine and roses for Jasmine. She had been attacked by thugs that the boyfriend had sent to teach her a lesson for leaving him.

All three were now in jail. But Jaz had spent time in the hospital over it.

Jasmine pushed her chin-length blond hair back before she answered. "I'm feeling pretty good." A smile lit up her face. "Good as new. A new group opened up: Yoga Rehab. Works wonders on injuries."

"Really?" asked Tyler, bright-eyed. That might interest her, too. *Someday,* she thought. "And how's my brother, Jake?"

A diamond seemed to sparkle in Jasmine's eye. "We're not engaged yet, though Jake would like that, and as soon as possible. But I'm quite content for him to live with me now."

"*Living* with you—"

"In grandma's house. She left to spend two weeks with a friend when last winter got cold and lonely, then decided to make it permanent. I'm living there now with my poodle, Rambo, so there was plenty of room for Jake."

Tyler was startled. *Jake engaged? As in, "to be married?" To Jasmine?*

Off her look, Jasmine said, "It's not so much a question of if we'll get married, but when. And whether Jake can pull off a proper marriage proposal." She grinned, the challenge in her eyes clear.

But Tyler was stuck on the ease that Jasmine had with the word *marriage.* "So, the small-town sheriff and the big-city vegetarian yoga instructor found a match made in heaven?"

"Seems like it."

Breakfast arrived. Jasmine had a veggie omelet. Tyler's poached eggs and dry toast came with add-ons. A platter of muffins was set down, along with organic jams, jellies and honey. Then came a platter of berries and fruit alongside a stack of flapjacks half a foot high.

"I didn't order all this—" Tyler began.

"Hello Miss Carter," a voice interrupted. "What brings you to West Cow Plop? Aren't you awfully far away from Sin City, excuse me, the Holy City of Las Vegas?"

It was a voice she had known since childhood. She turned to see the shrunken but still dapper form of Mr. Wilkinson, the unofficial town mayor and patriarch. He wore a wide-brimmed western hat, a string tie, and a pair of handmade boots with big heels that made him five-foot-six if he didn't slouch. The hat added another four inches on top.

And you just spent the night at his house, Tyler's conscience whispered.

Tyler knew Mr. Wilkinson loved conversational banter, and Tyler had learned the art in Vegas. "Mr. Wilkinson! If I wasn't married to my job, you could tempt me."

"I'm too young for you, my dear. But my older brother might be interested."

Tyler's mouth fell open. She didn't have a comeback for that.

Mr. Wilkinson seized the moment. "My brother just wrote his will. It was one line. Want to hear it?" Without waiting for an answer he added, "Being of sound mind and body, I already spent all my money."

Tyler and Jasmine set their coffee cups down. Nobody, absolutely nobody else in the world could get away with these lines. But it was Mr. Wilkinson, beloved by all and ultimately harmless. When he was on a roll you didn't dare have a beverage near your mouth in case you spit it all over anyone sitting across from you.

"Seriously, though? I'm so old the doctor can check my age by counting the rings in my wrinkles."

Tyler put her hand up for mercy. "Kidding aside, how have you been?"

Mr. Wilkinson tweaked his string tie. "Haven't you heard? My old woodpile is getting a facelift. Thanks to a friend of Jasmine's. An architect all the way from See-attle."

And at that moment, Pat appeared at Mr. Wilkinson's elbow. "Hi," he said, looking a little sheepish. His hair was sticking up in places, and he looked like he'd just rolled out of bed.

Jasmine's face lit up. "Pat! What brings you here?"

"Ummm, actually..." he mumbled, and extended something in a plastic bag to Tyler. "I thought you might need this."

A pregnant pause fell over the table. Tyler felt the world shift to slow motion. If underwear was in the bag, everyone would know she and Pat had spent the night together. But she'd stowed her underwear back in her suitcase and put on fresh after this morning's shower. So what could be in there? She decided to gamble.

"What is it?" she said in a businesslike tone, and pulled the mystery item from the bag. It was a black spandex tube, of sorts.

"What's that?" Jasmine blurted.

"Same question crossed my mind," Mr. Wilkinson said, and turned knowing eyes from Jasmine to Tyler.

"Nobody knows what this is?" Tyler twirled the item on her finger. "Any guesses?"

"We're in a family place, remember," Mr. Wilkinson warned.

"It's an elastic knee sleeve," Tyler stated. "You pull it over the knee to support the muscles and ligaments. Dancers wear them."

Jasmine gave a hoot of relief. She pointed form Tyler to Pat. "You two know each other?" Astonishment was written all over her face.

"Not really," Tyler said.

"Since the Indie Rock Festival," Pat said at the same time.

Tyler glared at him. She balled the sleeve up and squashed it into her pocket.

"The old indie rock festival, huh?" Mr. Wilkinson said thoughtfully. "So that's what they're calling it nowadays." He rubbed his chin thoughtfully. "Well, I never!"

He attracted the attention of Minnie and Daisy, who tuned their ears to what was coming next. "I'll have no hanky-panky in my house, do you understand?" he broadcast loudly.

Jaws dropped around the table.

Across the room, Daisy and Minnie thrust out their chins in agreement. They really didn't know what was being discussed, but if Mr. Wilkinson had a moral opinion on it, they agreed.

Then he lowered his voice, winked at Pat and Tyler, and said, "Now you kids go and have fun."

Tyler stomped up the steps to the dance studio. She and Pat had fled the diner, but she'd said "no" to his offer of a lift anywhere she wanted to go and sent him away. They were both very embarrassed about the knee-sleeve incident. Pat groaned when she let him know a dozen knee sleeves were in her suitcase as backup. All that public humiliation for nothing.

At the door of the studio, she snapped an icicle off the frame and crunched it into pieces. Her mood was really not improving, but she had to make herself presentable before going to see her parents. It was as good a time as any. Putting the old key in the lock, she noticed a red stain on the ground. There was no snow here under the porch overhang. She frowned and bent down. Was that blood? Carefully, she touched the wet spot with one finger. At the same time, she felt a tingle on the back of her neck. She straightened up and looked around. She couldn't spot anyone. Tyler was about to smell the liquid on her finger when her eyes fell on the studio window. She drew a sharp breath, like a gasp.

Three jet-black feathers were stuck to the window, clotted with blood. Shiny black crow feathers. On the windowpane were more red streaks and spatters that appeared intentionally arranged. Was that blood? Who on earth did this? Was it meant for Jasmine? Or was it meant for her? *Only one of us performs as a blackbird onstage in front of ten thousand people every week. A crow is a black bird.* And yet anyone could have known Jasmine would soon show up at the yoga studio to see it. She had classes to teach. Perhaps the person who did it didn't care, just so long as the gruesome 'artwork' got seen.

Tyler pulled out her phone and took a picture of the display. Then she grabbed handfuls of snow and wiped the window clean. She threw the feathers over the side of the porch, walked around, and packed them down with her foot so they were buried. Then she stumbled off up the street.

ROCKY MOUNTAIN RECIPES

JASMINE'S PUMPKIN SOUP

INGREDIENTS

1 large red onion, chopped

1 large Russet or Yukon Gold potato, peeled, cut into pieces

1 large piece of pumpkin, recommend a cooking pumpkin or butternut squash (approx. 1 lb.), peeled, seeded, and cut into approx. 1-inch cubes

White wine (for deglazing and just maaaybe for a sip or two)

1–2 cups organic vegetable broth

Pinch salt

Pinch cayenne pepper

Pinch chili powder (for those who like it spicy)

Pinch nutmeg

Optional condiments:

> Bread croutons or toasted bruschetta crackers
>
> Pumpkin seed oil
>
> Manchego (Spanish sheep cheese), grated
>
> Parmesan cheese, grated
>
> Organic half cream
>
> Sour cream
>
> Bacon or sausages, if you have stubborn carnivores at the table

INSTRUCTIONS

Sauté onions in a saucepan. Add all remaining ingredients, and sauté for five minutes, stirring occasionally.

Deglaze with a little white wine. Wait until the alcohol has evaporated.

Add at least enough vegetable broth to cover the vegetables.

Simmer over low heat until the vegetables are soft. This will take about 15–25 minutes, depending on the thickness of the vegetable pieces. The vegetables are soft enough when they can be easily mashed on the edge of the pot with a fork. In principle, a soup can never be overcooked. According to Eastern beliefs, the heat generated during cooking is stored in the soup, warming and nourishing it all the more. This effect can be enhanced by hot spices.

When the vegetables are soft, it's time for the blender. Puree, season to taste with the chosen spices, and serve.

This soup goes well with homemade bread croutons, a few drops of organic pumpkin seed oil, or even grated sheep's cheese such as Manchego. The soup can be finished with cream or sour cream. I usually put all of these ingredients on the table so that everyone can prepare their soup just the way they like it best. If you have carnivores at the table who insist on meat being served, try bacon or sausages.

If you are not sure whether you prefer the soup thicker, you should add only the minimum amount of broth. After pureeing, you can easily add more hot water or additional vegetable broth if the soup becomes too thick. All others can quietly add more liquid from the beginning.

Of course, you can experiment with the addition of a wide variety of vegetables. I wish you a lot of fun with it.

Indian Kachari

INGREDIENTS

DOUGH:

3 cups + 2 tbsp. white flour

1 cup wheat semolina

1 stick + 1 tbsp. cooking butter

1 pinch salt

1 cup water, lukewarm

FILLING:

1 red bell pepper, finely chopped

1 cup peas, drained from a can or frozen

2 tbsp. peanut oil (alternatively, sesame oil works as well)

1 tsp. mustard seeds, light

1 tsp. cumin, whole

1 tsp. garam masala (a very specific curry mixture)

1 tsp. whole cane sugar or palm sugar

1 tsp. salt

1 tsp. curry, hot

1 pinch of Hing (This is also an Indian spice. Smells like garlic, but has a flatulence-relieving effect instead of the other way around. However, the kachari will be just as good without this exotic spice.)

Water for coating

INSTRUCTIONS

Mix the flour, wheat semolina, and salt together, add the butter and rub by hand to form a fine crumbly mass. Combine and make a well in the center. Pour in the water. Fold the edge over and knead thoroughly. Cover and let rest for one hour.

Now the dough is ready for further use as Indian flatbread (by rolling out about ⅛ inch flat and baking on both sides in a coated frying pan) or, as in our case, as dough for kachari, a type of Indian doughnut.

For the kachari, roll out the dough about ⅛ inch thin and cut out circles about 2 inches in diameter.

Sauté mustard seeds and cumin in oil. Sauté the bell pepper and peas. Add the rest of the spices. Mash the mixture in the pan with a fork. If the whole thing becomes very dry, you can add a little water.

Place a tablespoon of filling in the center of each dough circle. Leave ½ inch border free and brush with water. Fold the dough into a pocket and press the edges tightly.

Then it goes with the kachari for 15 minutes off in the oven which has been preheated to 375 degrees Fahrenheit.

(The kachari are very suitable for freezing. If needed, place frozen on a baking sheet and bake in a preheated oven for 30 minutes).

There is a great vegetarian restaurant in Zurich called "Hiltl," A few years ago they published the book *Hiltl. Vegetarisch nach Lust und Laune.* The original recipe for the Kachari comes from this book.

Provençal Vegetable Cake

The preparation takes quite a long time.
I have never made it under two and a half hours.
So plan enough time. But the work is definitely worth it!

INGREDIENTS

½ cup + 1 tbsp. olive oil

1 red bell pepper, peeled and cut into 1½-inch pieces

1 yellow bell pepper, peeled and cut into 1½-inch pieces

1 medium eggplant, cut into 1½-inch cubes

1 small sweet potato, peeled and cut into 1 inch cubes

1 small zucchini, cut into 1-inch cubes

2 large onions, cut into thin rings

2 bay leaves, dried

8 sprigs of thyme (or from the spice cupboard, but fresh herbs really do taste better here)

½ cup ricotta cheese, in small lumps

½ cup feta cheese, in small cubes

7 cherry tomatoes, halved

2 organic eggs

1 cup organic half cream

10 oz shortcrust pastry – a shortcrust pastry is a French-style dough with a crumbly, biscuit-like texture. A traditional pie crust may work if you can't find shortcrust at your local supermarket. Or feel free to make a shortcrust if you don't mind spending a little extra time in the kitchen.

INSTRUCTIONS

Preheat the oven to 450°F and start roasting the vegetables. Place the sliced peppers in an ovenproof dish, drizzle with a little olive oil, and place in the oven on the top rack.

Put the eggplant cubes in a bowl, mix with 4 tablespoons of olive oil, salt, and pepper. Place in an ovenproof dish and place in the oven next to the peppers.

After 12 minutes, mix the sweet potatoes, also tossed in oil, salt, and pepper, into the eggplant and return to the oven.

After another 12 minutes, add the equally prepared zucchini, and leave in the oven for another 10 minutes. Then remove everything and lower the oven temperature to 325°F.

While the vegetables are roasting in the oven, heat 2 tbsp. of olive oil in a frying pan over medium heat. Add the onions and bay leaves to the hot oil and season with herb salt. Turn down the heat and roast the onion rings for 25 minutes, until golden, soft, and sweet. Remove bay leaves and remove from heat.

If using batter or making from scratch, pour the batter into a shallow cake pan and blind bake weighted with dried beans for 10 minutes. Remove beans, and bake the cake base for another 10 minutes.

Spread the fried onions first and then the roasted vegetables evenly on the pastry base. Sprinkle with half the thyme leaves. Spread the pieces of ricotta and feta. Then place the tomatoes in between, cut-side up.

Whisk the eggs and cream, and season with salt and pepper. Pour over the cake and sprinkle with the remaining thyme. Bake at 325°F for about 35 minutes. Remove and let rest for 10 minutes. Enjoy your meal.

This recipe is originally from the book *Genussvoll vegetarisch* by Yotam Ottolenghi. One of my favorite cookbooks.

Jasmine's Vegan, Lactose-free Ice Cream

I recently stumbled across this recipe on the Internet.
I tried it immediately and was very pleasantly surprised
by this almost healthy variant of ice cream.

INGREDIENTS (FOR 1–2 PEOPLE)

1 ripe banana, so that you almost don't want to eat it, but not yet so that it smells of alcohol, sliced

15–20 strawberries, cut into pieces

1 cup organic coconut milk (without additives)

INSTRUCTIONS

Freeze strawberries for two hours. Remove from freezer, allow to thaw for 5–10 minutes, and process with a blender until the individual crystals combine to form a smooth, ice cream–like mass. The fact that this works is due to the small amount of fat that the banana brings.

Add coconut milk to taste. Return to the refrigerator until mixture is firm. Allow to thaw 5–10 minutes before enjoying.

NOTES

This variant is not very sweet. This can be remedied with honey or even normal sugar.

In addition, of course, the mixture can be spiced up with chocolate spread, peanut butter, vanilla flavoring, or roasted nuts.

But remember: the more ingredients, the less "healthy" and the more calories. But if you do an hour of yoga afterwards, you can easily afford it.

If you prefer to enjoy a smoothie, simply omit the second freezing stage and add more coconut or almond milk (thinner).

BOOK CLUB QUESTIONS

1. There are several animals and pets in the book. Was there one you like the best? Why?

2. Did Jasmine's move to small-town Colorado shift her expectations of people and life? What changed?

3. Is a small-town lifestyle something that appeals to you? Why or why not?

4. Is Jake's overprotectiveness an issue for most women? Or is Jasmine unusual in that regard?

5. What about the relationship between Paula and the homeless girl, Leslie? Did Paula do the right thing for her?

6. Do you think Jasmine and Jake are well suited for one another? Will the relationship last?

7. If you could rewrite the ending, would it change? How?

ROCKY MOUNTAIN ROMANCES

Rocky Mountain Yoga

Rocky Mountain Star

Rocky Mountain Dogs

Rocky Mountain Kid

Rocky Mountain Secrets

COLLECT THE ENTIRE SERIES!

ABOUT THE AUTHOR

AUTHOR, MOTHER, HORSE WHISPERER, and part-time healthy food cook, Virginia Fox is a woman who cares deeply about family, animals, the environment, and friendships.

Creative from a young age, she turned her love of books into a prolific career as a writer. Her German-language Rocky Mountain series saw every volume enter the Top 50 of the Kindle charts on day one of launch. Now the bestselling Rocky Mountain Romances series breaks onto the US scene.

Virginia Fox lives on a small ranch near Zurich with her family, her Australian cattle dog, and two moody tomcats. When she isn't writing, she delights in caring for her horses and cooking for her family. Discover more on her website:

WWW.VIRGINIAFOX.COM